Full Length
Roof Framer

A series of tables giving the full length of all rafters for any span, for 48 different pitches.

Cuts and bevels for Common, Hip, Valley, Jack and Purlin rafters; also cuts and bevels for Gable and Cornice Mouldings, accompanying each of the 48 pitches with illustrations.

By

A. F. RIECHERS

Box 405

Palo Alto, California 94302

$6.00
~~Postpaid~~

INDEX

PREFACE

This book gives the ENTIRE *Length* of the Common, Hip, Valley and Jack Rafters for 48 different pitches.

The flattest pitch is a ½ inch rise to 12 inches of run. Pitches increase ½ inch of rise each time until they reach 24 inches of rise to 12 inches of run. There are 48 pitches, all told.

There are 2,400 different spans or widths of buildings given for *each* pitch. The smallest span is ¼ inch, and they increase ¼ inch each time until they reach a span of 50 feet. There is a different rafter length for each ¼ inch of span; therefore there are 2,400 Common and 2,400 Hip Rafter lengths, or 4,800 rafter lengths for each pitch; or 230,400 rafter lengths can be had for the 48 pitches.

By doubling or trebling the spans, the range of this book can be increased to meet the requirements of any building or bridge, even should the span run in the hundreds of feet.

The 144 Tables will give the ENTIRE length of the Common, Hip, Valley or Jack Rafter to ⅛ inch, for *positively* any span, be it in odd feet, odd inches, or odd fractions of an inch.

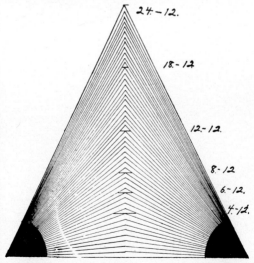

The cuts and bevels for all the roof work are given with each of the 48 pitches.

5

First determine the pitch and then the span of the rafters. Fig. 1 shows the pitch to be 8

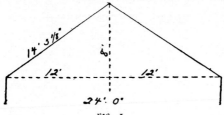

FIG. I

feet rise for 12 feet run, or 8 inch rise for 12 inch run, or 8 and 12 pitch.

The span is shown to be 24' 0".

Find the length of the rafters.

Turn to 8 and 12 pitch. Under the heading "Common Rafter—Span, Feet," locate 24'; opposite this is 14' 5⅛", which is the length of the Common Rafters.

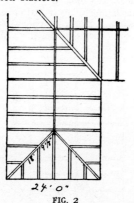

FIG. 2

Now suppose we wish a Hip or Valley Rafter for this roof as shown in Fig. 2. Under the heading "Hip or Valley Rafter—Span, Feet," locate 24'; opposite this is 18' 9⅛", which is the length of the Hip or Valley Rafter.

Now we will want some Jack Rafters to fit against the sides of the Hip and Valley Rafters.

Suppose we have them spaced 30" apart. Under the heading "Jack Rafters—Spaced,

Inches," locate 30"; opposite this is 3' 0", which is the length of the shortest one. The second one will be twice as long, or 6' 0". The third one will be thrice as long, or 9' 0", and so on.

SPANS OF ODD INCHES

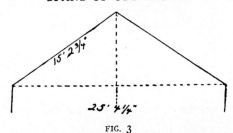

FIG. 3

Fig. 3 shows another 8 and 12 roof with an odd span of 25' 4¼". Find the Common Rafter length.

In the Span, Feet column......25' = 15'   0¼"
In the Span, Inch column....4¼" =   2½"

Total length of Common Rafter..15'   2¾"

Fig. 4 shows a Hip and Valley Rafter for the same roof. Find their length. In the Hip and Valley Rafter column:

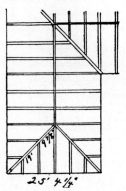

FIG. 4

Span, feet....................25' = 19'   6½"
Span, inches ....4¼" =   3⅜"

Total length Hip & Valley Rafter..19'   9⅞"
Our Jack Rafters are spaced 32" this time.
In the "spaced inches" column 32" = 3' 2½".

8

The shortest Jack will then be 3′ 2½″ long, and each of the others will be 3′ 2½″ longer than the next as they advance in length.

WHEN RAFTERS OVERHANG BUILDING

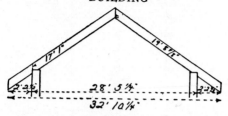

FIG. 5

An 8 and 12 overhang roof, which projects 2′ 2½″ (measuring out level) is shown in Fig. 5.

Overhang rafters must have a seat cut to set on buildings, as Fig 6 shows.

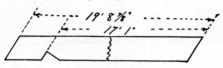

FIG. 6

Find location of plumb mark of the seat cut. Span or width of building is 28′ 5¼″.

Using the tables as before....28′ = 16′ 9⅞″
5¼″ =   3⅛″

Location of plumb mark of seat cut. 17′ 1   ″
As shown in Fig. 6.

Find the entire length of Common Rafters.

By adding the two overhangs to width of building we have a rafter span of 32′ 10¼″, as Fig. 5.

Using the tables as before.....32′ = 19′ 2¾″
10¼″ =   6⅛″

Total length of Common Rafters..19′ 8⅞″

Now find the location of seat cut and entire length of Hip or Valley Rafter for the same span roof as shown in Fig. 7.

Using the Hip and Valley table 28′ = 21′ 10⅝″
5¼″ =   4⅛″

Location of plumb mark of seat cut. 22′ 2¾″
As shown in Fig. 8.

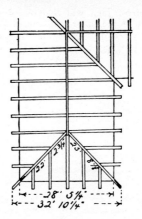

FIG. 7

Now the entire length.

Using table .... $32' = 25'$ $0\frac{1}{8}'$
                          $10\frac{1}{4}'' =$ 8

Total length of Hip or Valley......$25'$ $8\frac{1}{8}''$

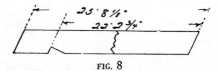

FIG. 8

Our Jack Rafters are spaced 24″ apart.

Using table for Jack Rafters, 24″ = 2′ 4⅞″;
2′ 4⅞″ is then the location of the plumb mark
of the seat cut. Add to this the same projec-

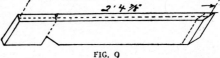

FIG. 9

tion of the Common Rafter overhang. Each
Jack will be 2′ 4⅞″ longer than the next, as
they advance in length.

Fig. 9 shows the correct way to measure a
Jack Rafter. The dotted lines at the top cut
show the allowance for half thickness of Hip
Rafter. This allowance for half thickness of

Hip Rafter is only deducted for the pattern or first Jack, then the other Jacks are measured full length as they step up 2' 4⅞" each time after the pattern length.

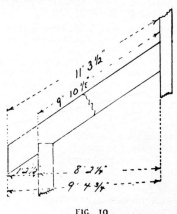

FIG. 10

To find the length of Common Rafter by its run or ½ span, as Fig. 10.

The first thing to do is to get the span, as if both sides of the roof were there. As in Fig. 10, double 8' 2¼" = 16' 4½"; 16' 4½" is then the span to look for in the table.

$$16' = 9' \quad 7⅜''$$
$$4½'' = \quad 2¾''$$

Location of seat cut .... 9' 10⅛"

Now for the length of Rafter. Get the whole span by doubling 9' 4¾", which = 18' 9½" span.

In the table .... 18' = 10' 9¾"
$$9½'' = \quad 5¾''$$

Total length of Common Rafter ... 11' 3½"

The Hip or Valley Rafter for this half roof is found by using the same span as the Common Rafter, as in all other cases.

The Length of Common, Hip or Valley, Lookout, or short finish Rafters which are fastened to the ends of the rough Rafters. is found by the same method, as above. Double the run and get the span, then proceed as for any other roof.

CUTS AND BEVELS FOR THE RAFTERS SO FAR DESCRIBED

So far we have used 8 and 12 pitch only. Not because it is easier to use by this book, but because it is the standard pitch.

It makes no difference whether you have ever framed, say a 17½-12 pitch roof or not, you can frame it as easy as any pitch you are most familiar with, by the aid of this book.

Looking back to Figs. 1 and 2, we have a Gable and Hip Roof of 8 and 12 pitch.

Turning to Table 8-12, and under the heading "Cuts for Steel Square," "The first figure is always the cut."

COMMON RAFTER

Plumb 8-12, see Figs. 11 and 12.
Level 12-8, see Fig. 12.

HIP OR VALLEY RAFTER

Plumb 8-17, see Fig. 13.
Level 17-8, see Fig. 13.
Side 9⅜-8½, see Figs. 14 and 15.
Backing 8-18¾, see Figs. 16 and 17.

JACK RAFTERS

Plumb 8-12, see Fig. 18.
Level 12-8, see Fig. 18.
Side 14⅜-12, see Figs 19 and 20.

The dotted line in Fig. 11, shows allowance for half thickness of Ridge.

The dotted line in Fig 15 shows allowance for half thickness of Ridge.

The dotted line in Fig. 20 shows allowance for half thickness of Hip.

PURLIN RAFTER OR ROOF SHEATHING

Plumb 8-14⅜, see Fig. 21.
Cross 12-14⅜, see Fig. 22.

VALLEY SHINGLES

Cross 12-14⅜, see Fig. 23.

MITRE-BOX CUTS FOR GABLE MOULDS

Plumb 8-12, see Figs. 24 and 25.
Mitre 14⅜-12, see Figs. 24 and 25.

BISECTION OF

8-12 = 7¼-24, see Fig. 26.
Mitre-box Cuts for Cornice Mouldings intersecting at Valley or Hip, Fig. 27. Always

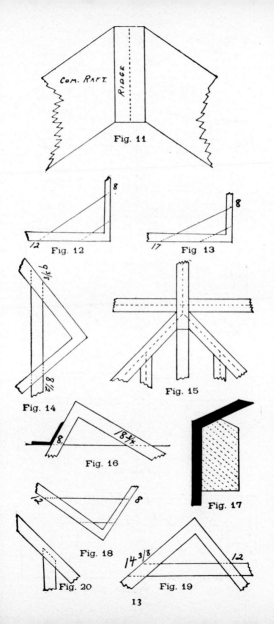

COM. RAFT.

RIDGE

Fig. 11

8

12 Fig. 12

8

17 Fig 13

3/8

8 1/2

Fig. 14

Fig. 15

8

18 1/4

Fig. 16

Fig. 17

12

8

Fig. 18

Fig. 20

14 3/8

12

Fig. 19

13

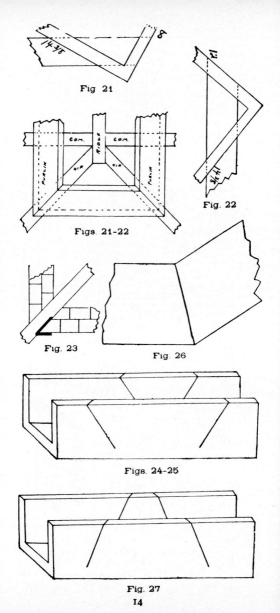

Fig 21

Fig. 22

Figs. 21-22

Fig. 23

Fig. 26

Figs. 24-25

Fig. 27

14

use the same cuts as for the Purlin Rafter or Roof Sheathing.

When Hip Rafters are Backed or Beveled on Top Edge they are marked and cut to the length as given by the tables. If they overhang, they must have a seat cut.

The plumb marks of the Common and Hip Rafter seat cut are of the same height, as Figs. 28 and 29.

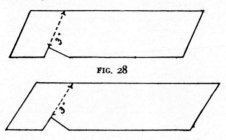

FIG. 28

FIG. 29

The amount of Backing to be beveled off the top edge depends on the thickness and pitch of the Hip Rafter.

The quickest and easiest way to mark the backing is as follows (Fig. 30):

Suppose the pitch is 8-12, the thickness of Hip Rafter 2".

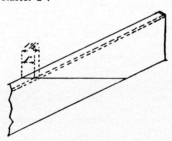

FIG. 30

Draw a level mark (17-8) anywhere on the side of the rafter. Measure on this level mark, half the rafter's thickness, or 1" in this case. The first dotted line shows the backing mark. For a Hip Rafter 3" thick measure 1½" on the level mark, which meets the second backing mark, and so on for a Hip Rafter of any thickness.

After the rafter has been completely laid out, mark back the half thickness of Ridge.

15

When Hip Rafters are not Backed (not beveled on top edge) they are marked and cut to the length given by the tables, and are the same as the Backed Hip Rafter, with but one exception, as follows:

When a Hip Rafter is to be Backed (top edge beveled) the plumb marks of the Common and Hip Rafter seat cuts are the same, as shown in Figs. 31 and 32.

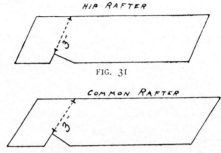

HIP RAFTER

FIG. 31

COMMON RAFTER

FIG. 32

When a Hip Rafter is not to be Backed (top edge left square) the plumb mark of the Common and Hip Rafter seat cut are not the same. The seat cut of the Hip Rafter is cut in deeper to allow the top corner edges to come down to the line of the Common and Jack Rafters. In this case the plumb mark of the Common Rafter seat cut is 3" and the plumb mark of the Hip Rafter seat cut is 2½", and they both line up with each other to a level line on top.

The extra amount to be cut out of the seat cut is found as follows:

The pitch is 8-12. The thickness of Hip Rafter is 2". The rafter is not going to be backed or the top edge is to remain as it is, or square.

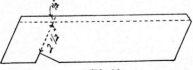

FIG. 33

We will use Fig. 33 for an example. First put a backing mark along the top edge, over the seat cut. It will cut off ½" off the plumb mark for this rafter. This will leave the plumb mark 2½" high at the seat cut. The way the

16

rafter looks now, it is ready to have the top corner beveled off. But instead of beveling the top corners off, which are sticking up ½" too high, we will cut ½" out of the seat cut,

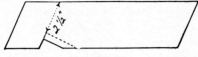

FIG. 34

as shown in Fig. 34. This will drop the corner edges down to a line with the Common and Jack Rafters and save the unnecessary work of chopping off the top edge of the Hip Rafter.

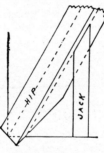

FIG. 35

Fig. 35 shows the proper position of Hip Rafter before the ½" allowance for backing has been made. It can be seen that the top corner edges of the Hip are too high.

Fig. 36 shows this same rafter after the ½" allowance for backing has been removed from the level seat cut. The rafter now lines up correctly with the building line and the top corner edges line up with the Common and Jack Rafters.

Fig. 37 shows the proper way to measure and mark the Hip Rafter. If the building span is 17' the location of the seat cut is 13' 3½", measuring along the center of the top edge, as shown by dotted line. If the Common Rafter overhang is 2', then the total span of Common Rafters is 21' and the Hip Rafter is 16' 5" long.

If the Hip is not to be Backed, mark the plumb mark of the seat cut the same height as for the Common Rafter. Then mark the allowance for backing as shown by the dotted level mark.

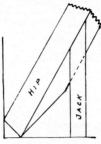

FIG. 36

Now mark the half thickness of ridge allowance shown by the dotted line and the

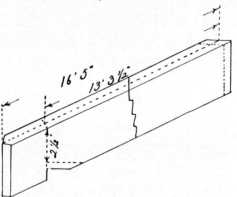

FIG. 37

rafter is ready to cut, and it will fit correctly when placed in position.

Use this Hip for a pattern and mark the others from it. Cut them in pairs.

VALLEY RAFTER

The length and bevels of the Valley Rafter are always the same as the Hip Rafter. Fig. 38 shows a Valley Rafter for the same roof as the Hip Rafter shown in Fig. 37.

Difference of an overhang Hip and Valley. A Hip Rafter is *notched* out deeper in the level mark of the seat cut to allow for backing. *The plumb mark is never moved.*

18

A *Valley Rafter is never notched* out deeper in the level mark of the seat cut to allow for backing (Fig. 39).

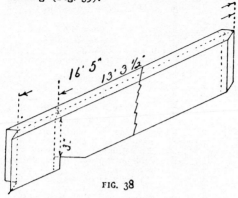

FIG. 38

The plumb mark is advanced to clear the crotch of the two building lines, as shown in

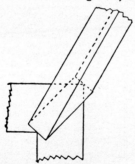

FIG. 39

Fig. 40. The same cut that fits the ridge will give the bevel for the crotch.

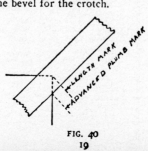

FIG. 40

Spaced In.	Length Ft. In.
1..	I
2..	2
3..	3
4..	4
5..	5
6..	6
7..	7
8..	8
9..	9
10..	10
11..	11
12..1	0
13..	1
14..	2
15..	3
16..	4
17..	5
18..	6
19..	7
20..	8
21..	9
22..	10
23..	11
24..2	0
25..	1
26..	2
27..	3
28..	4
29..	5
30..	6
31..	7
32..	8
33..	9
34..	10
35..	11
36..3	0
37..	1
38..	2
39..	3
40..	4
41..	5
42..	6
43..	7
44..	8
45..	9
46..	10
47..	11
48..4	0

$\frac{1}{2}$ & 12 — 2$\frac{1}{2}$°

EXPLANATION

Common Rafter

Width of building............ 40'6"
Find length of Common Rafter.
　Answer:

Under Span, ft. find　40'　= 20' 0¼"
　"　　　" in. "　　6" =　　3"

Total length Common Rft. 20' 3¼"

When rafters overhang, add both overhangs to width of building. Use total span as before.

To get length of rafter by its run: doubling the run gives the span. Proceed as before.

Tables give full length. Allow for half thickness of ridge.

Spans over 50', as 60', add lengths of 50' & 10' spans together.

Hip Rafter

If common rafter span is 40'6", Hip rafter is 28'7¾" long. Measure length of Hip on center of top edge. If Hip is unbacked (top edge square), see Index. If edge is backed (beveled), see Index.

Allow for half thickness of ridge.

Jack Rafters

Spaced 32" apart are 2'8" different in length. Measure length on center of top edge. Cut short equal to half thickness of hip.

CUTS FOR STEEL SQUARE.

The first figure is always the cut.

Common Rafter	Purlin Rafter Roof Sheathing
Plumb　½- 12	
Level.　12 -　½	Plumb　½- 12
	Cross. 12 - 12

Hip Rafter	Valley Shingles
Plumb　½- 17	
Level.　17 -　½	Cross. 12 - 12
Side..　8½- 8½	Set bevel on
Backing　½- 17	butt end

Set bevel to last named.

	Mitre-Box Cuts for Gable Moulds
	Plumb　½- 12
Jack Rafter	Mitre. 12 - 12
Plumb　½- 12	
Level.　12 -　½	Bisection of
Side..　12 - 12	½- 12 = ½- 24

For full explanation see Index.

COMMON RAFTER					HIP OR VALLEY RAFTER				
Span Ft.	Length Ft.	Length In.	Span In.	Lgth. In.	Span Ft.	Length Ft.	Length In.	Span In.	Lgth. In.
1		6	¼	⅛	1		8½	¼	⅛
2	1	0	½	¼	2	1	5	½	⅜
3	1	6	¾	⅜	3	2	1½	¾	½
4	2	0	1	½	4	2	10	1	¾
5	2	6	¼	⅝	5	3	6½	¼	⅞
6	3	0	½	¾	6	4	2⅞	½	1
7	3	6	¾	⅞	7	4	11⅜	¾	¼
8	4	0	2	1	8	5	7⅞	2	⅜
9	4	6	¼	⅛	9	6	4⅜	¼	⅝
10	5	0	½	¼	10	7	0⅞	½	¾
11	5	6	¾	⅜	11	7	9⅜	¾	2
12	6	0	3	½	12	8	5⅞	3	⅛
13	6	6⅛	¼	⅝	13	9	2⅜	¼	¼
14	7	0⅛	½	¾	14	9	10⅞	½	½
15	7	6⅛	¾	⅞	15	10	7⅜	¾	⅝
16	8	0⅛	4	2	16	11	3⅞	4	⅞
17	8	6⅛	¼	⅛	17	12	0⅜	¼	3
18	9	0⅛	½	¼	18	12	8¾	½	⅛
19	9	6⅛	¾	⅜	19	13	5¼	¾	⅜
20	10	0⅛	5	½	20	14	1¾	5	½
21	10	6⅛	¼	⅝	21	14	10¼	¼	¾
22	11	0⅛	½	¾	22	15	6¾	½	⅞
23	11	6⅛	¾	⅞	23	16	3¼	¾	4⅛
24	12	0⅛	6	3	24	16	11¾	6	¼
25	12	6⅛	¼	⅛	25	17	8¼	¼	⅜
26	13	0⅛	½	¼	26	18	4¾	½	⅝
27	13	6⅛	¾	⅜	27	19	1¼	¾	¾
28	14	0⅛	7	½	28	19	9¾	7	5
29	14	6⅛	¼	⅝	29	20	6⅛	¼	⅛
30	15	0⅛	½	¾	30	21	2⅝	½	¼
31	15	6⅛	¾	⅞	31	21	11⅛	¾	½
32	16	0⅛	8	4	32	22	7⅝	8	⅝
33	16	6⅛	¼	⅛	33	23	4⅛	¼	⅞
34	17	0⅛	½	¼	34	24	0⅝	½	6
35	17	6⅛	¾	⅜	35	24	9⅛	¾	¼
36	18	0⅛	9	½	36	25	5⅝	9	⅜
37	18	6⅛	¼	⅝	37	26	2⅛	¼	½
38	19	0¼	½	¾	38	26	10⅝	½	¾
39	19	6¼	¾	⅞	39	27	7⅛	¾	⅞
40	20	0¼	10	5	40	28	3½	10	7⅛
41	20	6¼	¼	⅛	41	29	0	¼	¼
42	21	0¼	½	¼	42	29	8½	½	⅜
43	21	6¼	¾	⅜	43	30	5	¾	⅝
44	22	0¼	11	½	44	31	1½	11	¾
45	22	6¼	¼	⅝	45	31	10	¼	8
46	23	0¼	½	¾	46	32	6½	½	⅛
47	23	6¼	¾	⅞	47	33	3	¾	¼
48	24	0¼	12	6	48	33	11½	12	½
49	24	6¼			49	34	8		
50	25	0¼			50	35	4½		

Spaced In.	Length Ft. In.
1..	1
2..	2
3..	3
4..	4
5..	5
6..	6
7..	7
8..	8
9..	9
10..	10
11..	11
12..1	0
13..	1
14..	2
15..	3
16..	4
17..	5
18..	6⅛
19..	7⅛
20..	8⅛
21..	9⅛
22..	10⅛
23..	11⅛
24..2	0⅛
25..	1⅛
26..	2⅛
27..	3⅛
28..	4⅛
29..	5⅛
30..	6⅛
31..	7⅛
32..	8⅛
33..	9⅛
34..	10⅛
35..	11⅛
36..3	0⅛
37..	1⅛
38..	2⅛
39..	3⅛
40..	4⅛
41..	5⅛
42..	6⅛
43..	7⅛
44..	8⅛
45..	9⅛
46..	10⅛
47..	11⅛
48..4	0⅛

1 & 12 — 4½°

EXPLANATION
Common Rafter
Width of building............24'4"
Find length of Common Rafter.
  Answer:

Under Span, ft. find	24'	= 12' 0½
" " in. "	4" =	2"

Total length Common Rft. 12' 2½"

When rafters overhang, add both
overhangs to width of building.
Use total span as before.

To get length of rafter by its run:
doubling the run gives the span.
Proceed as before.

Tables give full length. Allow for
half thickness of ridge.

Spans over 50', as 60', add lengths
of 50' & 10' spans together.

Hip Rafter
If common rafter span is 24'4",
Hip rafter is 17'2⅞" long. Measure length of Hip on center of top
edge. If Hip is unbacked (top edge
square), see Index. If edge is
backed (beveled), see Index.

Allow for half thickness of ridge.

Jack Rafters
Spaced 29" apart are 2'5⅛" different in length. Measure leng_
on center of top edge. Cut short
equal to half thickness of hip.

CUTS FOR STEEL SQUARE.
The first figure is always the cut.

Common Rafter	Purlin Rafter Roof Sheathing
Plumb 1 - 12	
Level. 12 - 1	Plumb 1 - 12
	Cross. 12 - 12

Hip Rafter	Valley Shingles
Plumb 1 - 17	Cross. 12 - 12
Level. 17 - 1	Set bevel on
Side.. 8½ - 8½	butt end
Backing 1 - 17	

Set bevel to
last named.

Mitre-Box Cut for Gable Moul_
Plumb 1 - 12
Mitre. 12 - 12

Jack Rafter	Bisection of
Plumb 1 - 12	1- 12 = 1- 24
Level. 12 - 1	
Side.. 12 - 12	

For full explanation see Index.

COMMON RAFTER

Span Ft.	Length Ft. In.	Span In.	Lgth In.
	. 6	¼ .. ⅛	
	1. 0	½ .. ¼	
3..	1. 6⅛	¾ .. ⅜	
4..	2. 0⅛	1 .. ½	
5..	2. 6⅛	¼ .. ⅝	
6..	3. 0⅛	½ .. ¾	
7..	3. 6⅛	¾ .. ⅞	
8..	4. 0⅛	2 .. 1	
9..	4. 6⅛	¼ .. ⅛	
10..	5. 0¼	½ .. ¼	
11..	5. 6¼	¾ .. ⅜	
12..	6. 0¼	3 .. ½	
13..	6. 6¼	¼ .. ⅝	
14..	7. 0¼	½ .. ¾	
15..	7. 6¼	¾ .. ⅞	
16..	8. 0⅜	4 .. 2	
17..	8. 6⅜	¼ .. ⅛	
18..	9. 0⅜	½ .. ¼	
19..	9. 6⅜	¾ .. ⅜	
20..	10. 0⅜	5 .. ½	
21..	10. 6⅜	¼ .. ⅝	
22..	11. 0½	½ .. ¾	
23..	11. 6½	¾ .. ⅞	
24..	12. 0½	6 .. 3	
25..	12. 6½	¼ .. ⅛	
26..	13. 0½	½ .. ¼	
27..	''. 6½	¾ .. ⅜	
28..	14. 0⅝	7 .. ½	
29..	14. 6⅝	¼ .. ⅝	
30..	15. 0⅝	½ .. ¾	
31..	15. 6⅝	¾ .. ⅞	
32..	16. 0⅝	8 .. 4	
33..	16. 6⅝	¼ .. ⅛	
34..	17. 0⅝	½ .. ¼	
35..	17. 6¾	¾ .. ⅜	
36..	18. 0¾	9 .. ½	
37..	18. 6¾	¼ .. ⅝	
38..	19. 0¾	½ .. ¾	
39..	19. 6¾	¾ .. ⅞	
40..	20. 0⅞	10 .. 5	
41..	20. 0⅞	¼ .. ⅛	
	. 0⅞	½ .. ¼	
	21. 6⅞	¾ .. ⅜	
	22. 0⅞	11 .. ½	
45..	22. 6⅞	¼ .. ⅝	
46..	23. 1	½ .. ¾	
47..	23. 7	¾ .. ⅞	
48..	24. 1	12 .. 6	
49..	24. 7		
50..	25. 1		

HIP OR VALLEY RAFTER

Span Ft.	Length Ft. In.	Span In.	Lgth In.
1..	. 8½	¼ .. ⅛	
2..	1. 5	½ .. ⅜	
3..	2. 1½	¾ .. ½	
4..	2.10	1 .. ¾	
5..	3. 6½	¼ .. ⅞	
6..	4. 3	½ ..1⅛	
7..	4.11½	¾ .. ¼	
8..	5. 8	2 .. ⅜	
9..	6. 4½	¼ .. ⅝	
10..	7. 1	½ .. ¾	
11..	7. 9½	¾ ..2	
12..	8. 6	3 .. ⅛	
13..	9. 2½	¼ .. ¼	
14..	9.11	½ .. ½	
15..	10. 7½	¾ .. ⅝	
16..	11. 4	4 .. ⅞	
17..	12. 0½	¼ ..3	
18..	12. 9	½ .. ⅛	
19..	13. 5½	¾ .. ⅜	
20..	14. 2	5 .. ½	
21..	14.10½	¼ .. ¾	
22..	15. 7	½ .. ⅞	
23..	16. 3½	¾ ..4⅛	
24..	17. 0	6 .. ¼	
25..	17. 8½	¼ .. ⅜	
26..	18. 5	½ .. ⅝	
27..	19. 1½	¾ .. ¾	
28..	19.10	7 ..5	
29..	20. 6½	¼ .. ⅛	
30..	21. 3	½ .. ¼	
31..	21.11½	¾ .. ⅜	
32..	22. 8	8 .. ⅝	
33..	23. 4½	¼ .. ⅞	
34..	24. 1	½ ..6	
35..	24. 9½	¾ .. ¼	
36..	25. 6	9 .. ⅜	
37..	26. 2½	¼ .. ½	
38..	26.11	½ .. ¾	
39..	27. 7½	¾ .. ⅞	
40..	28. 4	10 ..7⅛	
41..	29. 0½	¼ .. ¼	
42..	29. 9	½ .. ½	
43..	30. 5½	¾ .. ⅝	
44..	31. 2	11 .. ¾	
45..	31.10½	¼ ..8	
46..	32. 7	½ .. ⅛	
47..	33. 3½	¾ .. ⅜	
48..	34. 0	12 .. ½	
49..	34. 8½		
50..	35. 5		

JACK RAFTER

Spaced In.	Length Ft. In.
1..	1
2..	2
3..	3
4 .	4
5..	5
6..	6
7..	7
8..	8
9..	9⅛
10..	10⅛
11..	11⅛
12..1	0⅛
13..	1⅛
14..	2⅛
15..	3⅛
16..	4⅛
17..	5⅛
18..	6⅛
19..	7⅛
20..	8⅛
21..	9⅛
22..	10⅛
23..	11⅛
24..2	0⅛
25..	1¼
26..	2¼
27.	3¼
28 .	4¼
29..	5¼
30..	6¼
31..	7¼
32..	8¼
33..	9¼
34..	10¼
35..	11¼
36..3	0¼
37..	1¼
38..	2¼
39..	3¼
40..	4¼
41..	5⅜
42..	6⅜
43..	7⅜
44..	8⅜
45..	9⅜
46..	10⅜
47..	11⅜
48..4	0⅜

1½ & 12--7°

EXPLANATION

Common Rafter

Width of building...........28′8¼″
Find length of Common Rafter.

Answer:

Under **Span, ft.** find 28′ = 14′ 1¼″
" " **in.** " 8¼″ = 4⅛″

Total length Common Rft. 14′ 5⅜″

When rafters overhang, add both overhangs to width of building. Use total span as before.

To get length of rafter by its run: doubling the run gives the span. Proceed as before.

Tables give full length. Allow for half thickness of ridge.

Spans over 50′, as 60′, add lengths of 50′ & 10′ spans together.

Hip Rafter

If common rafter span is 28′8¼″, Hip rafter is 20′4⅜″ long. Measure length of Hip on center of top edge. If Hip is unbacked (top edge square), see Index. If edge is backed (beveled), see Index.

Allow for half thickness of ridge.

Jack Rafters

Spaced 30″ apart are 2′6¼″ different in length. Measure length on center of top edge. Cut short equal to half thickness of hip.

CUTS FOR STEEL SQUARE.

The first figure is always the cut.

Common Rafter

Plumb 1½- 12
Level. 12 - 1½

Hip Rafter

Plumb 1½- 17
Level. 17 - 1½
Side.. 8½- 8½
Backing 1½- 17

Set bevel to last named.

Jack Rafter

Plumb 1½- 12
Level. 12 - 1½
Side.. 12⅛- 12

Purlin Rafter Roof Sheathing

Plumb 1½- 12⅛
Cross. 12 - 12⅛

Valley Shingles

Cross. 12 - 12⅛

Set bevel on butt end.

Mitre-Box Cuts for Gable Moulds

Plumb 1½- 12
Mitre. 12⅛- 12

Bisection of

1½- 12=1½- 24

For full explanation see Index.

COMMON RAFTER

Span Ft.	Length Ft. In.	Span In.	Lgth. In.
1..	. 6	¼..	⅛
2..	1. 0⅛	½..	¼
3..	1. 6⅛	¾..	⅜
4..	2. 0⅛	1 ..	½
5..	2. 6¼	¼..	⅝
6..	3. 0¼	½..	¾
7..	3. 6⅜	¾..	⅞
8..	4. 0⅜	2 ..	1
9..	4. 6⅜	¼..	⅛
10..	5. 0½	½..	¼
11..	5. 6½	¾..	⅜
12..	6. 0½	3 ..	½
13..	6. 6⅝	¼..	⅝
14..	7. 0⅝	½..	¾
15..	7. 6¾	¾..	⅞
16..	8. 0¾	4 ..	2
17..	8. 6¾	¼..	⅛
18..	9. 0⅞	½..	¼
19..	9. 6⅞	¾..	⅜
20..	10. 0⅞	5 ..	½
21..	10. 7	¼..	⅝
22..	11. 1	½..	¾
23..	11. 7⅛	¾..	⅞
24..	12. 1⅛	6 ..	3
25..	12. 7⅛	¼..	⅛
26..	13. 1¼	½..	¼
27..	13. 7¼	¾..	⅜
28..	14. 1¼	7 ..	½
29..	14. 7⅜	¼..	⅝
30..	15. 1⅜	½..	¾
31..	15. 7½	¾..	⅞
32..	16. 1½	8 ..	4
33..	16. 7½	¼..	⅛
34..	17. 1⅝	½..	¼
35..	17. 7⅝	¾..	⅜
36..	18. 1⅝	9 ..	½
37..	18. 7¾	¼..	⅝
38..	19. 1¾	½..	¾
39..	19. 7⅞	¾..	⅞
40..	20. 1⅞	10 ..	5
41..	20. 7⅞	¼..	⅛
42..	21. 2	½..	¼
43..	21. 8	¾..	⅜
44..	22. 2	11 ..	½
45..	22. 8⅛	¼..	⅝
46..	23. 2⅛	½..	¾
47..	23. 8⅛	¾..	⅞
48..	24. 2¼	12 ..	6
49..	24. 8¼		
50..	25. 2⅜		

HIP OR VALLEY RAFTER

Span Ft.	Length Ft. In.	Span In.	Lgth. In.
1..	. 8½	¼..	⅛
2..	1. 5	½..	⅜
3..	2. 1½	¾..	½
4..	2. 10⅛	1 ..	¾
5..	3. 6⅝	¼..	⅞
6..	4. 3⅛	½..	1⅛
7..	4. 11⅝	¾..	¼
8..	5. 8⅛	2 ..	⅜
9..	6. 4⅝	¼..	⅝
10..	7. 1⅛	½..	¾
11..	7. 9¾	¾..	2
12..	8. 6¼	3 ..	⅛
13..	9. 2¾	¼..	¼
14..	9. 11¼	½..	½
15..	10. 7¾	¾..	⅝
16..	11. 4¼	4 ..	⅞
17..	12. 0¾	¼..	3
18..	12. 9⅜	½..	¼
19..	13. 5⅞	¾..	⅜
20..	14. 2⅜	5 ..	½
21..	14. 10⅞	¼..	¾
22..	15. 7⅜	½..	⅞
23..	16. 3⅞	¾	4⅛
24..	17. 0⅜	6 ..	¼
25..	17. 9	¼..	⅜
26..	18. 5½	½..	⅝
27..	19. 2	¾..	¾
28..	19. 10½	7 ..	5
29..	20. 7	¼..	⅛
30..	21. 3½	½..	⅜
31..	22. 0	¾..	½
32..	22. 8⅝	8 ..	⅝
33..	23. 5⅛	¼..	⅞
34..	24. 1⅝	½..	6
35..	24. 10⅛	¾..	¼
36..	25. 6⅝	9 ..	⅜
37..	26. 3⅛	¼..	⅝
38..	26. 11⅝	½..	¾
39..	27. 8¼	¾..	⅞
40..	28. 4¾	10 ..	7⅛
41..	29. 1¼	¼..	¼
42..	29. 9¾	½..	½
43..	30. 6¼	¾..	⅝
44..	31. 2¾	11 ..	¾
45..	31. 11¼	¼..	8
46..	32. 7⅞	½..	⅛
47..	33. 4⅜	¾..	⅜
48..	34. 0⅞	12 ..	½
49..	34. 9⅜		
50..	35. 5⅞		

JACK RAFTER	
Spaced	Length
In.	Ft. In.
1..	1
2..	2
3..	3
4..	4
5..	5⅛
6..	6⅛
7..	7⅛
8..	8⅛
9..	9⅛
10..	10⅛
11..	11⅛
12..1	0⅛
13..	1⅛
14..	2¼
15..	3¼
16..	4¼
17..	5¼
18..	6¼
19..	7¼
20..	8¼
21..	9¼
22..	10¼
23..	11⅜
24..2	0⅜
25..	1⅜
26..	2⅜
27..	3⅜
28..	4⅜
29..	5⅜
30..	6⅜
31..	7⅜
32..	8½
33..	9½
34..	10½
35..	11½
36..3	0½
37..	1½
38..	2½
39..	3½
40..	4½
41..	5⅝
42..	6⅝
43..	7⅝
44..	8⅝
45..	9⅝
46..	10⅝
47..	11⅝
48..4	0⅝

2 & 12 — 9½°

EXPLANATION
Common Rafter
Width of building..........36'9¾"
Find length of Common Rafter.

Answer:

Under **Span**, ft. find 36' = 18' 3"
    "   " in. " 9¾" = 5"

Total length Common Rft. 18' 8"

When rafters overhang, add both overhangs to width of building. Use total span as before.

To get length of rafter by its run: doubling the run gives the span. Proceed as before.

Tables give full length. Allow for half thickness of ridge.

Spans over 50', as 60', add lengths of 50' & 10' spans together.

Hip Rafter
If common rafter span is 36'9¾", Hip rafter is 26'2⅝" long. Measure length of Hip on center of top edge. If Hip is unbacked (top edge square), see Index. If edge is backed (beveled), see Index.

Allow for half thickness of ridge.

Jack Rafters
Spaced **33"** apart are **2'9½"** different in length. Measure length on center of top edge. Cut short equal to half thickness of hip.

CUTS FOR STEEL SQUARE.
The first figure is always the cut.

Common Rafter	Purlin Rafter
	Roof Sheathing
Plumb 2 - 12	
Level. 12 - 2	Plumb 2 - 12⅛
	Cross. 12 - 12⅛

Hip Rafter	Valley Shingles
Plumb 2 - 17	Cross. 12 - 12⅛
Level. 17 - 2	Set bevel on
Side.. 8½ - 8½	butt end.
Backing 2 - 17⅛	

Set bevel to last named.

	Mitre-Box Cuts
	for Gable Moulds
	Plumb 2 - 12
Jack Rafter	Mitre. 12⅛ - 12

Jack Rafter	
Plumb 2 - 12	**Bisection of**
Level. 12 - 2	2- 12=1⅞- 24
Side.. 12⅛ - 12	

For full explanation see Index.

COMMON RAFTER   HIP or VALLEY RAFTER

Span Ft.	Length Ft. In.	Span in.	Lgth. In.	Span Ft.	Length Ft. In.	Span In.	Lgth. In.
1	. 6⅛	¼	⅛	1	. 8½	¼	⅛
2	1. 0⅛	½	¼	2	1. 5⅛	½	⅜
3	1. 6¼	¾	⅜	3	2. 1⅝	¾	½
4	2. 0⅜	1	½	4	2.10⅛	1	¾
5	2. 6⅜	¼	⅝	5	3. 6¾	¼	⅞
6	3. 0½	½	¾	6	4. 3¼	½	1⅛
7	3. 6⅝	¾	⅞	7	4.11¾	¾	¼
8	4. 0⅝	2	1	8	5. 8⅜	2	⅜
9	4. 6¾	¼	⅛	9	6. 4⅞	¼	⅝
10	5. 0⅞	½	¼	10	7. 1½	½	¾
11	5. 6⅞	¾	⅜	11	7.10	¾	2
12	6. 1	3	½	12	8. 6½	3	⅛
13	6. 7⅛	¼	⅝	13	9. 3⅛	¼	⅜
14	7. 1⅛	½	¾	14	9.11⅝	½	½
15	7. 7¼	¾	⅞	15	10. 8⅛	¾	⅝
16	8. 1⅜	4	2	16	11. 4¾	4	⅞
17	8. 7⅜	¼	⅛	17	12. 1¼	¼	3
18	9. 1½	½	¼	18	12. 9¾	½	¼
19	9. 7⅝	¾	⅜	19	13. 6⅜	¾	⅜
20	10. 1⅝	5	½	20	14. 2⅞	5	½
21	10. 7¾	¼	⅝	21	14.11⅜	¼	¾
22	11. 1⅞	½	¾	22	15. 8	½	⅞
23	11. 7⅞	¾	⅞	23	16. 4½	¾	4⅛
24	12. 2	6	3	24	17. 1	6	¼
25	12. 8⅛	¼	⅛	25	17. 9⅝	¼	½
26	13. 2⅛	½	¼	26	18. 6⅛	½	⅝
27	13. 8¼	¾	⅜	27	19. 2¾	¾	¾
28	14. 2⅜	7	½	28	19.11¼	7	5
29	14. 8⅜	¼	⅝	29	20. 7¾	¼	⅛
30	15. 2½	½	¾	30	21. 4⅜	½	⅜
31	15. 8⅝	¾	⅞	31	22. 0⅞	¾	½
32	16. 2⅝	8	4	32	22. 9⅜	8	¾
33	16. 8¾	¼	⅛	33	23. 6	¼	⅞
34	17. 2⅞	½	¼	34	24. 2½	½	6
35	17. 8⅞	¾	½	35	24.11	¾	¼
36	18. 3	9	⅝	36	25. 7⅝	9	⅜
37	18. 9⅛	¼	¾	37	26. 4⅛	¼	⅝
38	19. 3⅛	½	⅞	38	27. 0⅝	½	¾
39	19. 9¼	¾	5	39	27. 9¼	¾	7
40	20. 3⅜	10	⅛	40	28. 5¾	10	⅛
41	20. 9⅜	¼	¼	41	29. 2¼	¼	¼
42	21. 3½	½	⅜	42	29.10⅞	½	½
43	21. 9½	¾	½	43	30. 7⅜	¾	⅝
44	22. 3⅝	11	⅝	44	31. 3⅞	11	⅞
45	22. 9¾	¼	¾	45	32. 0½	¼	8
46	23. 3¾	½	⅞	46	32. 9	½	¼
47	23. 9⅞	¾	6	47	33. 5⅝	¾	⅜
48	24. 4	12	⅛	48	34. 2⅛	12	½
49	24.10			49	34.10⅝		
50	25. 4⅛			50	35. 7¼		

27

Spaced In.	Length Ft. In.
1..	1
2..	2
3..	3⅛
4..	4⅛
5..	5⅛
6..	6⅛
7..	7⅛
8..	8⅛
9..	9¼
10..	10¼
11..	11¼
12..1	0¼
13..	1¼
14..	2¼
15..	3⅜
16..	4⅜
17..	5⅜
18..	6⅜
19..	7⅜
20..	8⅜
21..	9½
22..	10½
23..	11½
24..2	0½
25..	1½
26..	2½
27..	3⅝
28..	4⅝
29..	5⅝
30..	6⅝
31..	7⅝
32..	8⅝
33..	9¾
34..	10¾
35..	11¾
36 3..	0¾
37..	1¾
38..	2⅞
39..	3⅞
40..	4⅞
41..	5⅞
42..	6⅞
43..	7⅞
44..	9
45..	10
46..	11
47..4	0
48..	1

2½ & 12 — 11¾°

EXPLANATION

Common Rafter

Width of building..........32'7¾"
Find length of Common Rafter.
Answer:

Under **Span**, ft. find 32' = 16' 4⅛"
"   "   in. "   7¾" = 4"

Total length Common Rft. 16' 8⅛"

When rafters overhang, add both overhangs to width of building. Use total span as before.

To get length of rafter by its run: doubling the run gives the span. Proceed as before.

Tables give full length. Allow for half thickness of ridge.

Spans over 50', as 60', add lengths of 50' & 10' spans together.

Hip Rafter

If common rafter span is 32'7¾", Hip rafter is 23'4" long. Measure length of Hip on center of top edge. If Hip is unbacked (top edge square), see Index. If edge is backed (beveled), see Index.

Allow for half thickness of ridge.

Jack Rafters

Spaced 40" apart are 3'4⅞" different in length. Measure length on center of top edge. Cut short equal to half thickness of hip.

CUTS FOR STEEL SQUARE.

The first figure is always the cut

Common Rafter	Purlin Rafter Roof Sheathing
Plumb 2½- 12	
Level. 12 - 2½	Plumb 2½- 12¼
	Cross. 12 - 12¼

Hip Rafter	Valley Shingles
Plumb 2½- 17	
Level. 17 - 2½	Cross. 12 - 12¼
Side.. 8⅝- 8½	Set bevel on
Backing 2½- 17⅛	butt end.

Set bevel to last named.

Jack Rafter	Mitre-Box Cuts for Gable Moulds
	Plumb 2½- 12
Plumb 2½- 12	Mitre. 12¼- 12
Level. 12 - 2½	
Side.. 12¼- 12	**Bisection of**
	2½- 12=2⅜ - 24

For full explanation see Index.

28

COMMON RAFTER

Span Ft.	Length Ft. In.	Span In.	Lgth. In.
1	6⅛	¼	⅛
2	1. 0¼	½	¼
3	1. 6⅜	¾	⅜
4	2. 0½	1	½
5	2. 6⅝	¼	⅝
6	3. 0¾	½	¾
7	3. 6⅞	¾	⅞
8	4. 1	2	1
9	4. 7⅛	¼	⅛
10	5. 1¼	½	¼
11	5. 7⅜	¾	⅜
12	6. 1½	3	½
13	6. 7⅝	¼	⅝
14	7. 1¾	½	¾
15	7. 7⅞	¾	⅞
16	8. 2	4	2
17	8. 8¼	¼	⅛
18	9. 2⅜	½	¼
19	9. 8½	¾	⅜
20	10. 2⅝	5	½
21	10. 8¾	¼	⅝
22	11. 2⅞	½	¾
23	11. 9	¾	⅞
24	12. 3⅛	6	3
25	12. 9¼	¼	¼
26	13. 3⅜	½	⅜
27	13. 9½	¾	½
28	14. 3⅝	7	⅝
29	14. 9¾	¼	¾
30	15. 3⅞	½	⅞
31	15. 10	¾	4
32	16. 4⅛	8	⅛
33	16 10¼	¼	¼
34	17. 4⅜	½	⅜
35	17. 10½	¾	½
36	18. 4⅝	9	⅝
37	18. 10¾	¼	¾
38	19. 4⅞	½	⅞
39	19. 11	¾	5
40	20 5⅛	10	⅛
41	20 11¼	¼	¼
42	21. 5⅜	½	⅜
43	21 11½	¾	½
44	22. 5⅝	11	⅝
45	22 11¾	¼	¾
46	23 5⅞	½	⅞
47	24. 0	¾	6
48	24. 6⅛	12	⅛
49	25. 0¼		
50	25. 6½		

HIP OR VALLEY RAFTER

Span Ft.	Length Ft. In.	Span In.	Lgth. In.
1	8⅝	¼	⅛
2	1. 5⅛	½	⅜
3	2. 1¾	¾	½
4	2. 10¼	1	¾
5	3. 6⅞	¼	⅞
6	4. 3½	½	1⅛
7	5. 0	¾	¼
8	5. 8⅝	2	⅜
9	6. 5¼	¼	⅝
10	7. 1¾	½	¾
11	7. 10⅜	¾	2
12	8. 6⅞	3	⅛
13	9. 3½	¼	⅜
14	10. 0⅛	½	½
15	10. 8⅝	¾	⅝
16	11. 5¼	4	⅞
17	12. 1¾	¼	3
18	12. 10⅜	½	¼
19	13. 7	¾	⅜
20	14. 3½	5	⅝
21	15. 0⅛	¼	¾
22	15. 8¾	½	⅞
23	16. 5¼	¾	4⅛
24	17. 1⅞	6	¼
25	17. 10⅜	¼	½
26	18. 7	½	⅝
27	19. 3⅝	¾	⅞
28	20. 0⅛	7	5
29	20. 8¾	¼	⅛
30	21. 5¼	½	⅜
31	22. 1⅞	¾	½
32	22. 10½	8	¾
33	23. 7	¼	⅞
34	24. 3⅝	½	6⅛
35	25. 0¼	¾	¼
36	25. 8¾	9	⅜
37	26. 5⅜	¼	⅝
38	27. 1⅞	½	¾
39	27. 10½	¾	7
40	28. 7⅛	10	⅛
41	29. 3⅜	¼	⅜
42	30. 0¼	½	½
43	30. 8¾	¾	⅝
44	31. 5⅜	11	⅞
45	32. 2	¼	8
46	32. 10½	½	¼
47	33. 7⅛	¾	⅜
48	34. 3⅝	12	⅝
49	35. 0¼		
50	35. 8⅞		

Spaced In.	Length Ft. In.
1..	1
2..	2
3..	3⅛
4..	4⅛
5..	5⅛
6..	6⅛
7..	7¼
8..	8¼
9..	9¼
10..	10¼
11..	11⅜
12..1	0⅜
13..	1⅜
14..	2⅜
15..	3½
16..	4½
17..	5½
18..	6½
19..	7⅝
20..	8⅝
21..	9⅝
22..	10⅝
23..	11¾
24..2	0¾
25..	1¾
26..	2¾
27..	3⅞
28..	4⅞
29..	5⅞
30..	6⅞
31..	8
32..	9
33..	10
34..	11
35 3.	0⅛
36..	1⅛
37..	2⅛
38..	3⅛
39..	4¼
40..	5¼
41..	6¼
42..	7¼
43..	8⅜
44..	9⅜
45..	10⅜
46..	11⅜
47..4	0½
48..	1½

3 & 12 — 14°

EXPLANATION

Common Rafter

Width of building..........38'8¾"
Find length of Common Rafter.
Answer:

Under Span, ft. find	38'	= 19' 7"
" " in. "	8¾" =	4½"

Total length Common Rft. 19'11½"

When rafters overhang, add both overhangs to width of building. Use total span as before.
To get length of rafter by its run: doubling the run gives the span. Proceed as before.

Tables give full length. Allow for half thickness of ridge.

Spans over 50', as 60', add lengths of 50' & 10' spans together.

Hip Rafter

If common rafter span is 38'8¾", Hip rafter is 27'9¾" long. Measure length of Hip on center of top edge. If Hip is unbacked (top edge square), see Index. If edge is backed (beveled), see Index.

Allow for half thickness of ridge.

Jack Rafters

Spaced 38" apart are 3'3⅛" different in length. Measure length on center of top edge. Cut short equal to half thickness of hip.

CUTS FOR STEEL SQUARE.

The first figure is always the cut.

Common Rafter		Purlin Rafter Roof Sheathing	
Plumb 3 - 12			
Level. 12 - 3		Plumb 3 - 12⅜	
		Cross. 12 - 12⅜	

Hip Rafter	
Plumb 3 - 17	
Level. 17 - 3	
Side.. 8⅝- 8½	
Backing 3 - 17¼	
Set bevel to last named.	

Valley Shingles

Cross. 12 - 12⅜
Set bevel on butt end.

Mitre-Box Cuts for Gable Moulds

Plumb 3 - 12
Mitre. 12⅜- 12

Jack Rafter	
Plumb 3 - 12	
Level. 12 - 3	
Side.. 12⅜- 12	

Bisection of
3 - 12=2⅞- 24

COMMON RAFTER Span Ft.	Length Ft. In.	Span In.	Lgth. In.
1	. 6⅛	¼	⅛
2	1. 0⅜	½	¼
3	1. 6½	¾	⅜
4	2. 0¾	1	½
5	2. 6⅞	¼	⅝
6	3. 1⅛	½	¾
7	3. 7¼	¾	⅞
8	4. 1½	2	1
9	4. 7⅝	¼	⅛
10	5. 1⅞	½	¼
11	5. 8	¾	⅜
12	6. 2¼	3	½
13	6. 8⅜	¼	⅝
14	7. 2⅝	½	¾
15	7. 8¾	¾	⅞
16	8. 3	4	2
17	8. 9⅛	¼	¼
18	9. 3⅜	½	⅜
19	9. 9½	¾	½
20	10. 3¾	5	⅝
21	10. 9⅞	¼	¾
22	11. 4⅛	½	⅞
23	11. 10¼	¾	3
24	12. 4⅜	6	⅛
25	12. 10⅝	¼	¼
26	13. 4¾	½	⅜
27	13. 11	¾	½
28	14. 5⅛	7	⅝
29	14. 11⅜	¼	¾
30	15. 5½	½	⅞
31	15. 11¾	¾	4
32	16. 5⅞	8	⅛
33	17. 0⅛	¼	¼
34	17. 6¼	½	⅜
35	18. 0½	¾	½
36	18. 6⅝	9	⅝
37	19. 0⅞	¼	¾
38	19. 7	½	⅞
39	20. 1¼	¾	5
40	20. 7⅜	10	⅛
41	21. 1⅝	¼	¼
42	21. 7¾	½	⅜
43	22. 2	¾	½
44	22. 8⅛	11	⅝
45	23. 2¼	¼	¾
46	23. 8½	½	⅞
47	24. 2⅝	¾	6
48	24. 8⅞	12	⅛
49	25. 3		
50	25. 9¼		

HIP OR VALLEY RAFTER Span Ft.	Length Ft. In.	Span In.	Lgth. In.
1	. 8⅝	¼	⅛
2	1. 5¼	½	⅜
3	2. 1⅞	¾	½
4	2. 10½	1	¾
5	3. 7⅛	¼	⅞
6	4. 3¾	½	1⅛
7	5. 0⅜	¾	¼
8	5. 8⅞	2	⅜
9	6. 5½	¼	⅝
10	7. 2⅛	½	¾
11	7. 10¾	¾	2
12	8. 7⅜	3	⅛
13	9. 4	¼	⅜
14	10. 0⅝	½	½
15	10. 9¼	¾	¾
16	11. 5⅞	4	⅞
17	12. 2½	¼	3
18	12. 11⅛	½	¼
19	13. 7¾	¾	⅜
20	14. 4⅜	5	⅝
21	15. 1	¼	¾
22	15. 9⅝	½	4
23	16. 6¼	¾	⅛
24	17. 2¾	6	¼
25	17. 11⅜	¼	½
26	18 .8	½	⅝
27	19. 4⅝	¾	⅞
28	20. 1¼	7	5
29	20. 9⅞	¼	¼
30	21. 6½	½	⅜
31	22. 3⅛	¾	⅝
32	22. 11¾	8	¾
33	23. 8⅜	¼	⅞
34	24. 5	½	6⅛
35	25. 1⅝	¾	¼
36	25. 10¼	9	½
37	26. 6⅞	¼	⅝
38	27. 3½	½	⅞
39	28. 0	¾	7
40	28. 8⅝	10	⅛
41	2c 5¼	¼	⅜
42	30. 1⅞	½	½
43	30. 10½	¾	¾
44	31. 7⅛	11	⅞
45	32. 3¾	¼	8⅛
46	33. 0⅜	½	¼
47	33. 9	¾	⅜
48	34. 5⅝	12	⅝
49	35. 2¼		
50	35. 10⅞		

JACK RAFTER

Spaced In.	Length Ft.	In.
1.		1
2..		2⅛
3..		3⅛
4..		4⅛
5..		5¼
6..		6¼
7..		7¼
8..		8⅜
9..		9⅜
10..		10⅜
11..		11½
12..	1	0½
13..		1½
14..		2⅝
15..		3⅝
16..		4⅝
17..		5¾
18..		6¾
19..		7¾
20..		8⅞
21..		9⅞
22..		10⅞
23..	2	0
24..		1
25..		2
26..		3⅛
27..		4⅛
28..		5⅛
29..		6¼
30..		7¼
31..		8¼
32..		9⅜
33..		10⅜
34..		11⅜
35..	3	0½
36..		1½
37..		2½
38..		3⅝
39..		4⅝
40..		5⅝
41..		6¾
42..		7¾
43..		8¾
44..		9⅞
45..		10⅞
46..		11⅞
47..	4	1
48..		2

3½ & 12 — 16¼°

EXPLANATION

Common Rafter

Width of building...........32′8¼″
Find length of Common Rafter.

Answer:

Under **Span, ft.** find **32′** = 16′ 8″
" " **in.** " **8¼″** = 4¼″

Total length Common Rft. 17′ 0¼″

When rafters overhang, add both overhangs to width of building. Use total span as before.

To get length of rafter by its run: doubling the run gives the span. Proceed as before.

Tables give full length. Allow for half thickness of ridge.

Spans over 50′, as 60′, add lengths of 50′ & 10′ spans together.

Hip Rafter

If common rafter span is 32′8¼″, Hip rafter is 23′7¼″ long. Measure length of Hip on center of top edge. If Hip is unbacked (top edge square), see Index. If edge is backed (beveled), see Index.

Allow for half thickness of ridge.

Jack Rafters

Spaced 30″ apart are 2′7¼″ different in length. Measure length on center of top edge. Cut short equal to half thickness of hip.

CUTS FOR STEEL SQUARE.

The first figure is always the cut.

Common Rafter

Plumb 3½- 12
Level. 12 - 3½

Hip Rafter

Plumb 3½- 17
Level. 17 - 3½
Side.. 8⅝- 8½
Backing 3½- 17⅜
Set bevel to last named.

Jack Rafter

Plumb 3½- 12
Level. 12 - 3½
Side.. 12½- 12

Purlin Rafter Roof Sheathing

Plumb 3½- 12½
Cross. 12 - 12½

Valley Shingles

Cross. 12 - 12½
Set bevel on butt end.

Mitre-Box Cuts for Gable Moulds

Plumb 3½- 12
Mitre. 12½- 12

Bisection of
3½- 12=3⅜- 24

For full explanation see Index.

COMMON RAFTER

Span Ft.	Length Ft. In.	Span In.	Lgth. In.
1..	. 6¼	¼..	⅛
2..	1. 0½	½..	¼
3..	1. 6¾	¾..	⅜
4..	2. 1	1 ..	½
5..	2. 7¼	¼..	⅝
6..	3. 1½	½..	¾
7..	3. 7¾	¾..	⅞
8..	4. 2	2 ..	1
9..	4. 8¼	¼..	⅛
10..	5. 2½	½..	¼
11..	5. 8¾	¾..	⅜
12..	6. 3	3 ..	⅝
13..	6. 9¼	¼..	¾
14..	7. 3½	½..	⅞
15..	7. 9¾	¾..	2
16..	8. 4	4 ..	⅛
17..	8.10¼	¼..	¼
18..	9. 4½	½..	⅜
19..	9.10¾	¾..	½
20..	10. 5	5 ..	⅝
21..	10.11¼	¼..	¾
22..	11. 5½	½..	⅞
23..	11.11¾	¾..	3
24..	12. 6	6 ..	⅛
25..	13. 0¼	¼..	¼
26..	13. 6½	½..	⅜
27..	14. 0¾	¾..	½
28..	14. 7	7 ..	⅝
29..	15. 1¼	¼..	¾
30..	15. 7½	½..	⅞
31..	16. 1¾	¾..	4
32..	16. 8	8 ..	⅛
33..	17. 2¼	¼..	¼
34..	17. 8½	½..	⅜
35..	18. 2¾	¾..	½
36..	18. 9	9 ..	¾
37..	19. 3¼	¼..	⅞
38..	19. 9½	½..	5
39..	20. 3¾	¾..	⅛
40..	20.10	10 ..	¼
41..	21. 4¼	¼..	⅜
42..	21.10½	½..	½
43..	22. 4¾	¾..	⅝
44..	22.11	11 ..	¾
45..	23. 5¼	¼..	⅞
46..	23.11½	½..	6
47..	24. 5¾	¾..	⅛
48..	25. 0	12 ..	¼
49..	25. 6¼		
50..	26. 0½		

HIP or VALLEY RAFTER

Span Ft.	Length Ft. In.	Span In.	Lgth. In.
1..	. 8⅝	¼..	⅛
2..	1. 5⅜	½..	⅜
3..	2. 2	¾..	½
4..	2.10⅝	1 ..	¾
5..	3. 7⅜	¼..	⅞
6..	4. 4	½..	1⅛
7..	5. 0⅝	¾..	¼
8..	5. 9¼	2 ..	½
9..	6. 6	¼..	⅝
10..	7. 2⅝	½..	¾
11..	7.11¼	¾..	2
12..	8. 8	3 ..	⅛
13..	9. 4⅝	¼..	⅜
14..	10. 1¼	½..	½
15..	10.10	¾..	¾
16..	11. 6⅝	4 ..	⅞
17..	12. 3¼	¼..	3⅛
18..	13. 0	½..	¼
19..	13. 8⅝	¾..	⅜
20..	14. 5¼	5 ..	⅝
21..	15. 2	¼..	¾
22..	15.10⅝	½..	4
23..	16. 7¼	¾..	⅛
24..	17. 3⅞	6 ..	⅜
25..	18. 0⅝	¼..	½
26..	18. 9¼	½..	¾
27..	19. 5⅞	¾..	⅞
28..	20. 2⅝	7 ..	5
29..	20.11¼	¼..	¼
30..	21. 7⅞	½..	⅜
31..	22. 4⅝	¾..	⅝
32..	23. 1¼	8 ..	¾
33..	23. 9⅞	¼..	6
34..	24. 6⅝	½..	⅛
35..	25. 3¼	¾..	⅜
36..	25'11⅞	9 ..	½
37..	26. 8⅝	¼..	⅝
38..	27. 5¼	½..	⅞
39..	28. 1⅞	¾..	7
40..	28.10½	10 ..	¼
41..	29. 7¼	¼..	⅜
42..	30. 3⅞	½..	⅝
43..	31. 0½	¾..	¾
44..	31. 9¼	11 ..	8
45..	32. 5⅞	¼..	⅛
46..	33. 2½	½..	¼
47..	33.11¼	¾..	½
48..	34. 7⅞	12 ..	⅝
49..	35. 4½		
50..	36. 1¼		

JACK RAFTER Spaced In.	Length Ft. In.
1..	1
2..	2⅛
3..	3⅛
4..	4¼
5..	5¼
6..	6⅜
7..	7⅜
8..	8⅜
9..	9½
10..	10½
11..	11⅝
12..1	0⅝
13..	1¾
14..	2¾
15..	3¾
16..	4⅞
17..	5⅞
18..	7
19..	8
20..	9⅛
21..	10⅛
22..	11¼
23..2	0¼
24..	1¼
25..	2⅜
26..	3⅜
27..	4½
28..	5½
29..	6⅝
30..	7⅝
31..	8⅝
32..	9¾
33..	10¾
34..	11⅞
35..3	0⅞
36..	2
37..	3
38..	4
39..	5⅛
40..	6⅛
41..	7¼
42..	8¼
43..	9⅜
44..	10⅜
45..	11⅜
46..4	0½
47..	1½
48..	2⅝

4 & 12 — 18½°

EXPLANATION

Common Rafter

Width of building...........31′4¾″
Find length of Common Rafter.

Answer:

Under **Span, ft.** find **31′** = **16′ 4″**
" " **in.** " **4¾″** = **2½″**

Total length Common Rft. **16′ 6½″**

When rafters overhang, add both overhangs to width of building. Use total span as before.

To get length of rafter by its run: doubling the run gives the span. Proceed as before.

Tables give full length. Allow for half thickness of ridge.

Spans over 50′, as 60′, add lengths of 50′ & 10′ spans together.

Hip Rafter

If common rafter span is 31′4¾″, Hip rafter is 22′9¾″ long. Measure length of Hip on center of top edge. If Hip is unbacked (top edge square), see Index. If edge is backed (beveled), see Index.

Allow for half thickness of ridge.

Jack Rafters

Spaced 28″ apart are 2′5½″ different in length. Measure length on center of top edge. Cut short equal to half thickness of hip.

CUTS FOR STEEL SQUARE.

The first figure is always the cut.

Common Rafter

Plumb	4	- 12
Level.	12	4

Hip Rafter

Plumb	4	- 17
Level.	17	- 4
Side..	8¾	- 8½
Backing	4	- 17⅜

Set bevel to last named.

Jack Rafter

Plumb	4	- 12
Level.	12	4
Side..	12⅝	- 12

Purlin Rafter Roof Sheathing

Plumb	4	- 12⅝
Cross.	12	- 12⅝

Valley Shingles

Cross.	12	- 12⅝

Set bevel on butt end.

Mitre-Box Cuts for Gable Moulds

Plumb	4	- 12
Mitre.	12⅝	- 12

Bisection of
4- 12=3⅞- 24

For full explanation see Index.

COMMON RAFTER			
Span Ft.	Length Ft. In.	Span In.	Lgth. In.
1	. 6⅜	¼	⅛
2	1. 0⅝	½	¼
3	1. 7	¾	⅜
4	2. 1¼	1	½
5	2. 7⅝	¼	⅝
6	3. 2	½	¾
7	3. 8¼	¾	⅞
8	4. 2⅝	2	1
9	4. 8⅞	¼	⅛
10	5. 3¼	½	⅜
11	5. 9⅝	¾	½
12	6. 3⅞	3	⅝
13	6. 10¼	¼	¾
14	7. 4½	½	⅞
15	7. 10⅞	¾	2
16	8. 5¼	4	⅛
17	8. 11½	¼	¼
18	9. 5⅞	½	⅜
19	10. 0⅛	¾	½
20	10. 6½	5	⅝
21	11. 0⅞	¼	¾
22	11. 7⅛	½	⅞
23	12. 1½	¾	3
24	12. 7¾	6	⅛
25	13. 2⅛	¼	¼
26	13. 8½	½	⅜
27	14. 2¾	¾	½
28	14. 9⅛	7	¾
29	15. 3⅜	¼	⅞
30	15. 9¾	½	4
31	16. 4	¾	⅛
32	16. 10⅜	8	¼
33	17. 4¾	¼	⅜
34	17. 11	½	½
35	18. 5⅜	¾	⅝
36	18. 11⅝	9	¾
37	19. 6	¼	⅞
38	20. 0⅜	½	5
39	20. 6⅝	¾	⅛
40	21. 1	10	¼
41	21. 7¼	¼	⅜
42	22. 1⅝	½	½
43	22. 8	¾	⅝
44	23. 2¼	11	¾
45	23. 8⅝	¼	⅞
46	24. 3	½	6
47	24. 9¼	¾	¼
48	25. 3⅝	12	⅜
49	25. 9⅞		
50	26. 4¼		

HIP OR VALLEY RAFTER			
Span Ft.	Length Ft. In.	Span In.	Lgth. In.
1	. 8¾	¼	⅛
2	1. 5⅜	½	⅜
3	2. 2⅛	¾	½
4	2. 10⅞	1	¾
5	3. 7⅝	¼	⅞
6	4. 4¼	½	1⅛
7	5. 1	¾	¼
8	5. 9¾	2	½
9	6. 6½	¼	⅝
10	7. 3⅛	½	⅞
11	7. 11⅞	¾	2
12	8. 8⅝	3	⅛
13	9. 5⅜	¼	⅜
14	10. 2	½	½
15	10. 10¾	¾	¾
16	11. 7½	4	⅞
17	12. 4¼	¼	3⅛
18	13. 0⅞	½	¼
19	13. 9⅝	¾	½
20	14. 6⅜	5	⅝
21	15. 3⅛	¼	⅞
22	15. 11¾	½	4
23	16. 8½	¾	⅛
24	17. 5¼	6	⅜
25	18. 2	¼	½
26	18. 10⅝	½	¾
27	19. 7⅜	¾	⅞
28	20. 4⅛	7	5⅛
29	21. 0⅞	¼	¼
30	21. 9½	½	½
31	22. 6¼	¾	⅝
32	23. 3	8	¾
33	23. 11¾	¼	6
34	24. 8⅜	½	⅛
35	25. 5⅛	¾	⅜
36	26. 1⅞	9	½
37	26. 10½	¼	¾
38	27. 7¼	½	⅞
39	28. 4	¾	7⅛
40	29. 0¾	10	¼
41	29. 9⅜	¼	½
42	30. 6⅛	½	⅝
43	31. 2⅞	¾	¾
44	31. 11⅝	11	8
45	32. 8¼	¼	⅛
46	33. 5	½	⅜
47	34. 1¾	¾	½
48	34. 10½	12	¾
49	35. 7⅛		
50	36. 3⅞		

JACK RAFTER

Spaced In.	Length Ft.	In.
1..		1⅛
2..		2⅛
3..		3¼
4..		4¼
5..		5⅜
6..		6⅜
7..		7½
8..		8½
9..		9⅝
10..		10⅝
11..		11¾
12..	1	0⅞
13..		1⅞
14..		3
15..		4
16..		5⅛
17..		6⅛
18..		7¼
19..		8¼
20..		9⅜
21..		10⅜
22..		11½
23..	2	0⅝
24..		1⅝
25..		2¾
26..		3¾
27..		4⅞
28..		5⅞
29..		7
30..		8
31..		9⅛
32..		10⅛
33..		11¼
34	3	0⅜
35..		1⅜
36..		2½
37..		3½
38..		4⅝
39..		5⅝
40..		6¾
41..		7¾
42..		8⅞
43..		9⅞
44..		11
45..	4	0
46..		1⅛
47..		2¼
48..		3¼

4½ & 12 — 20½°

EXPLANATION

Common Rafter

Width of building...........27′5½″
Find length of Common Rafter.

Answer:

Under **Span, ft.** find 27′ = 14′ 5″
" " **in.** " 5½″ = 3″

Total length Common Rft. 14′ 8″

When rafters overhang, add both overhangs to width of building. Use total span as before.

To get length of rafter by its run: doubling the run gives the span. Proceed as before.

Tables give full length. Allow for half thickness of ridge.

Spans over 50′, as 60′, add lengths of 50′ & 10′ spans together.

Hip Rafter

If common rafter span is 27′5½″, Hip rafter is 20′1″ long. Measure length of Hip on center of top edge. If Hip is unbacked (top edge square), see Index. If edge is backed (beveled), see Index.

Allow for half thickness of ridge.

Jack Rafters

Spaced 35″ apart are 3′1⅜″ different in length. Measure length on center of top edge. Cut short equal to half thickness of hip.

CUTS FOR STEEL SQUARE.

The first figure is always the cut.

Common Rafter

Plumb 4½- 12
Level. 12 - 4½

Hip Rafter

Plumb 4½- 17
Level. 17 - 4½
Side.. 8¾- 8½
Backing 4½- 17½
Set bevel to last named.

Jack Rafter

Plumb 4½- 12
Level. 12 - 4½
Side.. 12⅞- 12

Purlin Rafter Roof Sheathing

Plumb 4½- 12⅞
Cross. 12 - 12⅞

Valley Shingles

Cross. 12 - 12⅞
Set bevel on butt end.

Mitre-Box Cuts for Gable Moulds

Plumb 4½- 12
Mitre. 12⅞- 12

Bisection of

4½- 12=4¼ - 24

For full explanation see Index.

COMMON RAFTER

Span Ft.	Length Ft. In.	Span In.	Lgth. In.
1	. 6⅜	¼	⅛
2	1. 0⅞	½	¼
3	1. 7¼	¾	⅜
4	2. 1⅝	1	½
5	2. 8	¼	⅝
6	3. 2½	½	¾
7	3. 8⅞	¾	⅞
8	4. 3¼	2	1⅛
9	4. 9⅝	¼	¼
10	5. 4⅛	½	⅜
11	5.10½	¾	½
12	6. 4⅞	3	⅝
13	6.11¼	¼	¾
14	7. 5¾	½	⅞
15	8. 0⅛	¾	2
16	8. 6½	4	⅛
17	9. 0⅞	¼	¼
18	9. 7⅜	½	⅜
19	10. 1¾	¾	½
20	10. 8⅛	5	⅝
21	11. 2⅝	¼	¾
22	11. 9	½	3
23	12. 3⅜	¾	⅛
24	12. 9¾	6	¼
25	13. 4¼	¼	⅜
26	13.10⅝	½	½
27	14. 5	¾	⅝
28	14.11⅜	7	¾
29	15. 5⅞	¼	⅞
30	16. 0¼	½	4
31	16. 6⅝	¾	⅛
32	17. 1	8	¼
33	17. 7½	¼	⅜
34	18. 1⅞	½	½
35	18. 8¼	¾	⅝
36	19. 2¾	9	¾
37	19. 9⅛	¼	5
38	20. 3½	½	⅛
39	20. 9⅞	¾	¼
40	21. 4⅜	10	⅜
41	21.10¾	¼	½
42	22. 5⅛	½	⅝
43	22.11½	¾	¾
44	23. 6	11	⅞
45	24. 0⅜	¼	6
46	24. 6¾	½	⅛
47	25. 1⅛	¾	¼
48	25. 7⅝	12	⅜
49	26. 2		
50	26. 8⅜		

HIP OR VALLEY RAFTER

Span Ft.	Length Ft. In.	Span In.	Lgth. In.
1	. 8¾	¼	⅛
2	1. 5½	½	⅜
3	2. 2⅜	¾	½
4	2.11⅛	1	¾
5	3. 7⅞	¼	⅞
6	4. 4⅝	½	1⅛
7	5. 1½	¾	¼
8	5.10¼	2	½
9	6. 7	¼	⅝
10	7. 3¾	½	⅞
11	8. 0⅝	¾	2
12	8. 9⅜	3	¼
13	9. 6⅛	¼	⅜
14	10. 2⅞	½	½
15	10.11⅝	¾	¾
16	11. 8½	4	⅞
17	12. 5¼	¼	3⅛
18	13. 2	½	¼
19	13.10¾	¾	½
20	14. 7⅝	5	⅝
21	15. 4⅜	¼	⅞
22	16. 1⅛	½	4
23	16. 9⅞	¾	¼
24	17. 6⅝	6	⅜
25	18. 3½	¼	⅝
26	19. 0¼	½	¾
27	19. 9	¾	⅞
28	20. 5¾	7	5⅛
29	21. 2⅝	¼	¼
30	21.11⅜	½	½
31	22. 8⅛	¾	⅝
32	23. 4⅞	8	⅞
33	24. 1¾	¼	6
34	24.10½	½	¼
35	25. 7¼	¾	⅜
36	26. 4	9	⅝
37	27. 0¾	¼	¾
38	27. 9⅝	½	7
39	28. 6⅜	¾	⅛
40	29. 3⅛	10	⅜
41	29.11⅞	¼	½
42	30. 8¾	½	⅝
43	31. 5½	¾	⅞
44	32. 2¼	11	8
45	32.11	¼	¼
46	33. 7¾	½	⅜
47	34. 4⅝	¾	⅝
48	35. 1⅜	12	¾
49	35.10⅛		
50	36. 6⅞		

5 & 12 — 22½°

EXPLANATION

Common Rafter

Width of building..........26' 5½"
Find length of Common Rafter.

Answer:

Under Span, ft. find	26'	= 14' 1"
" " in. "	5½" =	3"

Total length Common Rft. 14' 4"

When rafters overhang, add both overhangs to width of building. Use total span as before.

To get length of rafter by its run: doubling the run gives the span. Proceed as before.

Tables give full length. Allow for half thickness of ridge.

Spans over 50', as 60', add lengths of 50' & 10' spans together.

Hip Rafter

If common rafter span is 26'5½", Hip rafter is 19'6" long. Measure length of Hip on center of top edge. If Hip is unbacked (top edge square), see Index. If edge is backed (beveled), see Index.

Allow for half thickness of ridge.

Jack Rafters

Spaced 37" apart are 3'4⅛" different in length. Measure length on center of top edge. Cut short equal to half thickness of hip.

CUTS FOR STEEL SQUARE.

The first figure is always the cut.

Common Rafter		Purlin Rafter Roof Sheathing
Plumb 5 - 12		
Level. 12 - 5		Plumb 5 - 13
		Cross. 12 - 13

Hip Rafter		Valley Shingles
Plumb 5 - 17		
Level. 17 - 5		Cross. 12 - 13
Side.. 8⅞- 8½		Set bevel on
Backing 5 - 17¾		butt end.
Set bevel to		Mitre-Box Cuts
last named.		for Gable Moulds
		Plumb 5 - 12
Jack Rafter		Mitre. 13 - 12
Plumb 5 - 12		
Level. 12 - 5		Bisection of
Side.. 13 - 12		5- 12=47⅝- 24

For full explanation see Index.

COMMON RAFTER				HIP or VALLEY RAFTER			
Span Ft.	Length Ft. In.	Span In.	Lgth. In.	Span Ft.	Length Ft. In.	Span In.	Lgth. In.
1..	.6½	¼..	⅛	1..	.8⅞	¼..	⅛
2..	1. 1	½..	¼	2..	1. 5¾	½..	⅜
3..	1. 7½	¾..	⅜	3..	2. 2½	¾..	½
4..	2. 2	1 ..	½	4..	2.11⅜	1 ..	¾
5..	2. 8½	¼..	⅝	5..	3. 8¼	¼..	⅞
6..	3. 3	½..	⅞	6..	4. 5⅛	½..	1⅛
7..	3. 9½	¾..	1	7..	5. 1⅞	¾..	¼
8..	4. 4	2 ..	⅛	8..	5.10¾	2 ..	½
9..	4.10½	¼..	¼	9..	6. 7⅝	¼..	⅝
10..	5. 5	½..	⅜	10..	7. 4½	½..	⅞
11..	5.11½	¾..	½	11..	8. 1¼	¾..	2
12..	6. 6	3 ..	⅝	12..	8.10⅛	3 ..	¼
13..	7. 0½	¼..	¾	13..	9. 7	¼..	⅜
14..	7. 7	½..	⅞	14..	10. 3⅞	½..	⅝
15..	8. 1½	¾..	2	15..	11. 0¾	¾..	¾
16..	8. 8	4 ..	⅛	16..	11. 9½	4 ..	3
17..	9. 2½	¼..	¼	17..	12. 6⅜	¼..	⅛
18..	9. 9	½..	½	18..	13. 3¼	½..	⅜
19..	10. 3½	¾..	⅝	19..	14. 0⅛	¾..	½
20..	10.10	5 ..	¾	20..	14. 8⅞	5 ..	⅝
21..	11. 4½	¼..	⅞	21..	15. 5¾	¼..	⅞
22..	11.11	½..	3	22..	16. 2⅝	½..	4
23..	12. 5½	¾..	⅛	23..	16.11½	¾..	¼
24..	13. 0	6 ..	¼	24..	17. 8¼	6 ..	⅜
25..	13. 6½	¼..	⅜	25..	18. 5⅛	¼..	⅝
26..	14. 1	½..	½	26..	19. 2	½..	¾
27..	14. 7½	¾..	⅝	27..	19.10⅞	¾..	5
28..	15. 2	7 ..	¾	28..	20. 7⅝	7 ..	⅛
29..	15. 8½	¼..	⅞	29..	21. 4½	¼..	⅜
30..	16. 3	½..	4½	30..	22. 1⅜	½..	½
31..	16. 9½	¾..	¼	31..	22.10¼	¾..	¾
32..	17. 4	8 ..	⅜	32..	23. 7⅛	8 ..	⅞
33..	17.10½	¼..	½	33..	24. 3⅞	¼..	6⅛
34..	18. 5	½..	⅝	34..	25. 0¾	½..	¼
35..	18.11½	¾..	¾	35..	25. 9⅝	¾..	½
36..	19. 6	9 ..	⅞	36..	26. 6½	9 ..	⅝
37..	20. 0½	¼..	5	37..	27. 3¼	¼..	⅞
38..	20. 7	½..	⅛	38..	28. 0⅛	½..	7
39..	21. 1½	¾..	¼	39..	28. 9	¾..	⅛
40..	21. 8	10 ..	⅜	40..	29. 5⅞	10 ..	⅜
41..	22. 2½	¼..	½	41..	30. 2⅝	¼..	½
42..	22. 9	½..	⅝	42..	30.11½	½..	¾
43..	23. 3½	¾..	⅞	43..	31. 8⅜	¾..	⅞
44..	23.10	11 ..	6	44..	32. 5¼	11 ..	8⅛
45..	24. 4½	¼..	⅛	45..	33. 2⅛	¼..	¼
46..	24.11	½..	¼	46..	33.10⅞	½..	½
47..	25. 5½	¾..	⅜	47..	34. 7¾	¾..	⅝
48..	26. 0	12 ..	½	48..	35. 4⅝	12 ..	⅞
49..	26. 6½			49..	36. 1½		
50..	27. 1			50..	36.10¼		

JACK RAFTER Spaced In.	Length Ft. In.
1..	1⅛
2..	2¼
3..	3¼
4..	4⅜
5..	5½
6..	6⅝
7..	7¾
8..	8¾
9..	9⅞
10..	11
11	1..0⅛
12..	1¼
13..	2¼
14..	3⅜
15..	4½
16..	5⅝
17..	6¾
18..	7¾
19..	8⅞
20..	10
21..	11⅛
22..2	0¼
23..	1¼
24..	2⅜
25..	3½
26..	4⅝
27..	5¾
28..	6¾
29..	7⅞
30..	9
31..	10⅛
32..	11¼
33..3	0¼
34..	1⅜
35..	2½
36..	3⅝
37..	4¾
38..	5¾
39..	6⅞
40..	8
41..	9⅛
42..	10¼
43..	11¼
44..4	0⅜
45..	1½
46..	2⅝
47..	3¾
48..	4¾

5½ & 12—24½°

EXPLANATION

Common Rafter

Width of building...........25′7¼″
Find length of Common Rafter.

Answer:

Under **Span, ft.** find **25′** = 13′ 9″
" " **in.** " **7¼″** = 4″

Total length Common Rft. 14′ 1″

When rafters overhang, add both overhangs to width of building. Use total span as before.

To get length of rafter by its run: doubling the run gives the span. Proceed as before.

Tables give full length. Allow for half thickness of ridge.

Spans over 50′, as 60′, add lengths of 50′ & 10′ spans together.

Hip Rafter

If common rafter span is 25′7¼″, Hip rafter is 19′0⅜″ long. Measure length of Hip on center of top edge. If Hip is unbacked (top edge square), see Index. If edge is backed (beveled), see Index.

Allow for half thickness of ridge.

Jack Rafters

Spaced 20′ apart are 1′10″ different in length. Measure length on center of top edge. Cut short equal to half thickness of hip.

CUTS FOR STEEL SQUARE.

The first figure is always the cut.

Common Rafter

Plumb 5½- 12
Level. 12 - 5½

Hip Rafter

Plumb 5½- 17
Level. 17 - 5½
Side.. 8⅞- 8½
Backing 5½- 17⅞
Set bevel to last named.

Jack Rafter

Plumb 5½- 12
Level. 12 - 5½
Side.. 13¼- 12

Purlin Rafter Roof Sheathing

Plumb 5½- 13¼
Cross. 12 - 13¼

Valley Shingles

Cross. 12 - 13¼
Set bevel on butt end.

Mitre-Box Cuts for Gable Moulds

Plumb 5½- 12
Mitre. 13¼- 12

Bisection of

5½- 12=5¼- 24

For full explanation see Index.

COMMON RAFTER

Span Ft.	Length Ft. In.	Span In.	Lgth. In.
1..	6⅝	¼..	⅛
2..	1. 1¼	½..	¼
3..	1. 7¾	¾..	⅜
4..	2. 2⅜	1 ..	½
5..	2. 9	¼..	¾
6..	3. 3⅝	½..	⅞
7..	3. 10¼	¾..	1
8..	4. 4¾	2 ..	⅛
9..	4. 11⅜	¼..	¼
10..	5. 6	½..	⅜
11..	6. 0⅝	¾..	½
12..	6. 7¼	3 ..	⅝
13..	7. 1¾	¼..	¾
14..	7. 8⅜	½..	⅞
15..	8. 3	¾..	2
16..	8. 9⅝	4 ..	¼
17..	9. 4¼	¼..	⅜
18..	9. 10¾	½..	½
19..	10. 5⅜	¾..	⅝
20..	11. 0	5 ..	¾
21..	11. 6⅝	¼..	⅞
22..	12. 1¼	½..	3
23..	12. 7¾	¾..	⅛
24..	13. 2⅜	6 ..	¼
25..	13. 9	¼..	⅜
26..	14. 3⅝	½..	⅝
27..	14. 10¼	¾..	¾
28..	15. 4¾	7 ..	⅞
29..	15. 11⅜	¼..	4
30..	16. 6	½..	⅛
31..	17. 0⅝	¾..	¼
32..	17. 7¼	8 ..	⅜
33..	18. 1¾	¼..	½
34..	18. 8⅜	½..	⅝
35..	19. 3	¾..	¾
36..	19. 9⅝	9 ..	5
37..	20. 4¼	¼..	⅛
38..	20. 10¾	½..	¼
39..	21. 5⅜	¾..	⅜
40..	22. 0	10 ..	½
41..	22. 6⅝	¼..	⅝
42..	23. 1¼	½..	¾
43..	23. 7¾	¾..	⅞
44..	24. 2⅜	11 ..	6
45..	24. 9	¼..	⅛
46..	25. 3⅝	½..	⅜
47..	25. 10¼	¾..	½
48..	26. 4¾	12 ..	⅝
49..	26. 11⅜		
50..	27. 6		

HIP or VALLEY RAFTER

Span Ft.	Length Ft. In.	Span In.	Lgth. In.
1..	8⅞	¼..	⅛
2..	1. 5⅞	½..	⅜
3..	2. 2¾	¾..	½
4..	2.11⅝	1 ..	¾
5..	3. 8⅝	¼..	⅞
6..	4. 5½	½..	1⅛
7..	5. 2½	¾..	¼
8..	5. 11⅜	2 ..	½
9..	6. 8¼	¼..	⅝
10..	7. 5¼	½..	⅞
11..	8. 2⅛	¾..	2
12..	8.11	3 ..	¼
13..	9. 8	¼..	⅜
14..	10. 4⅞	½..	⅝
15..	11. 1¾	¾..	¾
16..	11.10¾	4 ..	3
17..	12. 7⅝	¼..	⅛
18..	13. 4½	½..	⅜
19..	14. 1½	¾..	½
20..	14.10⅜	5 ..	¾
21..	15. 7⅜	¼..	⅞
22..	16. 4¼	½..	4⅛
23..	17. 1⅛	¾..	¼
24..	17.10⅛	6 ..	½
25..	18. 7	¼..	⅝
26..	19. 3⅞	½..	⅞
27..	20. 0⅞	¾..	5
28..	20. 9¾	7 ..	¼
29..	21. 6⅝	¼..	⅜
30..	22. 3⅝	½..	⅝
31..	23. 0½	¾..	¾
32..	23. 9⅜	8 ..	6
33..	24. 6⅜	¼..	⅛
34..	25. 3¼	½..	⅜
35..	26. 0¼	¾..	½
36..	26. 9⅛	9 ..	¾
37..	27. 6	¼..	⅞
38..	28. 3	½..	7
39..	28.11⅞	¾..	¼
40..	29. 8¾	10 ..	⅜
41..	30. 5¾	¼..	⅝
42..	31. 2⅝	½..	¾
43..	31.11½	¾..	8
44..	32. 8½	11 ..	⅛
45..	33. 5⅜	¼..	⅜
46..	34. 2¼	½..	½
47..	34.11¼	¾..	¾
48..	35. 8⅛	12 ..	⅞
49..	36. 5⅛		
50..	37. 2		

JACK RAFTER

Spaced In.	Length Ft.	In.
1..		1⅛
2..		2¼
3..		3⅜
4..		4½
5..		5⅝
6..		6¾
7..		7⅞
8..		9
9..		10⅛
10..		11⅛
11..	1	0¼
12..		1⅜
13..		2½
14..		3⅝
15..		4¾
16..		5⅞
17..		7
18..		8⅛
19..		9¼
20..		10⅜
21..		11½
22	2..	0⅝
23..		1¾
24..		2⅞
25..		4
26..		5⅛
27..		6⅛
28..		7¼
29..		8⅜
30..		9½
31..		10⅝
32..		11¾
33	3..	0⅞
34..		2
35..		3⅛
36..		4¼
37..		5⅜
38..		6½
39..		7⅝
40..		8¾
41..		9⅞
42..		11
43	4..	0⅛
44..		1¼
45..		2¼
46..		3⅜
47..		4½
48..		5⅝

6 & 12 — 26½°

EXPLANATION

Common Rafter

Width of building...........24′6¼″
Find length of Common Rafter.

Answer:

Under **Span, ft.** find 24′ = 13′ 5″
" " **in.** " 6¼″ = 3½″

Total length Common Rft. 13′ 8½″

When rafters overhang, add both overhangs to width of building. Use total span as before.

To get length of rafter by its run: doubling the run gives the span. Proceed as before.

Tables give full length. Allow for half thickness of ridge.

Spans over 50′, as 60′, add lengths of 50′ & 10′ spans together.

Hip Rafter

If common rafter span is 24′6¼″, Hip rafter is 18′4⅝″ long. Measure length of Hip on center of top edge. If Hip is unbacked (top edge square), see Index. If edge is backed (beveled), see Index.

Allow for half thickness of ridge.

Jack Rafters

Spaced 24″ apart are 2′2⅞″ different in length. Measure length on center of top edge. Cut snort equal to half thickness of hip.

CUTS FOR STEEL SQUARE.

The first figure is always the cut.

Common Rafter

Plumb 6 - 12
Level. 12 - 6

Hip Rafter

Plumb 6 - 17
Level. 17 - 6
Side.. 9 - 8½
Backing 6 - 18
Set bevel to last named.

Jack Rafter

Plumb 6 - 12
Level. 12 - 6
Side.. 13⅜- 12

Purlin Rafter Roof Sheathing

Plumb 6 - 13⅜
Cross. 12 - 13⅜

Valley Shingles

Cross. 12 - 13⅜
Set bevel on butt end.

Mitre-Box Cuts for Gable Moulds

Plumb 6 - 12
Mitre. 13⅜- 12

Bisection of
6- 12=5⅝- 24

For full explanation see **Index.**

COMMON RAFTER

Span Ft.	Length Ft.	Length In.	Span In.	Lgth. In.
1		6¾	¼	⅛
2	1	1⅜	½	¼
3	1	8⅛	¾	⅜
4	2	2⅞	1	½
5	2	9½	¼	¾
6	3	4¼	½	⅞
7	3	11	¾	1
8	4	5⅝	2	⅛
9	5	0⅜	¼	¼
10	5	7⅛	½	⅜
11	6	1¾	¾	½
12	6	8½	3	⅝
13	7	3¼	¼	⅞
14	7	9⅞	½	2
15	8	4⅝	¾	⅛
16	8	11⅜	4	¼
17	9	6	¼	⅜
18	10	0¾	½	½
19	10	7½	¾	⅝
20	11	2⅛	5	¾
21	11	8⅞	¼	⅞
22	12	3⅝	½	3⅛
23	12	10¼	¾	¼
24	13	5	6	⅜
25	13	11¾	¼	½
26	14	6⅜	½	⅝
27	15	1⅛	¾	¾
28	15	7⅞	7	⅞
29	16	2½	¼	4
30	16	9¼	½	¼
31	17	4	¾	⅜
32	17	10⅝	8	½
33	18	5⅜	¼	⅝
34	19	0⅛	½	¾
35	19	6¾	¾	⅞
36	20	1½	9	5
37	20	8¼	¼	⅛
38	21	2⅞	½	¼
39	21	9⅝	¾	½
40	22	4⅜	10	⅝
41	22	11	¼	¾
42	23	5¾	½	⅞
43	24	0½	¾	6
44	24	7⅛	11	⅛
45	25	1⅞	¼	¼
46	25	8⅝	½	⅜
47	26	3¼	¾	½
48	26	10	12	¾
49	27	4¾		
50	27	11⅜		

HIP OR VALLEY RAFTER

Span Ft.	Length Ft.	Length In.	Span In.	Lgth. In.
1		9	¼	¼
2	1	6	½	⅜
3	2	3	¾	⅝
4	3	0	1	¾
5	3	9	¼	1
6	4	6	½	⅛
7	5	3	¾	¼
8	6	0	2	½
9	6	9	¼	⅝
10	7	6	½	⅞
11	8	3	¾	2
12	9	0	3	¼
13	9	9	¼	⅜
14	10	6	½	⅝
15	11	3	¾	¾
16	12	0	4	3
17	12	9	¼	⅛
18	13	6	½	⅜
19	14	3	¾	½
20	15	0	5	¾
21	15	9	¼	⅞
22	16	6	½	4⅛
23	17	3	¾	¼
24	18	0	6	½
25	18	9	¼	⅝
26	19	6	½	⅞
27	20	3	¾	5
28	21	0	7	¼
29	21	9	¼	⅜
30	22	6	½	⅝
31	23	3	¾	¾
32	24	0	8	6
33	24	9	¼	⅛
34	25	6	½	⅜
35	26	3	¾	½
36	27	0	9	¾
37	27	9	¼	⅞
38	28	6	½	7⅛
39	29	3	¾	¼
40	30	0	10	½
41	30	9	¼	⅝
42	31	6	½	⅞
43	32	3	¾	8
44	33	0	11	¼
45	33	9	¼	⅜
46	34	6	½	⅝
47	35	3	¾	¾
48	36	0	12	9
49	36	9		
50	37	6		

Spaced In.	Length Ft. In.
1..	1⅛
2..	2¼
3..	3⅜
4..	4½
5..	5⅝
6..	6⅞
7..	8
8..	9⅛
9..	10¼
10..	11⅜
11..1	0½
12..	1⅝
13..	2¾
14..	3⅞
15..	5
16..	6¼
17..	7⅜
18..	8½
19..	9⅝
20..	10¾
21..	11⅞
22..2	1
23..	2⅛
24..	3¼
25..	4⅜
26..	5⅝
27..	6¾
28..	7⅞
29..	9
30..	10⅛
31..	11¼
32..3	0⅜
33..	1½
34..	2⅝
35..	3¾
36..	4⅞
37..	6⅛
38..	7¼
39..	8⅜
40..	9½
41..	10⅝
42..	11¾
43..4	0⅞
44..	2
45..	3⅛
46..	4¼
47..	5½
48..	6⅝

6½ & 12 — 28¼°

EXPLANATION

Common Rafter

Width of building...........23′5¼″
Find length of Common Rafter.
Answer:
Under Span, ft. find 23′ = 13′ 1″
" " in. " 5¼″ = 3″

Total length Common Rft. 13′ 4″

When rafters overhang, add both overhangs to width of building. Use total span as before.

To get length of rafter by its run: doubling the run gives the span. Proceed as before.

Tables give full length. Allow for half thickness of ridge.

Spans over 50′, as 60′, add lengths of 50′ & 10′ spans together.

Hip Rafter

If common rafter span is 23′5¼″, Hip rafter is 17′9″ long. Measure length of Hip on center of top edge. If Hip is unbacked (top edge square), see Index. If edge is backed (beveled), see Index.

Allow for half thickness of ridge.

Jack Rafters

Spaced 22″ apart are 2′1″ different in length. Measure length on center of top edge. Cut short equal to half thickness of hip.

CUTS FOR STEEL SQUARE.

The first figure is always the cut.

Common Rafter	Purlin Rafter Roof Sheathing
Plumb 6½- 12	Plumb 6½- 13⅝
Level. 12 - 6½	Cross. 12 - 13⅝

Hip Rafter	Valley Shingles
Plumb 6½- 17	Cross. 12 - 13⅝
Level. 17 - 6½	Set bevel on
Side.. 9⅛- 8½	butt end.
Backing 18⅛- 18½	
Set bevel to	Mitre-Box Cuts
last named.	for Gable Moulds
	Plumb 6½- 12
Jack Rafter	Mitre. 13⅝- 12
Plumb 6½- 12	
Level. 12 - 6½	Bisection of
Side.. 13⅝- 12	6½· 12=6 - 24

For full explanation see Index.

44

COMMON RAFTER

Span Ft.	Length Ft. In.	Span In.	Lgth. In.
1..	. 6⅞	¼..	⅛
2..	1. 1⅝	½..	¼
3..	1. 8½	¾..	⅜
4..	2. 3¼	1 ..	⅝
5..	2.10⅛	¼..	¾
6..	3. 5	½..	⅞
7..	3.11¾	¾..	1
8..	4. 6⅝	2 ..	⅛
9..	5. 1⅜	¼..	¼
10..	5. 8¼	½..	⅜
11..	6. 3	¾..	⅝
12..	6. 9⅞	3 ..	¾
13..	7. 4¾	¼..	⅞
14..	7.11½	½..	2
15..	8. 6⅜	¾..	⅛
16..	9. 1⅛	4 ..	¼
17..	9. 8	¼..	⅜
18..	10. 2⅞	½..	½
19..	10. 9⅝	¾..	¾
20..	11. 4½	5 ..	⅞
21..	11.11¼	¼..	3
22..	12. 6⅛	½..	⅛
23..	13. 1	¾..	¼
24..	13. 7¾	6 ..	⅜
25..	14. 2⅝	¼..	½
26..	14. 9⅜	½..	¾
27..	15. 4¼	¾..	⅞
28..	15.11	7 ..	4
29..	16. 5⅞	¼..	⅛
30..	17. 0¾	½..	¼
31..	17. 7½	¾..	⅜
32..	18. 2⅜	8 ..	½
33..	18. 9⅛	¼..	⅝
34..	19. 4	½..	⅞
35..	19.10⅞	¾..	5
36..	20. 5⅝	9 ..	⅛
37..	21. 0½	¼..	¼
38..	21. 7¼	½..	⅜
39..	22. 2⅛	¾..	½
40..	22. 9	10 ..	⅝
41..	23. 3¾	¼..	⅞
42..	23.10⅝	½..	6
43..	24. 5⅜	¾..	⅛
44..	25. 0¼	11 ..	¼
45..	25. 7⅛	¼..	⅜
46..	26. 1⅞	½..	½
47..	26. 8¾	¾..	⅝
48..	27. 3½	12 ..	⅞
49..	27.10⅜		
50..	28. 5⅛		

HIP OR VALLEY RAFTER

Span Ft.	Length Ft. In.	Span In.	Lgth. In.
1..	. 9⅛	¼..	¼
2..	1. 6⅛	½..	⅜
3..	2. 3¼	¾..	⅝
4..	3. 0⅜	1 ..	¾
5..	3. 9⅜	¼..	1
6..	4. 6½	½..	⅛
7..	5. 3⅝	¾..	⅜
8..	6. 0¾	2 ..	½
9..	6. 9¾	¼..	¾
10..	7. 6⅞	½..	⅞
11..	8. 4	¾..	2⅛
12..	9. 1	3 ..	¼
13..	9.10⅛	¼..	½
14..	10. 7¼	½..	⅝
15..	11. 4¼	¾..	⅞
16..	12. 1⅜	4 ..	3
17..	12.10½	¼..	¼
18..	13. 7½	½..	⅜
19..	14. 4⅝	¾..	⅝
20..	15. 1¾	5 ..	¾
21..	15.10¾	¼..	4
22..	16. 7⅞	½..	⅛
23..	17. 5	¾..	⅜
24..	18. 2⅛	6 ..	½
25..	18.11⅛	¼..	¾
26..	19. 8¼	½..	⅞
27..	20. 5⅜	¾..	5⅛
28..	21. 2⅜	7 ..	¼
29..	21.11½	¼..	½
30..	22. 8⅝	½..	⅝
31..	23. 5⅝	¾..	⅞
32..	24. 2¾	8 ..	6
33..	24.11⅞	¼..	¼
34..	25. 8⅞	½..	⅜
35..	26. 6	¾..	⅝
36..	27. 3⅛	9 ..	¾
37..	28. 0⅛	¼..	7
38..	28. 9¼	½..	⅛
39..	29. 6⅜	¾..	⅜
40..	30. 3½	10 ..	½
41..	31. 0½	¼..	¾
42..	31. 9⅝	½..	8
43..	32. 6¾	¾..	⅛
44..	33. 3¾	11 ..	⅜
45..	34. 0⅞	¼..	½
46..	34.10	½..	¾
47..	35. 7	¾..	⅞
48..	36. 4⅛	12 ..	9⅛
49..	37. 1¼		
50..	37.10¼		

Spaced In.	Length Ft. In.
1..	1⅛
2..	2⅜
3..	3½
4..	4⅝
5..	5¾
6..	7
7..	8⅛
8..	9¼
9..	10⅜
10..	11⅝
11..1	0¾
12..	1⅞
13..	3
14..	4¼
15..	5⅜
16..	6½
17..	7⅝
18..	8⅞
19..	10
20..	11⅛
21..2	0¼
22..	1½
23..	2⅝
24..	3¾
25..	5
26..	6⅛
27..	7¼
28..	8⅜
29..	9⅝
30..	10¾
31..	11⅞
32..3	1
33..	2¼
34..	3⅜
35..	4½
36..	5⅝
37..	6⅞
38..	8
39..	9⅛
40..	10¼
41..	11½
42..4	0⅝
43..	1¾
44..	3
45..	4⅛
46..	5¼
47..	6⅜
48..	7⅝

7 & $12 - 30\frac{1}{4}°$

EXPLANATION

Common Rafter

Width of building..........19'5¼"
Find length of Common Rafter.
Answer:

Under Span, ft. find	19	= 11' 0"
" " In. "	5¼" =	3"

Total length Common Rft. 11' 3"

When rafters overhang, add both overhangs to width of building. Use total span as before.

To get length of rafter by its run: doubling the run gives the span. Proceed as before.

Tables give full length. Allow for half thickness of ridge.

Spans over 50', as 60', add lengths of 50' & 10' spans together.

Hip Rafter

If common rafter span is 19'5¼", Hip rafter is 14'10⅜" long. Measure length of Hip on top edge. If Hip is unbacked (top edge square), see Index. If edge is backed (beveled), see Index.

Allow for half thickness of ridge.

Jack Rafters

Spaced 28" apart are 2'8⅜" different in length. Measure length on center of top edge. Cut short equal to half thickness of hip.

CUTS FOR STEEL SQUARE.

The first figure is always the cut.

Common Rafter		Purlin Rafter Roof Sheathing	
Plumb	7 - 12		
Level.	12 - 7	Plumb 7 - 13⅞	
		Cross. 12 - 13⅞	

Hip Rafter		Valley Shingles	
Plumb	7 - 17	Cross. 12 - 13⅞	
Level.	17 - 7		
Side..	9⅛- 8½	Set bevel on butt end.	
Backing 7 - 18⅜			
Set bevel to last named.		Mitre-Box-Cut for Gable Mould₃	

Jack Rafter		Plumb 7 - 12	
Plumb	7 - 12	Mitre. 13⅞- 12	
Level.	12 - 7	**Bisection of**	
Side..	13⅞- 12	7- 12=6½- 24	

For full explanation see Index.

46

COMMON RAFTER				HIP or VALLEY RAFTER			
Span Ft.	Length Ft. In.	Span In.	Lgth. In.	Span Ft.	Length Ft. In.	Span In.	Lgth. In.
1..	. 7	¼ ..	⅛	1..	. 9⅛	¼ ..	¼
2..	I. 1⅞	½ ..	¼	2..	I. 6⅜	½ ..	⅜
3..	I. 8⅞	¾ ..	⅜	3..	2. 3½	¾ ..	⅝
4..	2. 3¾	1 ..	⅝	4..	3. 0⅝	1 ..	¾
5..	2.10¾	¼ ..	¾	5..	3. 9⅞	¼ ..	I
6..	3. 5⅝	½ ..	⅞	6..	4.. 7⅛	½ ..	⅛
7..	4. 0⅝	¾ ..	1	7..	5. 4¼	¾ ..	⅜
8..	4. 7⅝	2 ..	⅛	8..	6. 1⅜	2 ..	½
9..	5. 2½	¼ ..	¼	9..	6.10⅝	¼ ..	¾
10..	5. 9½	½ ..	½	10..	7. 7¾	½ ..	⅞
11..	6. 4⅜	¾ ..	⅝	11..	8. 5	¾ ..	2⅛
12..	6.11⅜	3 ..	¾	12..	9. 2⅛	3 ..	¼
13..	7. 6¼	¼ ..	⅞	13..	9.11⅜	¼ ..	½
14..	8. 1¼	½ ..	2	14..	10. 8½	½ ..	⅝
15..	8. 8¼	¾ ..	⅛	15..	11. 5⅝	¾ ..	⅞
16..	9. 3⅛	4 ..	⅜	16..	12. 2⅞	4 ..	3
17..	9.10⅛	¼ ..	½	17..	13. 0	¼ ..	¼
18..	10. 5	½ ..	⅝	18..	13. 9¼	½ ..	½
19..	11. 0	¾ ..	¾	19..	14. 6⅜	¾ ..	⅝
20..	11. 6⅞	5 ..	⅞	20..	15. 3⅝	5 ..	⅞
21..	12. 1⅞	¼ ..	3	21..	16. 0¾	¼ ..	4
22..	12. 8⅞	½ ..	⅛	22..	16. 9⅞	½ ..	⅛
23..	13. 3¾	¾ ..	⅜	23..	17. 7⅛	¾ ..	⅜
24..	13.10¾	6 ..	½	24..	18. 4¼	6 ..	⅝
25..	14. 5⅝	¼ ..	⅝	25..	19. 1½	¼ ..	¾
26..	15. 0⅝	½ ..	¾	26..	19.10⅝	½ ..	5
27..	15. 7½	¾ ..	⅞	27..	20. 7⅞	¾ ..	⅛
28..	16. 2½	7 ..	4	28..	21. 5	7 ..	⅜
29..	16. 9⅜	¼ ..	⅛	29..	22. 2⅛	¼ ..	½
30..	17. 4⅜	½ ..	¼	30..	22.11⅜	½ ..	¾
31..	17.11⅜	¾ ..	½	31..	23. 8½	¾ ..	⅞
32..	18. 6¼	8 ..	⅝	32..	24. 5¾	8 ..	6⅛
33..	19. 1¼	¼ ..	¾	33..	25. 2⅞	¼ ..	¼
34..	19. 8¼	½ ..	⅞	34..	26. 0	½ ..	½
35..	20. 3⅛	¾ ..	5	35..	26. 9¼	¾ ..	¾
36..	20.10	9 ..	¼	36..	27. 6⅜	9..	.⅞
37..	21. 5	¼ ..	⅜	37..	28. 3⅝	¼ ..	7⅛
38..	22. 0	½ ..	½	38..	29. 0¾	½ ..	¼
39..	22. 6⅞	¾ ..	⅝	39..	29.10	¾ ..	½
40..	23. 1⅞	10 ..	¾	40..	30. 7⅛	10 ..	⅝
41..	23. 8¾	¼ ..	⅞	41..	31. 4⅜	¼ ..	⅞
42..	24. 3¾	½ ..	6⅛	42..	32. 1½	½ ..	8
43..	24.10⅝	¾ ..	¼	43..	32.10⅝	¾ ..	¼
44..	25. 5⅝	11 ..	⅜	44..	33. 7⅞	11 ..	⅜
45..	26. 0⅝	¼ ..	½	45..	34. 5	¼ ..	⅝
46..	26. 7½	½ ..	⅝	46..	35. 2¼	½ ..	¾
47..	27. 2½	¾ ..	¾	47..	35.11⅜	¾ ..	9
48..	27. 9⅜	12 ..	⅞	48..	36. 8⅝	12 ..	⅛
49..	28. 4⅜			49..	37. 5¾		
50..	28.11¼			50..	38. 2⅞		

Spaced In.	Length Ft. In.
1..	1⅛
2..	2⅜
3..	3½
4..	4¾
5..	5⅞
6..	7⅛
7..	8¼
8..	9⅜
9..	10⅝
10..	11¾
11..1	1
12..	2⅛
13..	3⅜
14..	4½
15..	5⅝
16..	6⅞
17..	8
18..	9¼
19..	10⅜
20..	11⅝
21..2	0¾
22..	2
23..	3⅛
24..	4¼
25..	5½
26..	6⅝
27..	7⅞
28..	9
29..	10¼
30..	11⅜
31..3	0½
32..	1¾
33..	2⅞
34..	4⅛
35..	5¼
36..	6½
37..	7⅝
38..	8¾
39..	10
40..	11⅛
41..4	0⅜
42..	1½
43..	2¾
44..	3⅞
45..	5
46..	6¼
47..	7⅜
48..	8⅝

7½ & 12 — 32°

EXPLANATION

Common Rafter

Width of building..........27'1¼"
Find length of Common Rafter.
Answer:
Under **Span**, ft. find 27' = 15'11"
"   "   in. "   1¼" = 0¾"

Total length Common Rft. 15'11¾"

When rafters overhang, add both overhangs to width of building. Use total span as before.
To get length of rafter by its run: doubling the run gives the span. Proceed as before.
Tables give full length. Allow for half thickness of ridge.
Spans over 50', as 60', add lengths of 50' & 10' spans together.

Hip Rafter

If common rafter span is 27'1¼", Hip rafter is 20'11½" long. Measure length of Hip on center of top edge. If Hip is unbacked (top edge square), see Index. If edge is backed (beveled), see Index.
Allow for half thickness of ridge.

Jack Rafters

Spaced 26" apart are 2'6⅝" different in length. Measure length on center of top edge. Cut short equal to half thickness of hip.

CUTS FOR STEEL SQUARE.

The first figure is always the cut.

Common Rafter	Purlin Rafter Roof Sheathing
Plumb 7½- 12	Plumb 7½- 14⅛
Level. 12 - 7½	Cross. 12 - 14⅛

Hip Rafter	Valley Shingles
Plumb 7½- 17	Cross. 12 - 14⅛
Level. 17 - 7½	Set bevel on
Side.. 9¼- 8½	butt end.
Backing 7½- 18½	
Set bevel to last named.	Mitre-Box Cuts for Gable Moulds

Jack Rafter	Plumb 7½- 12
	Mitre. 14⅛- 12
Plumb 7½- 12	Bisection of
Level. 12 - 7½	7½- 12=6⅞- 24
Side.. 14⅛- 12	

For full explanation see Index.

48

COMMON RAFTER

Span Ft.	Length Ft. In.	Span In.	Lgth. In.
1	7⅛	¼	⅛
2	1. 2⅛	½	¼
3	1. 9¼	¾	½
4	2. 4¼	1	⅝
5	2. 11⅜	¼	¾
6	3. 6½	½	⅞
7	4. 1½	¾	1
8	4. 8⅝	2	⅛
9	5. 3⅝	¼	⅜
10	5. 10¾	½	½
11	6. 5⅞	¾	⅝
12	7. 0⅞	3	¾
13	7. 8	¼	⅞
14	8. 3	½	2⅛
15	8. 10⅛	¾	¼
16	9. 5¼	4	⅜
17	10. 0¼	¼	½
18	10. 7⅜	½	⅝
19	11. 2⅜	¾	¾
20	11. 9½	5	3
21	12. 4⅝	¼	⅛
22	12. 11⅝	½	¼
23	13. 6¾	¾	⅜
24	14. 1¾	6	½
25	14. 8⅞	¼	⅝
26	15. 4	½	⅞
27	15. 11	¾	4
28	16. 6⅛	7	⅛
29	17. 1⅛	¼	¼
30	17. 8¼	½	⅜
31	18. 3⅜	¾	⅝
32	18. 10⅜	8	¾
33	19. 5½	¼	⅞
34	20. 0⅝	½	5
35	20. 7⅝	¾	⅛
36	21. 2¾	9	¼
37	21. 9¾	¼	½
38	22. 4⅞	½	⅝
39	23. 0	¾	¾
40	23. 7	10	⅞
41	24. 2⅛	¼	6
42	24. 9⅛	½	⅛
43	25. 4¼	¾	⅜
44	25. 11⅜	11	½
45	26. 6⅜	¼	⅝
46	27. 1½	½	¾
47	27. 8½	¾	⅞
48	28. 3⅝	12	7⅛
49	28. 10⅝		
50	29. 5¾		

HIP OR VALLEY RAFTER

Span Ft.	Length Ft. In.	Span In.	Lgth. In.
1	9¼	¼	¼
2	1. 6½	½	⅜
3	2. 3⅞	¾	⅝
4	3. 1⅛	1	¾
5	3. 10⅜	¼	1
6	4. 7⅝	½	⅛
7	5. 5	¾	⅜
8	6. 2¼	2	½
9	6. 11½	¼	¾
10	7. 8¾	½	⅞
11	8. 6	¾	2⅛
12	9. 3⅜	3	⅜
13	10. 0⅝	¼	½
14	10. 9⅞	½	¾
15	11. 7⅛	¾	⅞
16	12. 4⅜	4	3⅛
17	13. 1¾	¼	¼
18	13. 11	½	½
19	14. 8¼	¾	⅝
20	15. 5½	5	⅞
21	16. 2⅞	¼	4
22	17. 0⅛	½	¼
23	17. 9⅜	¾	½
24	18. 6⅝	6	⅝
25	19. 3⅞	¼	⅞
26	20. 1¼	½	5
27	20. 10½	¾	¼
28	21. 7¾	7	⅜
29	22. 5	¼	⅝
30	23. 2¼	½	¾
31	23. 11⅝	¾	6
32	24. 8⅞	8	⅛
33	25. 6⅛	¼	⅜
34	26. 3⅜	½	⅝
35	27. 0¾	¾	¾
36	27. 10	9	7
37	28. 7¼	¼	⅛
38	29. 4½	½	⅜
39	30. 1¾	¾	½
40	30. 11⅛	10	¾
41	31. 8⅜	¼	⅞
42	32. 5⅝	½	8⅛
43	33. 2⅞	¾	¼
44	34. 0⅛	11	½
45	34. 9½	¼	¾
46	35. 6¾	½	⅞
47	36. 4	¾	9⅛
48	37. 1¼	12	¼
49	37. 10⅝		
50	38. 7⅞		

Spaced In.	Length Ft. In.
1..	1¼
2..	2⅜
3..	3⅝
4..	4¾
5..	6
6..	7¼
7..	8⅜
8..	9⅝
9..	10⅞
10..1	0
11..	1¼
12..	2⅜
13..	3⅝
14..	4⅞
15..	6
16..	7¼
17..	8⅜
18..	9⅝
19..	10⅞
20..2	0
21..	1¼
22..	2½
23..	3⅝
24..	4⅞
25..	6
26..	7¼
27..	8½
28..	9⅝
29..	10⅞
30..3	0
31..	1¼
32..	2½
33..	3⅝
34..	4⅞
35..	6⅛
36..	7¼
37..	8½
38..	9⅝
39..	10⅞
40..4	0⅛
41..	1¼
42..	2½
43..	3⅝
44..	4⅞
45..	6⅛
46..	7¼
47..	8½
48..	9⅝

8 & 12 — 33¾°

EXPLANATION

Common Rafter

Width of building..........38'3¼"
Find length of Common Rafter.
Answer:

Under Span, ft. find 38'	= 22'10"
" " in. " 3¼" =	2"

Total length Common Rft. 23' 0"

When rafters overhang, add both overhangs to width of building. Use total span as before.

To get length of rafter by its run: doubling the run gives the span. Proceed as before.

Tables give full length. Allow for half thickness of ridge.

Spans over 50', as 60', add lengths of 50' & 10' spans together.

Hip Rafter

If common rafter span is 38'3¼", Hip rafter is 29'11" long. Measure length of Hip on center of top edge. If Hip is unbacked (top edge square), see Index. If edge is backed (beveled), see Index.

Allow for half thickness of ridge.

Jack Rafters

Spaced 32" apart are 3'2½" different in length. Measure length on center of top edge. Cut short equal to half thickness of hip.

CUTS FOR STEEL SQUARE.

The first figure is always the cut.

Common Rafter		Purlin Rafter Roof Sheathing	
Plumb	8 - 12		
Level.	12 - 8	Plumb 8 - 14⅜	
		Cross. 12 - 14⅜	

Hip Rafter		Valley Shingles	
Plumb	8 - 17	Cross. 12 - 14⅜	
Level.	17 - 8	Set bevel on	
Side..	9⅜- 8½	butt end.	
Backing 8 - 18¾			

Set bevel to last named.

Jack Rafter		Mitre-Box Cuts for Gable Moulds	
Plumb	8 - 12	Plumb 8 - 12	
Level.	12 - 8	Mitre. 14⅜- 12	
Side..	14⅜- 12		

Bisection of
8- 12=7¼- 24

For full explanation see Index.

COMMON RAFTER				HIP or VALLEY RAFTER			
Span Ft.	Length Ft. In.	Span In.	Lgth. In.	Span Ft.	Length Ft. In.	Span In.	Lgth. In.
1..	7¼	¼..	⅛	1..	9⅜	¼..	¼
2..	1. 2⅜	½..	¼	2..	1. 6¾	½..	⅜
3..	1. 9⅝	¾..	½	3..	2. 4⅛	¾..	⅝
4..	2. 4⅞	1 ..	⅝	4..	3. 1½	1 ..	¾
5..	3. 0	¼..	¾	5..	3.10⅞	¼..	1
6..	3. 7¼	½..	⅞	6..	4. 8¼	½..	⅛
7..	4. 2½	¾..	1	7..	5. 5⅝	¾..	⅜
8..	4. 9¾	2 ..	¼	8..	6. 3	2 ..	⅝
9..	5. 4⅞	¼..	⅜	9..	7. 0⅜	¼..	¾
10..	6. 0⅛	½..	½	10..	7. 9¾	½..	2
11..	6. 7⅜	¾..	⅝	11..	8. 7¼	¾..	⅛
12..	7. 2½	3 ..	¾	12..	9. 4⅝	3 ..	⅜
13..	7. 9¾	¼..	2	13..10. 2		¼..	½
14..	8. 5	½..	⅛	14..10.11⅜		½..	¾
15..	9. 0⅛	¾..	¼	15..11. 8¾		¾..	⅞
16..	9. 7⅜	4 ..	⅜	16..12. 6⅛		4 ..	3⅛
17..10. 2⅝		¼..	½	17..13. 3½		¼..	⅜
18 .10. 9¾		½..	¾	18..14. 0⅞		½..	½
19..11. 5		¾..	⅞	19..14.10¼		¾..	¾
20..12. 0⅛		5 ..	3	20..15. 7⅝		5 ..	⅞
21..12. 7½		¼..	⅛	21..16. 5		¼..	4⅛
22..13. 2⅝		½..	¼	22..17. 2⅜		½..	¼
23..13. 9⅞		¾..	½	23..17.11¾		¾..	½
24..14. 5⅛		6 ..	⅝	24..18. 9⅛		6 ..	¾
25..15. 0⅛		¼..	¾	25..19. 6⅛		¼..	⅞
26..15. 7½		½..	⅞	26..20. 3⅞		½..	5⅛
27..16. 2¾		¾..	4	27..21. 1¼		¾..	¼
28..16. 9⅞		7 ..	¼	28..21.10⅝		7 ..	½
29..17. 5⅛		¼..	⅜	29..22. 8		¼..	⅝
30..18. 0⅜		½..	½	30..23. 5⅜		½..	⅞
31..18. 7½		¾..	⅝	31..24. 2¾		¾..	6
32..19. 2¾		8 ..	¾	32..25. 0⅛		8 ..	¼
33..19.10		¼..	5	33..25. 9⅝		¼..	½
34..20. 5⅛		½..	⅛	34..26. 7		½..	⅝
35..21. 0⅜		¾..	¼	35..27. 4⅜		¾..	⅞
36..21. 7⅝		9 ..	⅜	36..28. 1¾		9 ..	7
37..22. 2¾		¼..	½	37..28.11⅛		¼..	¼
38..22.10		½..	¾	38..29. 8½		½..	⅜
39..23. 5¼		¾..	⅞	39..30. 5⅞		¾..	⅝
40..24. 0½		10 ..	6	40..31. 3¼		10 ..	⅞
41..24. 7⅝		¼..	⅛	41..32. 0⅝		¼..	8
42..25. 2⅞		½..	¼	42..32.10		½..	¼
43..25.10⅛		¾..	½	43..33. 7⅜		¾..	⅜
44..26. 5¼		11 ..	⅝	44..34. 4¾		11 ..	⅝
45..27. 0⅛		¼..	¾	45..35. 2⅛		¼..	¾
46..27. 7¾		½..	⅞	46..35.11½		½..	9
47..28. 2⅞		¾..	7	47..36. 8⅞		¾..	⅛
48..28.10⅛		12 ..	¼	48..37. 6¼		12 ..	⅜
49..29. 5⅜				49..38. 3⅝			
50..30. 0½				50..39 1			

JACK RAFTER

Spaced In.	Length Ft.	In.
1..		1¼
2..		2½
3..		3⅝
4..		4⅞
5..		6⅛
6..		7⅜
7..		8⅝
8..		9¾
9..		11
10..	1	0¼
11..		1½
12..		2¾
13..		3⅞
14..		5⅛
15..		6⅜
16..		7⅝
17..		8⅞
18..		10
19..		11¼
20..	2	0½
21..		1¾
22..		3
23..		4⅛
24..		5⅜
25..		6⅝
26..		7⅞
27..		9⅛
28..		10¼
29..		11½
30..	3	0¾
31..		2
32..		3¼
33..		4½
34..		5⅝
35..		6⅞
36..		8⅛
37..		9⅜
38..		10⅝
39..		11¾
40..	4	1
41..		2¼
42..		3½
43..		4¾
44..		5⅞
45..		7⅛
46..		8⅜
47..		9⅝
48..		10⅞

8½ & 12 — 35¼°

EXPLANATION

Common Rafter

Width of building...........34′6½″
Find length of Common Rafter.

Answer:

Under **Span, ft.** find **34′** = 20′10″
" " **in.** " 6½″ = 4″

Total length Common Rft. 21′ 2″

When rafters overhang, add both overhangs to width of building. Use total span as before.

To get length of rafter by its run: doubling the run gives the span. Proceed as before.

Tables give full length. Allow for half thickness of ridge.

Spans over 50′, as 60′, add lengths of 50′ & 10′ spans together.

Hip Rafter

If common rafter span is 34′6½″, Hip rafter is 27′3¾″ long. Measure length of Hip on center of top edge. If Hip is unbacked (top edge square), see Index. If edge is backed (beveled), see Index.

Allow for half thickness of ridge.

Jack Rafters

Spaced 38″ apart are 3′10⅝″ different in length. Measure length on center of top edge. Cut short equal to half thickness of hip.

CUTS FOR STEEL SQUARE.

The first figure is always the cut.

Common Rafter

Plumb 8½- 12
Level. 12 - 8½

Hip Rafter

Plumb 8½- 17
Level. 17 - 8½
Side.. 9½- 8½
Backing 8½- 19
Set bevel to last named.

Jack Rafter

Plumb 8½- 12
Level. 12 - 8½
Side.. 14¾- 12

Purlin Rafter Roof Sheathing

Plumb 8½- 14¾
Cross. 12 - 14¾

Valley Shingles

Cross. 12 - 14¾
Set bevel on butt end.

Mitre-Box Cuts for Gable Moulds

Plumb 8½- 12
Mitre. 14¾- 12

Bisection of

8½- 12=7½- 24

For full explanation see Index.

COMMON RAFTER

Span Ft.	Length Ft. In.	Span In.	Lgth. In.
1	. 7⅜	¼	⅛
2	1. 2¾	½	¼
3	1.10	¾	½
4	2. 5⅜	1	⅝
5	3. 0¾	¼	¾
6	3. 8⅛	½	⅞
7	4. 3½	¾	1⅛
8	4.10⅞	2	¼
9	5. 6⅛	¼	⅜
10	6. 1½	½	½
11	6. 8⅞	¾	¾
12	7. 4¼	3	⅞
13	7.11⅝	¼	2
14	8. 7	½	⅛
15	9. 2¼	¾	¼
16	9. 9⅝	4	½
17	10. 5	¼	⅝
18	11. 0⅜	½	¾
19	11. 7¾	¾	⅞
20	12. 3	5	3
21	12.10⅜	¼	¼
22	13. 5¾	½	⅜
23	14. 1⅛	¾	½
24	14. 8½	6	⅝
25	15. 3⅞	¼	⅞
26	15.11⅛	½	4
27	16. 6½	¾	⅛
28	17. 1⅞	7	¼
29	17. 9¼	¼	½
30	18. 4⅝	½	⅝
31	18.11⅞	¾	¾
32	19. 7¼	8	⅞
33	20. 2⅝	¼	5
34	20.10	½	¼
35	21. 5⅜	¾	⅜
36	22. 0¾	9	½
37	22. 8	¼	⅝
38	23. 3⅜	½	⅞
39	23.10¾	¾	6
40	24. 6⅛	10	⅛
41	25. 1½	¼	¼
42	25. 8⅞	½	⅜
43	26. 4⅛	¾	⅝
44	26.11½	11	¾
45	27. 6⅞	¼	⅞
46	28. 2¼	½	7
47	28. 9⅝	¾	¼
48	29. 5	12	⅜
49	30. 0¼		
50	30. 7⅝		

HIP OR VALLEY RAFTER

Span Ft.	Length Ft. In.	Span In.	Lgth. In.
1	. 9½	¼	¼
2	1. 7	½	⅜
3	2. 4½	¾	⅝
4	3. 2	1	¾
5	3.11½	¼	1
6	4. 9	½	⅛
7	5. 6½	¾	⅜
8	6. 3⅞	2	⅝
9	7. 1⅜	¼	¾
10	7.10⅞	½	2
11	8. 8⅜	¾	⅛
12	9. 5⅞	3	⅜
13	10. 3⅜	¼	⅝
14	11. 0⅞	½	¾
15	11.10⅜	¾	3
16	12. 7⅞	4	⅛
17	13. 5⅜	¼	⅜
18	14. 2⅞	½	½
19	15. 0⅜	¾	¾
20	15. 9¾	5	4
21	16. 7¼	¼	⅛
22	17. 4¾	½	⅜
23	18. 2¼	¾	½
24	18.11¾	6	¾
25	19. 9¼	¼	5
26	20. 6¾	½	⅛
27	21. 4¼	¾	⅜
28	22. 1¾	7	½
29	22.11¼	¼	¾
30	23. 8¾	½	⅞
31	24. 6¼	¾	6⅛
32	25. 3⅝	8	⅜
33	26. 1⅛	¼	½
34	26.10⅝	½	¾
35	27. 8⅛	¾	⅞
36	28. 5⅝	9	7⅛
37	29. 3⅛	¼	¼
38	30. 0⅝	½	½
39	30.10⅛	¾	¾
40	31. 7⅝	10	⅞
41	32. 5⅛	¼	8⅛
42	33. 2⅝	½	¼
43	34. 0⅛	¾	½
44	34. 9½	11	¾
45	35. 7	¼	⅞
46	36. 4½	½	9⅛
47	37. 2	¾	¼
48	37.11½	12	½
49	38. 9		
50	39. 6½		

Spaced In.	Length Ft. In.
1..	1¼
2..	2½
3..	3¾
4..	5
5..	6¼
6..	7½
7..	8¾
8..	10
9..	11¼
10..1	0½
11..	1¾
12..	3
13..	4¼
14..	5½
15..	6¾
16..	8
17..	9¼
18..	10½
19..	11¾
20..2	1
21..	2¼
22..	3½
23..	4¾
24..	6
25..	7¼
26..	8½
27..	9¾
28..	11
29..3	0¼
30..	1½
31..	2¾
32..	4
33..	5¼
34..	6½
35..	7¾
36..	9
37..	10¼
38..	11½
39..4	0¾
40..	2
41..	3¼
42..	4½
43..	5¾
44..	7
45..	8¼
46..	9½
47..	10¾
48..5	0

9 & 12 — 37°

EXPLANATION

Common Rafter

Width of building..........24′6½″
Find length of Common Rafter.
Answer:

Under **Span**, ft. find	24′	= 15′ 0″
" " in. "	6½″ =	4″

Total length Common Rft. 15′ 4″

When rafters overhang, add both overhangs to width of building. Use total span as before.

To get length of rafter by its run: doubling the run gives the span. Proceed as before.

Tables give full length. Allow for half thickness of ridge.

Spans over 50′, as 60′, add lengths of 50′ & 10′ spans together.

Hip Rafter

If common rafter span is 24′6½″, Hip rafter is 19′7¾″ long. Measure length of Hip on center of top edge. If Hip is unbacked (top edge square), see Index. If edge is backed (beveled), see Index.

Allow for half thickness of ridge.

Jack Rafters

Spaced 32″ apart are 3′4″ different in length. Measure length on center of top edge. Cut short equal to half thickness of hip.

CUTS FOR STEEL SQUARE.

The first figure is always the cut.

Common Rafter		Purlin Rafter Roof Sheathing	
Plumb	9 - 12		
Level.	12 - 9	Plumb	9 - 15
		Cross.	12 - 15

Hip Rafter		Valley Shingles	
Plumb	9 - 17	Cross.	12 - 15
Level.	17 - 9	Set bevel on
Side..	9⅝- 8½	butt end.
Backing 2 - 19¼		
Set bevel to		Mitre-Box Cuts
last named.		for Gable Moulds

		Plumb	9 - 12
Jack Rafter		Mitre.	15 - 12
Plumb	9 - 12		
Level.	12 - 9	Bisection of	
Side..	15 - 12	9- 12=7⅞- 24	

For full explanation see **Index.**

COMMON RAFTER

Span Ft.	Length Ft. In.	Span In.	Lgth. In.
1	. 7½	¼	⅛
2	1. 3	½	⅜
3	1.10½	¾	½
4	2. 6	1	⅝
5	3. 1½	¼	¾
6	3. 9	½	1
7	4. 4½	¾	⅛
8	5. 0	2	¼
9	5. 7½	¼	⅜
10	6. 3	½	⅝
11	6.10½	¾	¾
12	7. 6	3	⅞
13	8. 1½	¼	2
14	8. 9	½	⅛
15	9. 4½	¾	⅜
16	10. 0	4	½
17	10. 7½	¼	⅝
18	11. 3	½	¾
19	11.10½	¾	3
20	12. 6	5	⅛
21	13. 1½	¼	¼
22	13. 9	½	⅜
23	14. 4½	¾	⅝
24	15. 0	6	¾
25	15. 7½	¼	⅞
26	16. 3	½	4
27	16.10½	¾	¼
28	17. 6	7	⅜
29	18. 1½	¼	½
30	18. 9	½	⅝
31	19. 4½	¾	⅞
32	20. 0	8	5
33	20. 7½	¼	⅛
34	21. 3	½	¼
35	21.10½	¾	½
36	22. 6	9	⅝
37	23. 1½	¼	¾
38	23. 9	½	⅞
39	24. 4½	¾	6⅛
40	25. 0	10	¼
41	25. 7½	¼	⅜
42	26. 3	½	½
43	26.10½	¾	¾
44	27. 6	11	⅞
45	28. 1½	¼	7
46	28. 9	½	⅛
47	29. 4½	¾	⅜
48	30. 0	12	½
49	30. 7½		
50	31. 3		

HIP OR VALLEY RAFTER

Span Ft.	Length Ft. In.	Span In.	Lgth. In.
1	. 9⅝	¼	¼
2	1. 7¼	½	⅜
3	2. 4⅞	¾	⅝
4	3. 2⅜	1	¾
5	4. 0	¼	1
6	4. 9⅝	½	¼
7	5. 7¼	¾	⅜
8	6. 4⅞	2	⅝
9	7. 2½	¼	¾
10	8. 0	½	2
11	8. 9⅝	¾	¼
12	9. 7¼	3	⅜
13	10. 4⅞	¼	⅝
14	11. 2½	½	¾
15	12. 0⅛	¾	3
16	12. 9⅝	4	¼
17	13. 7¼	¼	⅜
18	14. 4⅞	½	⅝
19	15. 2½	¾	¾
20	16. 0⅛	5	4
21	16. 9¾	¼	¼
22	17. 7¼	½	⅜
23	18. 4⅞	¾	⅝
24	19. 2½	6	¾
25	20. 0⅛	¼	5
26	20. 9¾	½	¼
27	21. 7⅜	¾	⅜
28	22. 4⅞	7	⅝
29	23. 2½	¼	¾
30	24. 0⅛	½	6
31	24. 9¾	¾	¼
32	25. 7⅜	8	⅜
33	26. 5	¼	⅝
34	27. 2½	½	¾
35	28. 0⅛	¾	7
36	28. 9¾	9	¼
37	29. 7⅜	¼	⅜
38	30. 5	½	⅝
39	31. 2⅝	¾	¾
40	32. 0⅛	10	8
41	32. 9¾	¼	¼
42	33. 7⅜	½	⅜
43	34. 5	¾	⅝
44	35. 2⅝	11	¾
45	36. 0¼	¼	9
46	36. 9¾	½	¼
47	37. 7⅜	¾	⅜
48	38. 5	12	⅝
49	39. 2⅝		
50	40. 0¼		

9½ & 12 — 38½°

EXPLANATION

Common Rafter

Width of building..........17'2½"
Find length of Common Rafter.
Answer:

| Under **Span**, ft. find | 17' | = 10'10⅛" |
| " " in. " | 2½" = | 1⅝" |

Total length Common Rft. 10'11¾"

When rafters overhang, add both overhangs to width of building. Use total span as before.

To get length of rafter by its run: doubling the run gives the span. Proceed as before.

Tables give full length. Allow for half thickness of ridge.

Spans over 50', as 60', add lengths of 50' & 10' spans together.

Hip Rafter

If common rafter span is 17'2½", Hip rafter is 13'11¼" long. Measure length of Hip on center of top edge. If Hip is unbacked (top edge square), see Index. If edge is backed (beveled), see Index.

Allow for half thickness of ridge.

Jack Rafters

Spaced 28" apart are 2'11¾" different in length. Measure length on center of top edge. Cut short equal to half thickness of hip.

CUTS FOR STEEL SQUARE.

The first figure is always the cut.

Common Rafter	Purlin Rafter
Plumb 9½- 12	Roof Sheathing
Level. 12 - 9½	Plumb 9½- 15¼
	Cross. 12 - 15¼

Hip Rafter	Valley Shingles
Plumb 9½- 17	Cross. 12 - 15¼
Level. 17 - 9½	Set bevel on
Side.. 9¾- 8½	butt end.
Backing 9½- 19½	
Set bevel to	Mitre-Box Cuts
last named.	for Gable Moulds

Jack Rafter	Plumb 9½- 12
Plumb 9½- 12	Mitre. 15¼- 12
Level. 12 - 9½	Bisection of
Side.. 15¼- 12	9½- 12=8¼- 24

For full explanation see Index.

COMMON RAFTER

Span Ft.	Length Ft. In.	Span In.	Lgth. In.
1	7⅝	¼	⅛
2	1. 3¼	½	⅜
3	1.11	¾	½
4	2. 6⅝	1	⅝
5	3. 2¼	¼	¾
6	3. 9⅞	½	1
7	4. 5⅝	¾	⅛
8	5. 1¼	2	¼
9	5. 8⅞	¼	⅜
10	6. 4½	½	⅝
11	7. 0⅛	¾	¾
12	7. 7⅞	3	⅞
13	8. 3½	¼	2⅛
14	8.11⅛	½	¼
15	9. 6¾	¾	⅜
16	10. 2½	4	½
17	10.10⅛	¼	¾
18	11. 5¾	½	⅞
19	12. 1⅜	¾	3
20	12. 9	5	¼
21	13. 4¾	¼	⅜
22	14. 0⅜	½	½
23	14. 8	¾	⅝
24	15. 3⅝	6	⅞
25	15.11⅜	¼	4
26	16. 7	½	⅛
27	17. 2⅝	¾	¼
28	17.10¼	7	½
29	18. 5⅞	¼	⅝
30	19. 1⅝	½	¾
31	19. 9¼	¾	5
32	20. 4⅞	8	⅛
33	21. 0½	¼	¼
34	21. 8¼	½	⅜
35	22. 3⅞	¾	⅝
36	22.11½	9	¾
37	23. 7⅛	¼	⅞
38	24. 2¾	½	6
39	24.10½	¾	¼
40	25. 6⅛	10	⅜
41	26. 1¾	¼	½
42	26. 9⅜	½	¾
43	27. 5	¾	⅞
44	28. 0¾	11	7
45	28. 8⅜	¼	⅛
46	29. 4	½	⅜
47	29.11⅝	¾	½
48	30. 7⅜	12	⅝
49	31. 3		
50	31.10⅝		

HIP OR VALLEY RAFTER

Span Ft.	Length Ft. In.	Span In.	Lgth. In.
1	9¾	¼	¼
2	1. 7½	½	⅜
3	2. 5⅛	¾	⅝
4	3. 2⅞	1	¾
5	4. 0⅝	¼	1
6	4.10⅜	½	¼
7	5. 8⅛	¾	⅜
8	6. 5¾	2	⅝
9	7. 3½	¼	⅞
10	8. 1¼	½	2
11	8.11	¾	¼
12	9. 8¾	3	⅜
13	10. 6⅜	¼	⅝
14	11. 4⅛	½	⅞
15	12. 1⅞	¾	3
16	12.11⅝	4	¼
17	13. 9¼	¼	½
18	14. 7	½	⅝
19	15. 4¾	¾	⅞
20	16. 2½	5	4
21	17. 0¼	¼	¼
22	17. 9⅞	½	½
23	18. 7⅝	¾	⅝
24	19. 5⅜	6	⅞
25	20. 3⅛	¼	5⅛
26	21. 0⅞	½	¼
27	21.10½	¾	½
28	22. 8¼	7	⅝
29	23. 6	¼	⅞
30	24. 3¾	½	6⅛
31	25. 1½	¾	¼
32	25.11⅛	8	½
33	26. 8⅞	¼	⅝
34	27. 6⅝	½	⅞
35	28. 4⅜	¾	7⅛
36	29. 2⅛	9	¼
37	29.11¾	¼	½
38	30. 9½	½	¾
39	31. 7¼	¾	⅞
40	32. 5	10	8⅛
41	33. 2⅝	¼	¼
42	34. 0⅜	½	½
43	34.10⅛	¾	¾
44	35. 7⅞	11	⅞
45	36. 5⅝	¼	9⅛
46	37. 3¼	½	⅜
47	38. 1	¾	½
48	38.10¾	12	¾
49	39. 8½		
50	40. 6¼		

Spaced In.	Length Ft. In.
1..	1¼
2..	2⅝
3..	3⅞
4..	5¼
5..	6½
6..	7¾
7..	9⅛
8..	10⅜
9..	11¾
10..	1 1
11..	2⅜
12..	3⅝
13..	4⅞
14..	6¼
15..	7½
16..	8⅞
17..	10⅛
18..	11⅜
19..	2 0¾
20..	2
21..	3⅜
22..	4⅝
23..	6
24..	7¼
25..	8½
26..	9⅞
27..	11⅛
28..	3 0½
29..	1¾
30..	3
31..	4⅜
32..	5⅝
33..	7
34..	8¼
35..	9½
36..	10⅞
37..	4 0⅛
38..	1½
39..	2¾
40..	4⅛
41..	5⅜
42..	6⅝
43..	8
44..	9¼
45..	10⅝
46..	11⅞
47..	5 1⅛
48..	2½

10 & 12 — 40°

EXPLANATION

Common Rafter

Width of building.......... 20'7¼"
Find length of Common Rafter.
Answer:

Under Span, ft. find 20' = 13' 0¼"
"   "   in. "   7¼" =   4¾"

Total length Common Rft. 13' 5"

When rafters overhang, add both overhangs to width of building. Use total span as before.
To get length of rafter by its run: doubling the run gives the span. Proceed as before.

Tables give full length. Allow for half thickness of ridge.

Spans over 50', as 60', add lengths of 50' & 10' spans together.

Hip Rafter

If common rafter span is 20'7¼", Hip rafter is 6'11" long. Measure length of Hip on center of top edge. If Hip is unbacked (top edge square), see Index. If edge is backed (beveled), see Index.

Allow for half thickness of ridge.

Jack Rafters

Spaced 24" apart are 2'7¼" different in length. Measure length on center of top edge. Cut short equal to half thickness of hip.

CUTS FOR STEEL SQUARE.

The first figure is always the cut.

Common Rafter	Purlin Rafter Roof Sheathing
Plumb 10 - 12	
Level. 12 - 10	Plumb 10..-.15⅝
	Cross. 12 - 15⅝

Hip Rafter

Hip Rafter	Valley Shingles
Plumb 10 - 17	
Level. 17 - 10	Cross. 12 - 15⅝
Side.. 9⅞ - 8½	Set bevel on
Backing 10 - 19¾	butt end.

Set bevel to last named.

Mitre-Box Cuts for Gable Moulds

Jack Rafter	
Plumb 10 - 12	Plumb 10 - 12
Level. 12 - 10	Mitre. 15⅝ - 12
Side.. 15⅝ - 12	

Bisection of
10 - 12 = 8⅝ - 24

For full explanation see **Index.**

58

COMMON RAFTER					HIP or VALLEY RAFTER			
Span Ft.	Length ft. In.	Span In.	Lgth. In.		Span Ft.	Length Ft. In.	Span In.	Lgth. In.
1..	. 7¾	¼..	⅛		1..	. 9⅞	¼..	¼
2..	1. 3⅜	½..	⅜		2..	1. 7¾	½..	⅜
3..	1.11⅜	¾..	½		3..	2. 5½	¾..	⅝
4..	2. 7¼	1 ..	⅝		4..	3. 3⅜	1 ..	⅞
5..	3. 3	¼..	⅞		5..	4. 1¼	¼..	1
6..	3.10⅞	½..	1		6..	4.11⅛	½..	¼
7..	4. 6⅝	¾..	⅛		7..	5. 9	¾..	⅜
8..	5. 2½	2 ..	¼		8..	6. 6¾	2 ..	⅝
9..	5.10¼	¼..	½		9..	7. 4⅝	¼..	⅞
10..	6. 6⅛	½..	⅝		10..	8. 2½	½..	2
11..	7. 1⅞	¾..	¾		11..	9. 0⅜	¾..	¼
12..	7. 9¾	3 ..	2		12..	9.10¼	3 ..	½
13..	8. 5½	¼..	⅛		13..	10. 8	¼..	⅝
14..	9. 1⅜	½..	¼		14..	11. 5⅞	½..	⅞
15..	9. 9⅛	¾..	½		15..	12. 3¾	¾..	3⅛
16..	10. 5	4 ..	⅝		16..	13. 1⅝	4 ..	¼
17..	11. 0¾	¼..	¾		17..	13.11⅜	¼..	½
18..	11. 8⅝	½..	⅞		18..	14. 9¼	½..	¾
19..	12. 4⅜	¾..	3⅛		19..	15. 7⅛	¾..	4
20..	13. 0¼	5 ..	¼		20..	16. 5	5 ..	4⅛
21..	13. 8	¼..	⅜		21..	17. 2⅞	¼..	¼
22..	14. 3⅞	½..	⅝		22..	18. 0⅝	½..	½
23..	14.11⅝	¾..	¾		23..	18.10½	¾..	¾
24..	15. 7½	6 ..	⅞		24..	19. 8⅜	6 ..	⅞
25..	16. 3¼	¼..	4⅛		25..	20. 6¼	¼..	5⅛
26..	16.11	½..	¼		26..	21. 4⅛	½..	⅜
27..	17. 6⅞	¾..	⅜		27..	22. 1⅞	¾..	½
28..	18. 2⅝	7 ..	½		28..	22.11⅝	7 ..	¾
29..	18.10½	¼..	¾		29..	23. 9⅝	¼..	6
30..	19. 6¼	½..	⅞		30..	24. 7½	½..	⅛
31..	20. 2⅛	¾..	5		31..	25. 5⅜	¾..	⅜
32..	20.10	8 ..	¼		32..	26. 3⅛	8 ..	⅝
33..	21. 5¾	¼..	⅜		33..	27. 1	¼..	¾
34..	22. 1½	½..	½		34..	27.10⅞	½..	7
35..	22. 9⅜	¾..	¾		35..	28. 8¾	¾..	⅛
36..	23. 5⅛	9 ..	⅞		36..	29. 6⅝	9 ..	⅜
37..	24. 1	¼..	6		37..	30. 4⅜	¼..	⅝
38..	24. 8¾	½..	⅛		38..	31. 2¼	½..	¾
39..	25. 4⅝	¾..	⅜		39..	32. 0⅛	¾..	8
40..	26. 0⅜	10 ..	½		40..	32.10	10 ..	¼
41..	26. 8¼	¼..	⅝		41..	33. 7¾	¼..	⅜
42..	27. 4	½..	⅞		42..	34. 5⅝	½..	⅝
43..	27.11⅞	¾..	7		43..	35. 3½	¾..	⅞
44..	28. 7⅝	11 ..	⅛		44..	36. 1⅜	11 ..	9
45..	29. 3½	¼..	⅜		45..	36.11¼	¼..	¼
46..	29.11¼	½..	½		46..	37. 9	½..	½
47..	30. 7⅛	¾..	⅝		47..	38. 6⅞	¾..	⅝
48..	31. 2⅞	12 ..	¾		48..	39. 4¾	12 ..	⅞
49..	31.10¾				49..	40. 2⅝		
50..	32. 6½				50..	41. 0½		

JACK RAFTER

Spaced In.	Length Ft.	In.
1..		1⅜
2..		2⅝
3..		4
4..		5⅜
5..		6⅝
6..		8
7..		9¼
8..		10⅝
9..	1	0
10..		1¼
11..		2⅝
12..		4
13..		5¼
14..		6⅝
15..		7⅞
16..		9¼
17..		10⅝
18..		11⅞
19..	2	1¼
20..		2⅝
21..		3⅞
22..		5¼
23..		6½
24..		7⅞
25..		9¼
26..		10½
27..		11⅞
28..	3	1¼
29..		2½
30..		3⅞
31..		5¼
32..		6½
33..		7⅞
34..		9⅛
35..		10½
36..		11⅞
37..	4	1⅛
38..		2½
39..		3⅞
40..		5⅛
41..		6½
42..		7¾
43..		9⅛
44..		10½
45..		11¾
46..	5	1⅛
47..		2½
48..		3¾

10½ & 12 — 41¼°

EXPLANATION

Common Rafter

Width of building...........28′3¾″
Find length of Common Rafter.

Answer:

Under **Span, ft.** find	28′	= 18′ 7¼″
" " **in.** "	3¾″ =	2½″
Total length Common Rft.		18′ 9¾″

When rafters overhang, add both overhangs to width of building. Use total span as before.

To get length of rafter by its run: doubling the run gives the span. Proceed as before.

Tables give full length. Allow for half thickness of ridge.

Spans over 50′, as 60′, add lengths of 50′ & 10′ spans together.

Hip Rafter

If common rafter span is 28′3¾″, Hip rafter is 23′6½″ long. Measure length of Hip on center of top edge. If Hip is unbacked (top edge square), see Index. If edge is backed (beveled), see Index.

Allow for half thickness of ridge.

Jack Rafters

Spaced 21″ apart are 2′3⅞″ different in length. Measure length on center of top edge. Cut short equal to half thickness of hip.

CUTS FOR STEEL SQUARE.

The first figure is always the cut.

Common Rafter

Plumb 10½ - 12
Level. 12 - 10½

Hip Rafter

Plumb 10½ - 17
Level. 17 - 10½
Side.. 10 - 8½
Backing 10½ - 20
Set bevel to last named.

Jack Rafter

Plumb 10½ - 12
Level. 12 - 10½
Side.. 16 - 12

Purlin Rafter Roof Sheathing

Plumb 10½ - 16
Cross. 12 - 16

Valley Shingles

Cross. 12 - 16
Set bevel on butt end.

Mitre-Box Cuts for Gable Moulds

Plumb 10½ - 12
Mitre. 16 - 12

Bisection of

10½ - 12 = 8⅞ - 24

For full explanation see Index.

COMMON RAFTER

Span Ft.	Length Ft. In.	Span Lgth. In.	In.
1..	.8	1/4 ..	1/8
2..	1. 4	1/2 ..	3/8
3..	1.11 7/8	3/4 ..	1/2
4..	2. 7 7/8	1 ..	5/8
5..	3. 3 7/8	1/4 ..	7/8
6..	3.11 7/8	1/2 ..	1
7..	4. 7 3/4	3/4 ..	1/8
8..	5. 3 3/4	2 ..	3/8
9..	5.11 3/4	1/4 ..	1/2
10..	6. 7 3/4	1/2 ..	5/8
11..	7. 3 3/4	3/4 ..	7/8
12..	7.11 5/8	3 ..	2
13..	8. 7 5/8	1/4 ..	1/8
14..	9. 3 5/8	1/2 ..	3/8
15..	9.11 5/8	3/4 ..	1/2
16..	10. 7 1/2	4 ..	5/8
17..	11. 3 1/2	1/4 ..	7/8
18..	11.11 1/2	1/2 ..	3
19..	12. 7 1/2	3/4 ..	1/8
20..	13. 3 1/2	5 ..	3/8
21..	13.11 3/8	1/4 ..	1/2
22..	14. 7 3/8	1/2 ..	5/8
23..	15. 3 3/8	3/4 ..	7/8
24..	15.11 3/8	6 ..	4
25..	16. 7 3/8	1/4 ..	1/8
26..	17. 3 1/4	1/2 ..	3/8
27..	17.11 1/4	3/4 ..	1/2
28..	18. 7 1/4	7 ..	5/8
29..	19. 3 1/4	1/4 ..	7/8
30..	19.11 1/8	1/2 ..	5
31..	20. 7 1/8	3/4 ..	1/8
32..	21. 3 1/8	8 ..	3/8
33..	21.11 1/8	1/4 ..	1/2
34..	22. 7 1/8	1/2 ..	5/8
35..	23. 3	3/4 ..	3/4
36..	23.11	9 ..	6
37..	24. 7	1/4 ..	1/8
38..	25. 3	1/2 ..	1/4
39..	25.10 7/8	3/4 ..	1/2
40..	26. 6 7/8	10 ..	5/8
41..	27. 2 7/8	1/4 ..	3/4
42..	27.10 7/8	1/2 ..	7
43..	28. 6 7/8	3/4 ..	1/8
44..	29. 2 3/4	11 ..	1/4
45..	29.10 3/4	1/4 ..	1/2
46..	30. 6 3/4	1/2 ..	5/8
47..	31. 2 3/4	3/4 ..	3/4
48..	31.10 5/8	12 ..	8
49..	32. 6 5/8		
50..	33. 2 5/8		

HIP or VALLEY RAFTER

Span Ft.	Length Ft. In.	Span Lgth. In.	In.
1..	.10	1/4 ..	1/4
2..	1. 8	1/2 ..	3/8
3..	2. 5 7/8	3/4 ..	5/8
4..	3. 3 7/8	1 ..	7/8
5..	4. 1 7/8	1/4 ..	1
6..	4.11 7/8	1/2 ..	1/4
7..	5. 9 7/8	3/4 ..	1/2
8..	6. 7 7/8	2 ..	5/8
9..	7. 5 3/4	1/4 ..	7/8
10..	8. 3 3/4	1/2 ..	2 1/8
11..	9. 1 3/4	3/4 ..	1/4
12..	9.11 3/4	3 ..	1/2
13..	10. 9 3/4	1/4 ..	3/4
14..	11. 7 3/4	1/2 ..	7/8
15..	12. 5 5/8	3/4 ..	3 1/8
16..	13. 3 5/8	4 ..	3/8
17..	14. 1 5/8	1/4 ..	1/2
18..	14.11 5/8	1/2 ..	3/4
19..	15. 9 5/8	3/4 ..	4
20..	16. 7 1/2	5 ..	1/8
21..	17. 5 1/2	1/4 ..	3/8
22..	18. 3 1/2	1/2 ..	5/8
23..	19. 1 1/2	3/4 ..	3/4
24..	19.11 1/2	6 ..	5
25..	20. 9 1/2	1/4 ..	1/4
26..	21. 7 3/8	1/2 ..	3/8
27..	22. 5 3/8	3/4 ..	5/8
28..	23. 3 3/8	7 ..	7/8
29..	24. 1 3/8	1/4 ..	6
30..	24.11 3/8	1/2 ..	1/4
31..	25. 9 3/8	3/4 ..	1/2
32..	26. 7 1/4	8 ..	5/8
33..	27. 5 1/4	1/4 ..	7/8
34..	28. 3 1/4	1/2 ..	7 1/8
35..	29. 1 1/4	3/4 ..	1/4
36..	29.11 1/4	9 ..	1/2
37..	30. 9 1/8	1/4 ..	3/4
38..	31. 7 1/8	1/2 ..	7/8
39..	32. 5 1/8	3/4 ..	8 1/8
40..	33. 3 1/8	10 ..	3/8
41..	34. 1 1/8	1/4 ..	1/2
42..	34.11 1/8	1/2 ..	3/4
43..	35. 9	3/4 ..	9
44..	36. 7	11 ..	1/8
45..	37. 5	1/4 ..	3/8
46..	38. 3	1/2 ..	5/8
47..	39. 1	3/4 ..	3/4
48..	39.11	12 ..	10
49..	40. 8 7/8		
50..	41. 6 7/8		

JACK RAFTER

Spaced In.	Length Ft.	In.
1..		1⅜
2..		2¾
3..		4⅛
4..		5⅜
5..		6¾
6..		8⅛
7..		9½
8..		10⅞
9..	1	0¼
10..		1⅝
11..		2⅞
12..		4¼
13..		5⅝
14..		7
15..		8⅜
16..		9¾
17..		11
18..	2	0⅜
19..		1¾
20..		3⅛
21..		4½
22..		5⅞
23..		7¼
24..		8½
25..		9⅞
26..		11¼
27..	3	0⅝
28.		2
29..		3⅜
30..		4¾
31..		6
32..		7⅜
33..		8¾
34..		10⅛
35..		11½
36..	4	0⅞
37..		2¼
38..		3½
39..		4⅞
40..		6¼
41..		7⅝
42..		9
43..		10⅜
44..		11⅝
45..	5	1
46..		2⅜
47..		3¾
48..		5⅛

11 & 12—42½°

EXPLANATION

Common Rafter

Width of building...........18′2¼″
Find length of Common Rafter.

Answer:

Under **Span, ft.** find	18′	=12′ 2½″
" " **In.** "	2¼″ =	1½″

Total length Common Rft. 12′ 4″

When rafters overhang, add both overhangs to width of building. Use total span as before.

To get length of rafter by its run: doubling the run gives the span. Proceed as before.

Tables give full length. Allow for half thickness of ridge.

Spans over 50′, as 60′, add lengths of 50′ & 10′ spans together.

Hip Rafter

If common rafter span is 18′2¼″, Hip rafter is 15′3⅞″ long. Measure length of Hip on center of top edge. If Hip is unbacked (top edge square), see Index. If edge is backed (beveled), see Index.

Allow for half thickness of ridge.

Jack Rafters

Spaced 34″ apart are 3′10⅛″ different in length. Measure length on center of top edge. Cut short equal to half thickness of hip.

CUTS FOR STEEL SQUARE.

The first figure is always the cut.

Common Rafter

Plumb	11	- 12
Level.	12	- 11

Hip Rafter

Plumb	11	- 17
Level.	17	- 11
Side..	10⅛	- 8½
Backing	11	- 20¼

Set bevel to last named.

Jack Rafter

Plumb	11	- 12
Level.	12	- 11
Side..	16¼	- 12

Purlin Rafter Roof Sheathing

Plumb	11	- 16¼
Cross.	12	- 16¼

Valley Shingles

Cross.	12	- 16¼

Set bevel on Butt end.

Mitre-Box Cuts for Gable Moulds

Plumb	11	- 12
Mitre.	16¼	- 12

Bisection of
11- 12=9¼- 24

For full explanation see Index.

COMMON RAFTER

Span Ft.	Length Ft. In.	Span In.	Lgth. In.
1	. 8⅛	¼	¼
2	1. 4¼	½	⅜
3	2. 0⅜	¾	½
4	2. 8½	1	⅝
5	3. 4¾	¼	⅞
6	4. 0⅞	½	1
7	4. 9	¾	¼
8	5. 5⅛	2	⅜
9	6. 1¼	¼	½
10	6. 9⅜	½	¾
11	7. 5½	¾	⅞
12	8. 1⅝	3	2
13	8. 9¾	¼	¼
14	9. 6	½	⅜
15	10. 2⅛	¾	½
16	10. 10¼	4	¾
17	11. 6⅜	¼	⅞
18	12. 2½	½	3
19	12. 10⅝	¾	¼
20	13. 6¾	5	⅜
21	14. 2⅞	¼	½
22	14. 11	½	¾
23	15. 7¼	¾	⅞
24	16. 3⅜	6	4⅛
25	16. 11½	¼	¼
26	17. 7⅝	½	⅜
27	18. 3¾	¾	⅝
28	18. 11⅞	7	¾
29	19. 8	¼	⅞
30	20. 4⅛	½	5⅛
31	21. 0¼	¾	¼
32	21. 8½	8	⅜
33	22. 4⅝	¼	⅝
34	23. 0¾	½	¾
35	23. 8⅞	¾	⅞
36	24. 5	9	6⅛
37	25. 1⅛	¼	¼
38	25. 9¼	½	½
39	26. 5⅜	¾	⅝
40	27. 1½	10	¾
41	27. 9¾	¼	7
42	28. 5⅞	½	⅛
43	29. 2	¾	¼
44	29. 10⅛	11	½
45	30. 6¼	¼	⅝
46	31. 2⅜	½	¾
47	31. 10½	¾	8
48	32. 6⅝	12	⅛
49	33. 2¾		
50	33. 11		

HIP or VALLEY RAFTER

Span Ft.	Length Ft. In.	Span In.	Lgth. In.
1	. 10⅛	¼	¼
2	1. 8¼	½	⅜
3	2. 6⅜	¾	⅝
4	3. 4½	1	⅞
5	4. 2½	¼	1
6	5. 0⅝	½	¼
7	5. 10¾	¾	½
8	6. 8⅞	2	⅝
9	7. 7	¼	⅞
10	8. 5⅛	½	2⅛
11	9. 3¼	¾	⅜
12	10. 1⅜	3	½
13	10. 11½	¼	¾
14	11. 9⅝	½	3
15	12. 7⅝	¾	⅛
16	13. 5¾	4	⅜
17	14. 3⅞	¼	⅝
18	15. 2	½	¾
19	16. 0⅛	¾	4
20	16. 10¼	5	¼
21	17. 8⅜	¼	⅜
22	18. 6½	½	⅝
23	19. 4⅝	¾	⅞
24	20. 2¾	6	5
25	21. 0¾	¼	¼
26	21. 10⅞	½	½
27	22. 9	¾	⅝
28	23. 7⅛	7	⅞
29	24. 5¼	¼	6⅛
30	25. 3⅜	½	⅜
31	26. 1½	¾	½
32	26. 11⅝	8	¾
33	27. 9¾	¼	7
34	28. 7¾	½	⅛
35	29. 5⅞	¾	⅜
36	30. 4	9	⅝
37	31. 2⅛	¼	¾
38	32. 0¼	½	8
39	32. 10⅜	¾	¼
40	33. 8½	10	⅜
41	34. 6⅝	¼	⅝
42	35. 4¾	½	⅞
43	36. 2⅞	¾	9
44	37. 0⅞	11	¼
45	37. 11	¼	½
46	38. 9⅛	½	¾
47	39. 7¼	¾	⅞
48	40. 5⅜	12	10⅛
49	41. 3½		
50	42. 1⅝		

JACK RAFTER

Spaced In.	Length Ft.	In.
1..		1⅜
2..		2¾
3..		4⅛
4..		5½
5..		6⅞
6..		8¼
7..		9¾
8..		11⅛
9	1	0½
10..		1⅞
11..		3¼
12..		4⅝
13..		6
14..		7⅜
15..		8¾
16..		10⅛
17..		11½
18	2	1
19..		2⅜
20..		3¾
21..		5⅛
22..		6½
23..		7⅞
24..		9¼
25..		10⅝
26..	3	0
27..		1⅜
28..		2¾
29..		4⅛
30..		5½
31..		7
32..		8⅜
33..		9¾
34..		11⅛
35	4	0½
36..		1⅞
37..		3¼
38..		4⅝
39..		6
40..		7⅜
41..		8¾
42..		10⅛
43..		11½
44..	5	1
45..		2⅜
46..		3¾
47..		5⅛
48..		6½

11½ & 12—43¾°

EXPLANATION

Common Rafter

Width of building...........33′2½″
Find length of Common Rafter.

Answer:

Under **Span, ft.** find **33′** = 22′10¼″
" " **in.** " 2½″ = 1¾″

Total length Common Rft. 23′ 0″

When rafters overhang, add both overhangs to width of building. Use total span as before.

To get length of rafter by its run: doubling the run gives the span. Proceed as before.

Tables give full length. Allow for half thickness of ridge.

Spans over 50′, as 60′, add lengths of 50′ & 10′ spans together.

Hip Rafter

If common rafter span is 33′2½″, Hip rafter is 28′4⅜″ long. Measure length of Hip on center of top edge. If Hip is unbacked (top edge square), see Index. If edge is backed (beveled), see Index.

Allow for half thickness of ridge.

Jack Rafters

Spaced 28″ apart are 3′2¾″ different in length. Measure length on center of top edge. Cut short equal to half thickness of hip.

CUTS FOR STEEL SQUARE.

The first figure is always the cut.

Common Rafter

Plumb 11½- 12
Level. 12 - 11½

Hip Rafter

Plumb 11½- 17
Level. 17 - 11½
Side.. 10¼- 8½
Backing 11½- 20½
Set bevel to last named.

Jack Rafter

Plumb 11½- 12
Level. 12 - 11½
Side.. 16⅝- 12

Purlin Rafter Roof-Sheathing

Plumb 11½- 16⅝
Cross. 12 - 16⅝

Valley Shingles

Cross. 12 - 16⅝
Set bevel on butt end.

Mitre-Box Cuts for Gable Moulds

Plumb 11½- 12
Mitre. 16⅝- 12

Bisection of

11½ 12=9½- 24

For full explanation see Index.

COMMON RAFTER

Span Ft.	Length Ft. In.	Span In.	Lgth. In.
1..	. 8¼	¼..	¼
2..	1. 4⅝	½..	⅜
3..	2. 1	¾..	½
4..	2. 9¼	1 ..	¾
5..	3. 5½	¼..	⅞
6..	4. 1⅞	½..	1
7..	4.10⅛	¾..	¼
8..	5. 6½	2 ..	⅜
9..	6. 2¾	¼..	½
10..	6.11⅛	½..	¾
11..	7. 7⅜	¾..	⅞
12..	8. 3¾	3 ..	2⅛
13..	9. 0	¼..	¼
14..	9. 8⅜	½..	⅜
15..	10. 4⅝	¾..	⅝
16..	11. 1	4 ..	¾
17..	11. 9¼	¼..	3
18..	12. 5⅝	½..	⅛
19..	13. 1⅞	¾..	¼
20..	13.10¼	5 ..	½
21..	14. 6½	¼..	⅝
22..	15. 2⅞	½..	¾
23..	15.11⅛	¾..	4
24..	16. 7½	6 ..	⅛
25..	17. 3¾	¼..	⅜
26..	18. 0⅛	½..	½
27..	18. 8⅜	¾..	⅝
28..	19. 4¾	7 ..	⅞
29..	20. 1..	¼..	5
30..	20. 9⅜	½..	¼
31..	21. 5⅝	¾..	⅜
32..	22. 2	8 ..	½
33..	22.10¼	¼..	¾
34..	23. 6½	½..	⅞
35..	24. 2⅞	¾..	6
36..	24.11⅛	9 ..	¼
37..	25. 7½	¼..	⅜
38..	26. 3¾	½..	⅝
39..	27. 0⅛	¾..	¾
40..	27. 8⅜	10 ..	⅞
41..	28. 4¾	¼..	7⅛
42..	29. 1	½..	¼
43..	29. 9⅜	¾..	½
44..	30. 5⅝	11 ..	⅝
45..	31. 2	¼..	¾
46..	31.10¼	½..	8
47..	32. 6⅝	¾..	⅛
48..	33. 2⅞	12 ..	¼
49..	33.11¼		
50..	34. 7½		

HIP OR VALLEY RAFTER

Span Ft.	Length Ft. In.	Span In.	Lgth. In.
1..	.10¼	¼..	¼
2..	1. 8½	½..	⅜
3..	2. 6¾	¾..	⅝
4..	3. 5	1 ..	⅞
5..	4. 3¼	¼..	1⅛
6..	5. 1½	½..	¼
7..	5.11¾	¾..	½
8..	6.10	2 ..	¾
9..	7. 8¼	¼..	⅞
10..	8. 6½	½..	2⅛
11..	9. 4¾	¾..	⅜
12..	10. 3	3 ..	⅝
13..	11. 1¼	¼..	¾
14..	11.11½	½..	3
15..	12. 9¾	¾..	¼
16..	13. 8	4 ..	⅜
17..	14. 6¼	¼..	⅝
18..	15. 4½	½..	⅞
19..	16. 2¾	¾..	4
20..	17. 1	5 ..	¼
21..	17.11¼	¼..	½
22..	18. 9½	½..	¾
23..	19. 7¾	¾..	⅞
24..	20. 6	6 ..	5⅛
25..	21. 4¼	¼..	⅜
26..	22. 2½	½..	½
27..	23. 0¾	¾..	¾
28..	23.11	7 ..	6
29..	24. 9¼	¼..	¼
30..	25. 7½	½..	⅜
31..	26. 5¾	¾..	⅝
32..	27. 4	8 ..	⅞
33..	28. 2¼	¼..	7
34..	29. 0½	½..	¼
35..	29.10¾	¾..	½
36..	30. 9	9 ..	⅝
37..	31. 7¼	¼..	⅞
38..	32. 5½	½..	8⅛
39..	33. 3¾	¾..	⅜
40..	34. 2	10 ..	½
41..	35. 0¼	¼..	¾
42..	35.10½	½..	9
43..	36. 8¾	¾..	⅛
44..	37. 7	11 ..	⅜
45..	38. 5¼	¼..	⅝
46..	39. 3½	½..	⅞
47..	40. 1¾	¾.	10
48..	41. 0	12 ..	¼
49..	41.10¼		
50..	42. 8½		

Spaced In.	Length Ft. In.
1..	1⅜
2..	2⅞
3..	4¼
4..	5⅝
5..	7⅛
6..	8½
7..	9⅞
8..	11⅜
9	1 0¾
10..	2⅛
11..	3½
12..	5
13..	6⅜
14..	7¾
15..	9¼
16..	10⅝
17	2 0
18..	1½
19..	2⅞
20..	4¼
21..	5¾
22..	7⅛
23..	8½
24..	9⅞
25..	11⅜
26	3 0¾
27..	2¼
28..	3⅝
29..	5
30..	6⅜
31..	7⅞
32..	9¼
33..	10⅝
34	4 0⅛
35..	1½
36..	2⅞
37..	4⅜
38..	5¾
39..	7⅛
40..	8⅝
41..	10
42..	11⅜
43..5	0⅞
44..	2¼
45..	3⅝
46..	5
47..	6½
48..	7⅞

12 & 12 — 45°

EXPLANATION

Common Rafter

Width of building..........50′3½″
Find length of Common Rafter.
Answer:
Under **Span**, ft. find 50′ = 35′ 4¼″
"   "   in. "   3½″ = 2½″

Total length Common Rft. 35′ 6¾″

When rafters overhang, add both overhangs to width of building. Use total span as before.
To get length of rafter by its run: doubling the run gives the span Proceed as before.
Tables give full length. Allow for half thickness of ridge.
Spans over 50′, as 60′, add lengths of 50′ & 10′ spans together.

Hip Rafter

If common rafter span is 50′3½″, Hip rafter is 43′6⅝″ long. Measure length of Hip on center of top edge. If Hip is unbacked (top edge square), see Index. If edge is backed (beveled), see Index.
Allow for half thickness of ridge.

Jack Rafters

Spaced 32″ apart are 3′9¼″ different in length. Measure length on center of top edge. Cut short equal to half thickness of hip.

CUTS FOR STEEL SQUARE.

The first figure is always the cut.

Common Rafter	Purlin Rafter Roof Sheathing
Plumb 12 - 12	
Level. 12 - 12	Plumb 12 - 17
	Cross. 12 - 1

Hip Rafter	Valley Shingles
Plumb 12 - 17	
Level. 17 - 12	Cross. 12 - 17
Side.. 10⅜ - 8½	Set bevel on
Backing12 - 20¾	butt end.

Set bevel to last named.

Jack Rafter	Mitre-Box Cuts for Gable Moulds
	Plumb 12 - 12
Plumb 12 - 12	Mitre. 17 - 12
Level. 12 - 12	
Side.. 17 - 12	Bisection of
	12- 12=9⅞- 24

For full explanation see Index.

66

COMMON RAFTER

Span Ft.	Length Ft. In.	Span Lgth. In.	In.
1..	.8½	¼..	⅛
2..	1. 5	½..	⅜
3..	2. 1½	¾..	½
4..	2.10	1 ..	¾
5..	3. 6⅜	¼..	⅞
6..	4. 2⅞	½..	1
7..	4.11⅜	¾..	¼
8..	5. 7⅞	2 ..	⅜
9..	6. 4⅜	¼..	⅝
10..	7. 0⅞	½..	¾
11..	7. 9⅜	¾..	2
12..	8. 5⅞	3 ..	⅛
13..	9. 2¼	¼..	¼
14..	9.10¾	½..	½
15..	10. 7¼	¾..	⅝
16..	11. 3¾	4 ..	⅞
17..	12. 0¼	¼..	3
18..	12. 8¾	½..	⅛
19..	13. 5¼	¾..	⅜
20..	14. 1¾	5 ..	½
21..	14.10⅛	¼..	¾
22..	15. 6⅝	½..	⅞
23..	16. 3⅛	¾..	4⅛
24..	16.11⅝	6 ..	¼
25..	17. 8⅛	¼..	⅜
26..	18. 4⅝	½..	⅝
27..	19. 1⅛	¾..	¾
28..	19. 9⅝	7 ..	5
29..	20. 6⅛	¼..	⅛
30..	21. 2½	½..	¼
31..	21.11	¾..	½
32..	22. 7½	8 ..	⅝
33..	23. 4	¼..	⅞
34..	24. 0½	½..	6
35..	24. 9	¾..	¼
36..	25. 5½	9 ..	⅜
37..	26. 2	¼..	½
38..	26.10⅜	½..	¾
39..	27. 6⅞	¾..	⅞
40..	28. 3⅜	10 ..	7⅛
41..	28.11⅞	¼..	¼
42..	29. 8⅜	½..	⅜
43..	30. 4⅞	¾..	⅝
44..	31. 1⅜	11 ..	¾
45..	31. 9⅞	¼..	8
46..	32. 6¼	½..	⅛
47..	33. 2¾	¾..	¼
48..	33.11¼	12 ..	½
49..	34. 7¾		
50..	35. 4¼		

HIP or VALLEY RAFTER

Span Ft.	Length Ft. In.	Span Lgth. In.	In.
1..	.10⅜	¼..	¼
2..	1. 8¾	½..	⅜
3..	2. 7⅛	¾..	⅝
4..	3. 5⅝	1 ..	⅞
5..	4. 4	¼..	1⅛
6..	5. 2⅜	½..	¼
7..	6. 0¾	¾..	½
8..	6.11⅛	2 ..	¾
9..	7. 9½	¼..	2
10..	8. 7⅞	½..	⅛
11..	9. 6⅜	¾..	⅜
12..	10. 4¾	3 ..	⅝
13..	11. 3⅛	¼..	⅞
14..	12. 1½	½..	3
15..	12.11⅞	¾..	¼
16..	13.10¼	4 ..	½
17..	14. 8⅝	¼..	⅝
18..	15. 7	½..	⅞
19..	16. 5½	¾..	4⅛
20..	17. 3¾	5 ..	⅜
21..	18. 2¼	¼..	½
22..	19. 0⅝	½..	¾
23..	19.11	¾..	5
24..	20. 9⅜	6 ..	¼
25..	21. 7¾	¼..	⅜
26..	22. 6¼	½..	⅝
27..	23. 4⅝	¾..	⅞
28..	24. 3	7 ..	6
29..	25. 1⅜	¼..	¼
30..	25.11¾	½..	½
31..	26.10⅛	¾..	¾
32..	27. 8½	8 ..	⅞
33..	28. 6⅞	¼..	7⅛
34..	29. 5⅜	½..	⅜
35..	30. 3¾	¾..	⅝
36..	31. 2⅛	9 ..	¾
37..	32. 0½	¼..	8
38..	32.10⅞	½..	¼
39..	33. 9¼	¾..	½
40..	34. 7⅝	10 ..	⅝
41..	35. 6⅛	¼..	⅞
42..	36. 4½	½..	9⅛
43..	37. 2⅞	¾..	¼
44..	38. 1¼	11 ..	½
45..	38.11⅝	¼..	¾
46..	39.10	½..	10
47..	40. 8⅜	¾..	⅛
48..	41. 6⅞	12 ..	⅜
49..	42. 5¼		
50..	43. 3⅝		

Spaced In.	Length Ft. In.
1..	1½
2..	2⅞
3..	4⅜
4..	5¾
5..	7¼
6..	8⅝
7..	10⅛
8..	11½
9..1	1
10..	2½
11..	3⅞
12..	5⅜
13..	6¾
14..	8¼
15..	9⅝
16..	11⅛
17..2	0½
18..	2
19..	3⅜
20..	4⅞
21..	6⅜
22..	7¾
23..	9¼
24..	10⅝
25..3	0⅛
26..	1½
27..	3
28..	4⅜
29..	5⅞
30..	7⅜
31..	8¾
32..	10¼
33..	11⅝
34..4	1⅛
35..	2½
36..	4
37..	5⅜
38..	6⅞
39..	8⅜
40..	9¾
41..	11¼
42..5	0⅝
43..	2⅛
44..	3½
45..	5
46..	6⅜
47..	7⅞
48..	9⅜

12½ & 12 — 46¼°

EXPLANATION

Common Rafter

Width of building..........21'2¾"
Find length of Common Rafter.
Answer:

Under Span, ft. find	21'	= 15' 2"
" " in. "	2¾"	= 2"

Total length Common Rft. 15' 4"

When rafters overhang, add both overhangs to width of building. Use total span as before.
To get length of rafter by its run: doubling the run gives the span. Proceed as before.
Tables give full length. Allow for half thickness of ridge.
Spans over 50', as 60', add lengths of 50' & 10' spans together.

Hip Rafter

If common rafter span is 21'2¾", Hip rafter is 18'7⅝" long. Measure length of Hip on center of top edge. If Hip is unbacked (top edge square), see Index. If edge is backed (beveled), see Index.
Allow for half thickness of ridge.

Jack Rafters

Spaced 31" apart are 3'8¾" different in length. Measure length on center of top edge. Cut short equal to half thickness of hip.

CUTS FOR STEEL SQUARE.

The first figure is always the cut.

Common Rafter	Purlin Rafter Roof Sheathing
Plumb 12½- 12	
Level. 12 - 12½	Plumb 12½- 17⅜
	Cross. 12 - 17⅜
Hip Rafter	
Plumb 12½- 17	**Valley Shingles**
Level. 17 - 12½	Cross. 12 - 17⅜
Side.. 10½- 8½	Set bevel on
Backing12½- 8½	butt end.
Set bevel to last named.	**Mitre-Box Cuts for Gable Moulds**
Jack Rafter	Plumb 12½- 12
Plumb 12½- 12	Mitre. 17⅜- 12
Level. 12 - 12½	**Bisection of**
Side.. 17⅜- 12	12½- 12=10⅛- 24

For full explanation see Index.

68

COMMON RAFTER

Span Ft.	Length Ft. In.	Span In.	Lgth. In.
1..	. 8⅝	¼	.. ⅛
2..	1. 5⅜	½	.. ⅜
3..	2. 2	¾	.. ½
4..	2.10⅝	1	.. ¾
5..	3. 7⅜	¼	.. ⅞
6..	4. 4	½	..1⅛
7..	5. 0⅝	¾	.. ¼
8..	5. 9⅜	2	.. ½
9..	6. 6	¼	.. ⅝
10..	7. 2⅝	½	.. ¾
11..	7.11¼	¾	..2
12..	8. 8	3	.. ⅛
13..	9. 4⅝	¼	.. ⅜
14..	10. 1¼	½	.. ½
15..	10.10	¾	.. ¾
16..	11. 6⅝	4	.. ⅞
17..	12. 3¼	¼	..3⅛
18..	13. 0	½	.. ¼
19..	13. 8⅝	¾	.. ⅜
20..	14. 5¼	5	.. ⅝
21..	15. 2	¼	.. ¾
22..	15.10⅝	½	..4
23..	16. 7¼	¾	.. ⅛
24..	17. 3⅞	6	.. ⅜
25..	18. 0⅝	¼	.. ½
26..	18. 9¼	½	.. ¾
27..	19. 5⅞	¾	.. ⅞
28..	20. 2⅝	7	..5
29..	20.11¼	¼	.. ¼
30..	21. 7⅞	½	.. ⅜
31..	22. 4⅝	¾	.. ⅝
32..	23. 1¼	8	.. ¾
33..	23. 9⅞	¼	..6
34..	24. 6⅝	½	.. ⅛
35..	25. 3¼	¾	.. ⅜
36..	25.11⅞	9	.. ½
37..	26. 8⅝	¼	.. ⅝
38..	27. 5¼	½	.. ⅞
39..	28. 1⅞	¾	..7
40..	28.10½	10	.. ¼
41..	29. 7¼	¼	.. ⅜
42..	30. 3⅞	½	.. ⅝
43..	31. 0½	¾	.. ¾
44..	31. 9¼	11	..8
45..	32. 5⅞	¼	.. ⅛
46..	33. 2½	½	.. ¼
47..	33.11¼	¾	.. ½
48..	34. 7⅞	12	.. ⅝
49..	35. 4½		
50..	36. 1¼		

HIP OR VALLEY RAFTER

Span Ft.	Length Ft. In.	Span In.	Lgth. In.
1..	.10½	¼	.. ¼
2..	1. 9⅛	½	.. ½
3..	2. 7⅝	¾	.. ⅝
4..	3. 6⅛	1	.. ⅞
5..	4. 4¾	¼	..1⅛
6..	5. 3¼	½	.. ⅜
7..	6. 1¾	¾	.. ½
8..	7. 0¼	2	.. ¾
9..	7.10⅞	¼	..2
10..	8. 9⅜	½	.. ¼
11..	9. 7⅞	¾	.. ⅜
12..	10. 6½	3	.. ⅝
13..	11. 5	¼	.. ⅞
14..	12. 3½	½	..3⅛
15..	13. 2⅛	¾	.. ¼
16..	14. 0⅝	4	.. ½
17..	14.11⅛	¼	.. ¾
18..	15. 9¾	½	..4
19..	16. 8¼	¾	.. ⅛
20..	17. 6¾	5	.. ⅜
21..	18. 5¼	¼	.. ⅝
22..	19. 3⅞	½	.. ⅞
23..	20. 2⅜	¾	..5
24..	21. 0⅞	6	.. ¼
25..	21.11½	¼	.. ½
26..	22.10	½	.. ¾
27..	23. 8½	¾	.. ⅞
28..	24. 7⅛	7	..6⅛
29..	25. 5⅝	¼	.. ⅜
30..	26. 4⅛	½	.. ⅝
31..	27. 2¾	¾	.. ¾
32..	28. 1¼	8	..7
33..	28.11¾	¼	.. ¼
34..	29.10⅜	½	.. ½
35..	30. 8⅞	¾	.. ⅝
36..	31. 7⅜	9	.. ⅞
37..	32. 5⅞	¼	..8⅛
38..	33. 4½	½	.. ⅜
39..	34. 3	¾	.. ⅝
40..	35. 1½	10	.. ¾
41..	36. 0⅛	¼	..9
42..	36.10⅝	½	.. ¼
43..	37. 9⅛	¾	.. ½
44..	38. 7¾	11	.. ⅝
45..	39. 6¼	¼	.. ⅞
46..	40. 4¾	½	.10⅛
47..	41. 3⅜	¾	.. ⅜
48..	42. 1⅞	12	.. ½
49..	43. 0⅜		
50..	43.10⅞		

JACK RAFTER

Spaced In.	Length Ft.	In.
1..		1½
2..		3
3..		4⅜
4..		5⅞
5..		7⅜
6..		8⅞
7..		10⅜
8..		11¾
9..	1	1¼
10..		2¾
11..		4¼
12..		5¾
13..		7⅛
14..		8⅝
15..		10⅛
16..		11⅝
17..	2	1⅛
18..		2½
19..		4
20..		5½
21..		7
22..		8⅜
23..		9⅞
24..		11⅜
25..	3	0⅞
26..		2⅜
27..		3¾
28..		5¼
29..		6¾
30..		8¼
31..		9¾
32..		11⅛
33..	4	0⅝
34..		2⅛
35..		3⅝
36..		5⅛
37..		6½
38..		8
39..		9½
40..		11
41..	5	0½
42..		1⅞
43..		3⅜
44..		4⅞
45..		6⅜
46..		7⅞
47..		9¼
48..		10¾

13 & 12 — 47¼°

EXPLANATION

Common Rafter

Width of building...........13′2¼″

Find length of Common Rafter.

Answer:

Under **Span, ft.** find	13′ =	9′ 7″
" " **in.** "	2¼″ =	1⅝″
Total length Common Rft.		9′ 8⅝″

When rafters overhang, add both overhangs to width of building. Use total span as before.

To get length of rafter by its run: doubling the run gives the span. Proceed as before.

Tables give full length. Allow for half thickness of ridge.

Spans over 50′, as 60′, add lengths of 50′ & 10′ spans together.

Hip Rafter

If common rafter span is 13′2¼″, Hip rafter is 11′9″ long. Measure length of Hip on center of top edge. If Hip is unbacked (top edge square), see Index. If edge is backed (beveled), see Index.

Allow for half thickness of ridge.

Jack Rafters

Spaced 26″ apart are 3′2⅜″ different in length. Measure length on center of top edge. Cut short equal to half thickness of hip.

CUTS FOR STEEL SQUARE.

The first figure is always the cut.

Common Rafter

Plumb 13 - 12
Level. 12 - 13

Hip Rafter

Plumb 13 - 17
Level. 17 - 13
Side.. 10¾ - 8½
Backing 13 - 21⅜
Set bevel to last named.

Jack Rafter

Plumb 13 - 12
Level. 12 - 13
Side.. 17¾ - 12

Purlin Rafter Roof Sheathing

Plumb 13 - 17¾
Cross. 12 - 17¾

Valley Shingles

Cross. 12 - 17¾
Set bevel on butt end.

Mitre-Box Cuts for Gable Moulds

Plumb 13 - 12
Mitre. 17¾ - 12

Bisection of
13 - 12 = 10½ - 24

For full explanation see Index.

COMMON RAFTER

Span Ft.	Length Ft. In.	Span In.	Lgth. In.
1..	. 8⅞	¼	.. ⅛
2..	1. 5¾	½	.. ⅜
3..	2. 2½	¾	.. ½
4..	2.11⅜	1	.. ¾
5..	3. 8¼	¼	.. ⅞
6..	4. 5⅛	½	..1⅛
7..	5. 1⅞	¾	.. ¼
8..	5.10¾	2	.. ½
9..	6. 7⅝	¼	.. ⅝
10..	7. 4½	½	.. ⅞
11..	8. 1¼	¾	..2
12..	8.10⅛	3	.. ¼
13..	9. 7	¼	.. ⅜
14..	10. 3⅞	½	.. ⅝
15..	11. 0¾	¾	.. ¾
16..	11. 9½	4	..3
17..	12. 6⅜	¼	.. ⅛
18..	13. 3¼	½	.. ⅜
19..	14. 0⅛	¾	.. ½
20..	14. 8⅞	5	.. ⅝
21..	15. 5¾	¼	.. ⅞
22..	16. 2⅝	½	..4
23..	16.11½	¾	.. ¼
24..	17. 8⅜	6	.. ⅜
25..	18. 5⅛	¼	.. ⅝
26..	19. 2	½	.. ¾
27..	19.10⅞	¾	..5
28..	20. 7¾	7	.. ⅛
29..	21. 4½	¼	.. ⅜
30..	22. 1⅜	½	.. ½
31..	22.10¼	¾	.. ¾
32..	23. 7⅛	8	.. ⅞
33..	24. 3⅞	¼	..6⅛
34..	25. 0¾	½	.. ¼
35..	25. 9⅝	¾	.. ½
36..	26. 6½	9	.. ⅝
37..	27. 3¼	¼	.. ⅞
38..	28. 0⅛	½	..7
39..	28. 9	¾	.. ⅛
40..	29. 5⅞	10	.. ⅜
41..	30. 2⅝	¼	.. ½
42..	30.11½	½	.. ¾
43..	31. 8⅜	¾	.. ⅞
44..	32. 5¼	11	..8⅛
45..	33. 2⅛	¼	.. ¼
46..	33.10⅞	½	.. ½
47..	34. 7¾	¾	.. ⅝
48..	35. 4⅝	12	.. ⅝
49..	36. 1½		
50..	36.10¼		

HIP OR VALLEY RAFTER

Span Ft.	Length Ft. In.	Span In.	Lgth. In.
1..	.10¾	¼	.. ¼
2..	1. 9⅜	½	.. ½
3..	2. 8⅛	¾	.. ⅝
4..	3. 6¾	1	.. ⅞
5..	4. 5½	¼	..1⅛
6..	5. 4⅛	½	.. ⅜
7..	6. 2⅞	¾	.. ½
8..	7. 1½	2	.. ¾
9..	8. 0¼	¼	..2
10..	8.10⅞	½	.. ¼
11..	9. 9⅝	¾	.. ½
12..	10. 8¼	3	.. ⅝
13..	11. 7	¼	.. ⅞
14..	12. 5⅝	½	..3⅛
15..	13. 4⅜	¾	.. ⅜
16..	14. 3	4	.. ½
17..	15. 1¾	¼	.. ¾
18..	16. 0⅜	½	..4
19..	16.11⅛	¾	.. ¼
20..	17. 9¾	5	.. ½
21..	18. 8½	¼	.. ⅝
22..	19. 7⅛	½	.. ⅞
23..	20. 5⅞	¾	..5⅛
24..	21. 4½	6	.. ⅜
25..	22. 3¼	¼	.. ⅝
26..	23. 1⅞	½	.. ¾
27..	24. 0⅝	¾	..6
28..	24.11¼	7	.. ¼
29..	25.10	¼	.. ½
30..	26. 8⅝	½	.. ⅝
31..	27. 7⅜	¾	.. ⅞
32..	28. 6	8	..7⅛
33..	29. 4¾	¼	.. ⅜
34..	30. 3⅜	½	.. ⅝
35..	31. 2⅛	¾	.. ¾
36..	32. 0¾	9	..8
37..	32.11½	¼	.. ¼
38..	33.10⅛	½	.. ½
39..	34. 8⅞	¾	.. ⅝
40..	35. 7½	10	.. ⅞
41..	36. 6¼	¼	..9⅛
42..	37. 4⅞	½	.. ⅜
43..	38. 3⅝	¾	.. ⅝
44..	39. 2¼	11	.. ¾
45..	40. 1	¼	.10
46..	40.11⅝	½	.. ¼
47..	41.10⅜	¾	.. ½
48..	42. 9	12	.. ⅝
49..	43. 7¾		
50..	44. 6⅜		

JACK RAFTER

Spaced In.	Length Ft.	In.
1..		1½
2..		3
3..		4½
4..		6
5..		7½
6..		9
7..		10½
8..	1	0
9..		1½
10..		3
11..		4½
12..		6⅛
13..		7⅝
14..		9⅛
15..		10⅝
16..	2	0⅛
17..		1⅝
18..		3⅛
19..		4⅝
20..		6⅛
21..		7⅝
22..		9⅛
23..		10⅝
24..	3	0⅛
25..		1⅝
26..		3⅛
27..		4⅝
28..		6⅛
29..		7⅝
30..		9⅛
31..		10⅝
32..	4	0⅛
33..		1⅝
34..		3⅛
35..		4⅝
36..		6¼
37..		7¾
38..		9¼
39..		10¾
40	5	0¼
41 .		1¾
42..		3¼
43..		4¾
44..		6¼
45..		7¾
46..		9¼
47..		10¾
48..	6	0¼

13½ & 12—48½°

EXPLANATION

Common Rafter

Width of building...........**32′1¼″**
Find length of Common Rafter.
Answer:

Under **Span, ft.** find 32′ = **24′ 1″**
" " **in.** " 1¼″ = **1″**

Total length Common Rft. **24′ 2″**

When rafters overhang, add both overhangs to width of **building.** Use total span as before.

To get length of rafter by its run: doubling the run gives **the span.** Proceed as before.

Tables give full length. **Allow for** half thickness of ridge.

Spans over 50′, as 60′, **add lengths** of 50′ & 10′ spans together.

Hip Rafter

If common rafter span **is 32′1¼″.** Hip rafter is 29′0⅛″ long. **Measure** length of Hip on center **of top** edge. If Hip is unbacked **(top edge** square), see Index. **If edge is** backed (beveled), see Index.

Allow for half thickness **of ridge.**

Jack Rafters

Spaced 35″ apart are **4′4⅝″ different** in length. **Measure length** on center of top edge. **Cut short** equal to half thickness **of hip.**

CUTS FOR STEEL SQUARE.

The first figure is always **the cut.**

Common Rafter
Plumb 13½- 12
Level. 12 - 13½

Hip Rafter
Plumb 13½- 17
Level. 17 - 13½
Side.. 10⅞- 8½
Backing 13½- 21⅝
Set bevel to last named.

Jack Rafter
Plumb 13½- 12
Level. 12 - 13½
Side.. 18⅛- 12

Purlin Rafter Roof Sheathing
Plumb **13½- 18⅛**
Cross. **12 - 18⅛**

Valley Shingles
Cross. **12 - 18⅛**
Set bevel **on** butt end.

Mitre-Box Cuts for Gable Moulds
Mitre. **18⅛- 12**
Plumb **13½- 12**

Bisection of
13½- 12=10¾- 24

For full explanation see **Index.**

COMMON RAFTER				HIP or VALLEY RAFTER			
Span	Length	Span	Lgth.	Span	Length	Span	Lgth.
Ft.	Ft. In.	In.	In.	Ft.	Ft. In.	In.	In.
1..	.9	¼ ..	¼	1..	.10⅞	¼ ..	¼
2..	1. 6⅛	½ ..	⅜	2..	1. 9⅝	½ ..	½
3..	2. 3⅛	¾ ..	⅝	3..	2. 8½	¾ ..	⅝
4..	3. 0⅛	1 ..	¾	4..	3. 7⅜	1 ..	⅞
5..	3. 9⅛	¼ ..	1	5..	4. 6¼	¼ ..	1⅛
6..	4. 6¼	½ ..	1⅛	6..	5. 5	½ ..	⅜
7..	5. 3¼	¾ ..	1⅜	7..	6. 3⅞	¾ ..	⅝
8..	6. 0¼	2 ..	½	8..	7. 2¾	2 ..	¾
9..	6. 9¼	¼ ..	¾	9..	8. 1⅝	¼ ..	2
10..	7. 6⅜	½ ..	⅞	10..	9. 0⅜	½ ..	¼
11..	8. 3⅜	¾ ..	2⅛	11..	9.11¼	¾ ..	½
12..	9. 0⅜	3 ..	¼	12..	10.10⅛	3 ..	¾
13..	9. 9⅜	¼ ..	½	13..	11. 9	¼ ..	3
14..	10. 6⅜	½ ..	⅝	14..	12. 7¾	½ ..	⅛
15..	11. 3½	¾ ..	⅞	15..	13. 6⅝	¾ ..	⅜
16..	12. 0½	4 ..	3	16..	14. 5¼	4 ..	⅝
17..	12. 9½	¼ ..	¼	17..	15. 4⅜	¼ ..	⅞
18..	13. 6½	½ ..	⅜	18..	16. 3⅛	½ ..	4⅛
19..	14. 3⅝	¾ ..	⅝	19..	17. 2	¾ ..	¼
20..	15. 0⅝	5 ..	¾	20..	18. 0⅞	5 ..	½
21..	15. 9⅝	¼ ..	4	21..	18.11¾	¼ ..	¾
22..	16. 6⅝	½ ..	⅛	22..	19.10½	½ ..	5
23..	17. 3¾	¾ ..	⅜	23..	20. 9⅜	¾ ..	¼
24..	18. 0¾	6 ..	½	24..	21. 8¼	6 ..	⅜
25..	18. 9¾	¼ ..	¾	25..	22. 7⅛	¼ ..	⅝
26..	19. 6¾	½ ..	⅞	26..	23. 5⅞	½ ..	⅞
27..	20. 3⅞	¾ ..	5⅛	27..	24. 4¾	¾ ..	6⅛
28..	21. 0⅞	7 ..	¼	28..	25. 3⅝	7 ..	⅜
29..	21. 9⅞	¼ ..	½	29..	26. 2⅜	¼ ..	½
30..	22. 6⅞	½ ..	⅝	30..	27. 1¼	½ ..	¾
31..	23. 4	¾ ..	⅞	31..	28. 0⅛	¾ ..	7
32..	24. 1	8 ..	6	32..	28.11	8 ..	¼
33..	24.10	¼ ..	¼	33..	29. 9¾	¼ ..	½
34..	25. 7	½ ..	⅜	34..	30. 8⅝	½ ..	⅝
35..	26. 4⅛	¾ ..	⅝	35..	31. 7½	¾ ..	⅞
36..	27. 1⅛	9 ..	¾	36..	32. 6⅜	9 ..	8⅛
37..	27.10⅛	¼ ..	7	37..	33. 5⅛	¼ ..	⅜
38..	28. 7⅛	½ ..	⅛	38..	34. 4	½ ..	⅝
39..	29. 4¼	¾ ..	⅜	39..	35. 2⅞	¾ ..	⅞
40..	30. 1¼	10 ..	½	40..	36. 1¾	10 ..	9
41..	30.10¼	¼ ..	¾	41..	37. 0½	¼ ..	¼
42..	31. 7¼	½ ..	⅞	42..	37.11⅜	½ ..	½
43..	32. 4⅜	¾ ..	8⅛	43..	38.10¼	¾ ..	¾
44..	33. 1⅜	11 ..	¼	44..	39. 9¼	11 ..	⅞
45..	33.10⅜	¼ ..	½	45..	40. 7⅞	¼ ..	10⅛
46..	34. 7⅜	½ ..	⅝	46..	41. 6¾	½ ..	⅜
47..	35. 4½	¾ ..	⅞	47..	42. 5⅝	¾ ..	⅝
48..	36. 1½	12 ..	9	48..	43. 4½	12 ..	¾
49..	36.10½			49..	44. 3¼		
50..	37. 7½			50..	45. 2⅛		

JACK RAFTER

Spaced In.	Length Ft. In.
1..	1½
2..	3⅛
3..	4⅝
4..	6⅛
5..	7⅝
6..	9¼
7..	10¾
8..1	0¼
9..	1⅞
10..	3⅜
11..	4⅞
12..	6½
13..	8
14..	9½
15..	11
16..2	0⅝
17..	2⅛
18..	3⅝
19..	5¼
20..	6¾
21..	8¼
22..	9⅞
23..	11⅜
24..3	0⅞
25..	2⅜
26..	4
27..	5½
28..	7
29..	8⅝
30..	10⅛
31..	11⅝
32..4	1⅛
33..	2¾
34..	4¼
35..	5¾
36..	7⅜
37..	8⅞
38..	10⅜
39..5	0
40..	1½
41..	3
42..	4½
43..	6⅛
44..	7⅝
45..	9⅛
46..	10⅝
47..6	0¼
48..	1¾

14 & 12 — 49½°

EXPLANATION

Common Rafter

Width of building..........41'5½"

Find length of Common Rafter.

Answer:

Under **Span**, ft. find 41' = 31' 6"
"   "   in. "   5½" = 4¼"

Total length Common Rft. 31'10¼"

When rafters overhang, add both overhangs to width of building. Use total span as before.

To get length of rafter by its run: doubling the run gives the span. Proceed as before.

Tables give full length. Allow for half thickness of ridge.

Spans over 50', as 60', add lengths of 50' & 10' spans together.

Hip Rafter

If common rafter span is 41'5½", Hip rafter is 38'0" long. Measure length of Hip on center of top edge. If Hip is unbacked (top edge square), see Index. If edge is backed (beveled), see Index.

Allow for half thickness of ridge.

Jack Rafters

Spaced 38" apart are 4'10⅜" different in length. Measure length on center of top edge. Cut short equal to half thickness of hip.

CUTS FOR STEEL SQUARE.

The first figure is always the cut.

Common Rafter	Purlin Rafter Roof Sheathing
Plumb 14 - 12	
Level. 12 - 14	Plumb 14 - 18½
	Cross. 12 - 18½

Hip Rafter	Valley Shingles
Plumb 14 - 17	Cross. 12 - 18½
Level. 17 - 14	Set bevel on
Side.. 11 - 8½	butt end.
Backing14 - 22	
Set bevel to	
last named.	

Jack Rafter	Mitre-Box Cuts for Gable Moulds
Plumb 14 - 12	Plumb 14 - 12
Level. 12 - 14	Mitre. 18½- 12
Side.. 18½- 12	

Bisection of
14- 12=11 - 24

For full explanation see Index.

COMMON RAFTER

Span Ft.	Length Ft. In.	Span In.	Lgth. In.
1	. 9¼	¼	¼
2	1. 6½	½	⅜
3	2. 3⅝	¾	⅝
4	3. 0⅞	1	¾
5	3.10⅛	¼	1
6	4. 7⅜	½	1⅛
7	5. 4½	¾	⅜
8	6. 1¾	2	½
9	6.11	¼	¾
10	7. 8¼	½	⅞
11	8. 5⅜	¾	2⅛
12	9. 2⅝	3	¼
13	9.11⅞	¼	½
14	10. 9⅛	½	¾
15	11. 6¼	¾	⅞
16	12. 3½	4	3⅛
17	13. 0¾	¼	¼
18	13.10	½	½
19	14. 7⅛	¾	⅝
20	15. 4⅜	5	⅞
21	16. 1⅝	¼	4
22	16.10⅞	½	¼
23	17. 8	¾	⅜
24	18. 5¼	6	⅝
25	19. 2½	¼	¾
26	19.11¾	½	5
27	20. 8⅞	¾	⅛
28	21. 6⅛	7	⅜
29	22. 3⅜	¼	⅝
30	23. 0⅝	½	¾
31	23. 9¾	¾	6
32	24. 7	8	⅛
33	25. 4¼	¼	⅜
34	26. 1½	½	½
35	26.10⅝	¾	¾
36	27. 7⅞	9	⅞
37	28. 5⅛	¼	7⅛
38	29. 2⅜	½	¼
39	29.11½	¾	½
40	30. 8¾	10	⅝
41	31. 6	¼	⅞
42	32. 3⅛	½	8⅛
43	33. 0⅜	¾	¼
44	33. 9⅝	11	½
45	34. 6⅞	¼	⅝
46	35. 4⅛	½	⅞
47	36. 1⅜	¾	9
48	36.10½	12	¼
49	37. 7¾		
50	38. 5		

HIP or VALLEY RAFTER

Span Ft.	Length Ft. In.	Span In.	Lgth. In.
1	.11	¼	¼
2	1.10	½	½
3	2. 9	¾	¾
4	3. 8	1	⅞
5	4. 7	¼	1⅛
6	5. 6	½	⅜
7	6. 5	¾	⅝
8	7. 4	2	⅞
9	8. 3	¼	2
10	9. 2	½	¼
11	10. 1	¾	½
12	11. 0	3	¾
13	11.11	¼	3
14	12.10	½	¼
15	13. 9	¾	⅜
16	14. 8	4	⅝
17	15. 7	¼	⅞
18	16. 6	½	4⅛
19	17. 5	¾	⅜
20	18. 4	5	⅝
21	19. 3	¼	¾
22	20. 2	½	5
23	21. 1	¾	¼
24	22. 0	6	½
25	22.11	¼	¾
26	23.10	½	6
27	24. 9	¾	⅛
28	25. 8	7	⅜
29	26. 7	¼	⅝
30	27. 6	½	⅞
31	28. 5	¾	7⅛
32	29. 4	8	⅜
33	30. 3	¼	½
34	31. 2	½	¾
35	32. 1	¾	8
36	33. 0	9	¼
37	33.11	¼	½
38	34.10	½	¾
39	35. 9	¾	⅞
40	36. 8	10	9⅛
41	37. 7	¼	⅜
42	38. 6	½	⅝
43	39. 5	¾	⅞
44	40. 4	11	10⅛
45	41. 3	¼	¼
46	42. 2	½	½
47	43. 1	¾	¾
48	44. 0	12	11
49	44.11		
50	45.10		

JACK RAFTER Spaced In.	Length Ft.	In.
1..		1⅝
2..		3⅛
3..		4¾
4..		6¼
5..		7⅞
6..		9⅜
7..		11
8..	1	0½
9..		2⅛
10..		3⅝
11..		5¼
12..		6⅞
13..		8⅜
14..		10
15..		11½
16..	2	1⅛
17..		2⅝
18..		4¼
19..		5¾
20..		7⅜
21..		9
22..		10½
23..	3	0⅛
24..		1⅝
25..		3¼
26..		4¾
27..		6⅜
28..		7⅞
29..		9½
30..		11
31..	4	0⅝
32..		2¼
33..		3¾
34..		5⅜
35..		6⅞
36..		8½
37..		10
38..		11⅝
39..	5	1⅛
40..		2¾
41..		4⅜
42..		5⅞
43..		7½
44..		9
45..		10⅝
46..	6	0⅛
47..		1¾
48..		3¼

14½ & 12 — 50½°

EXPLANATION

Common Rafter

Width of building...........17′3¼″
Find length of Common Rafter.

Answer:

Under **Span, ft.** find 17′ = 13′ 4″
" " in. " 3¼″ = 2½″

Total length Common Rft. 13′ 6½″

When rafters overhang, add both overhangs to width of building. Use total span as before.

To get length of rafter by its run: doubling the run gives the span. Proceed as before.

Tables give full length. Allow for half thickness of ridge.

Spans over 50′, as 60′, add lengths of 50′ & 10′ spans together.

Hip Rafter

If common rafter span is 17′3¼″, Hip rafter is 16′0¾″ long. Measure length of Hip on center of top edge. If Hip is unbacked (top edge square), see Index. If edge is backed (beveled), see Index.

Allow for half thickness of ridge.

Jack Rafters

Spaced 36″ apart are 4′8½″ different in length. Measure length on center of top edge. Cut short equal to half thickness of hip.

CUTS FOR STEEL SQUARE.

The first figure is always the cut.

Common Rafter
Plumb 14½- 12
Level. 12 - 14½

Hip Rafter
Plumb 14½- 17
Level. 17 - 14½
Side.. 11⅛- 8½
Backing 14½- 22⅜
Set bevel to last named.

Jack Rafter
Plumb 14½- 12
Level. 12 - 14½
Side.. 18⅞- 12

Purlin Rafter Roof Sheathing
Plumb 14½- 18⅞
Cross. 12 - 18⅞

Valley Shingles
Cross. 12 - 18⅞
Set bevel on butt end.

Mitre-Box Cuts for Gable Moulds
Plumb 14½- 12
Mitre. 18⅞- 12

Bisection of
14½- 12=11¼- 24

For full explanation see **Index.**

COMMON RAFTER

Span Ft.	Length Ft. In.	Span In.	Lgth. In.
1..	9⅜	¼ ..	¼
2..	1. 6⅞	½ ..	⅜
3..	2. 4¼	¾ ..	⅝
4..	3. 1⅝	1 ..	¾
5..	3.11	¼ ..	1
6..	4. 8½	½ ..	1⅛
7..	5. 5⅞	¾ ..	1⅜
8..	6. 3¼	2 ..	1⅝
9..	7. 0¾	¼ ..	1¾
10..	7.10⅛	½ ..	2
11..	8. 7½	¾ ..	2⅛
12..	9. 4⅞	3 ..	2⅜
13..	10. 2⅜	¼ ..	2½
14..	10.11¾	½ ..	2¾
15..	11. 9⅛	¾ ..	3
16..	12. 6⅝	4 ..	3⅛
17..	13. 4	¼ ..	3⅜
18..	14. 1⅜	½ ..	3½
19..	14.10¾	¾ ..	3¾
20..	15. 8¼	5 ..	3⅞
21..	16. 5⅝	¼ ..	4⅛
22..	17. 3	½ ..	4¼
23..	18. 0½	¾ ..	4½
24..	18. 9⅞	6 ..	4¾
25..	19. 7¼	¼ ..	4⅞
26..	20. 4⅝	½ ..	5⅛
27..	21. 2⅛	¾ ..	5¼
28..	21.11½	7 ..	5½
29..	22. 8⅞	¼ ..	5⅝
30..	23. 6⅜	½ ..	5⅞
31..	24. 3¾	¾ ..	6⅛
32..	25. 1⅛	8 ..	6¼
33..	25.10½	¼ ..	6½
34..	26. 8	½ ..	6⅝
35..	27. 5⅜	¾ ..	6⅞
36..	28. 2¾	9 ..	7
37..	29. 0¼	¼ ..	7¼
38..	29. 9⅝	½ ..	7½
39..	30. 7	¾ ..	7⅝
40..	31. 4⅜	10 ..	7⅞
41..	32. 1⅞	¼ ..	8
42..	32.11¼	½ ..	8¼
43..	33. 8⅝	¾ ..	8½
44..	34. 6⅛	11 ..	8⅝
45..	35. 3½	¼ ..	8⅞
46..	36. 0⅞	½ ..	9
47..	36.10¼	¾ ..	9¼
48..	37. 7¾	12 ..	9⅜
49..	38. 5⅛		
50..	39. 2½		

HIP or VALLEY RAFTER

Span Ft.	Length Ft. In.	Span In.	Lgth. In.
1..	11⅛	¼ ..	¼
2..	1.10⅜	½ ..	½
3..	2. 9½	¾ ..	¾
4..	3. 8⅝	1 ..	⅞
5..	4. 7¾	¼ ..	1⅛
6..	5. 7	½ ..	1⅜
7..	6. 6⅛	¾ ..	1⅝
8..	7. 5¼	2 ..	1⅞
9..	8. 4½	¼ ..	2⅛
10..	9. 3⅝	½ ..	2⅜
11..	10. 2¾	¾ ..	2½
12..	11. 1⅞	3 ..	2¾
13..	12. 1⅛	¼ ..	3
14..	13. 0¼	½ ..	3¼
15..	13.11⅜	¾ ..	3½
16..	14.10⅝	4 ..	3¾
17..	15. 9¾	¼ ..	4
18..	16. 8⅞	½ ..	4⅛
19..	17. 8	¾ ..	4⅜
20..	18. 7¼	5 ..	4⅝
21..	19. 6⅜	¼ ..	4⅞
22..	20. 5½	½ ..	5⅛
23..	21. 4¾	¾ ..	5⅜
24..	22. 3⅞	6 ..	5⅝
25..	23. 3	¼ ..	5⅞
26..	24. 2⅛	½ ..	6
27..	25. 1⅜	¾ ..	6¼
28..	26. 0½	7 ..	6½
29..	26.11⅝	¼ ..	6¾
30..	27.10⅞	½ ..	7
31..	28.10	¾ ..	7¼
32..	29. 9⅛	8 ..	7½
33..	30. 8⅜	¼ ..	7⅝
34..	31. 7½	½ ..	7⅞
35..	32. 6⅝	¾ ..	8⅛
36..	33. 5¾	9 ..	8⅜
37..	34. 5	¼ ..	8⅝
38..	35. 4⅛	½ ..	8⅞
39..	36. 3¼	¾ ..	9⅛
40..	37. 2⅜	10 ..	9¼
41..	38. 1⅝	¼ ..	9½
42..	39. 0¾	½ ..	9¾
43..	39.11⅞	¾ ..	10
44..	40.11⅛	11 ..	10¼
45..	41.10¼	¼ ..	10½
46..	42. 9⅜	½ ..	10¾
47..	43. 8½	¾ ..	10⅞
48..	44. 7¾	12 ..	11⅛
49..	45. 6⅞		
50..	46. 6		

JACK RAFTER	
Spaced	Length
In.	Ft. In.
1..	1⅝
2..	3¼
3..	4¾
4..	6⅜
5..	8
6..	9⅝
7..	11¼
8..1	0¾
9..	2⅜
10..	4
11..	5⅝
12..	7¼
13..	8⅞
14..	10⅜
15..2	0
16..	1⅝
17..	3¼
18..	4⅞
19..	6⅜
20..	8
21..	9⅝
22..	11¼
23..3	0⅞
24..	2⅜
25..	4
26..	5⅝
27..	7¼
28..	8⅞
29..	10⅜
30..4	0
31..	1⅝
32..	3¼
33..	4⅞
34..	6⅜
35..	8
36..	9⅝
37..	11¼
38..5	0⅞
39..	2½
40..	4
41..	5⅝
42..	7¼
43..	8⅞
44..	10½
45..6	0
46..	1⅝
47..	3¼
48..	4⅞

15 & 12 — 51½°

EXPLANATION
Common Rafter
Width of building..........43'3¾"
Find length of Common Rafter.
Answer:

Under **Span**, ft. find 43' = 34' 5"
" " in. " 3¾" = 3"

Total length Common Rft. 34' 8"

When rafters overhang, add both overhangs to width of building. Use total span as before.

To get length of rafter by its run: doubling the run gives the span. Proceed as before.

Tables give full length. Allow for half thickness of ridge.

Spans over 50', as 60', add lengths of 50' & 10' spans together.

Hip Rafter
If common rafter span is 43'3¾", Hip rafter is 40'10½" long. Measure length of Hip on center of top edge. If Hip is unbacked (top edge square), see Index. If edge is backed (beveled), see Index.

Allow for half thickness of ridge.

Jack Rafters
Spaced 32" apart are 4'3¼" different in length. Measure length on center of top edge. Cut short equal to half thickness of hip.

CUTS FOR STEEL SQUARE.
The first figure is always the cut.

Common Rafter	Purlin Rafter Roof Sheathing
Plumb 15 - 12	
Level. 12 · 15	Plumb 15 - 19¼
	Cross. 12 - 19¼

Hip Rafter	Valley Shingles
Plumb 15 - 17	Cross. 12 - 19¼
Level. 17 - 15	Set bevel on
Side.. 11⅜- 8½	butt end.
Backing15 - 22⅝	
Set bevel to	Mitre-Box Cuts
last named.	for Gable Moulds
	Plumb 15 - 12
Jack Rafter	Mitre. 19¼- 12
Plumb 15 - 12	
Level. 12 - 15	Bisection of
Side.. 19¼- 12	15- 12=11½- 24

For full explanation see Index.

COMMON RAFTER				HIP or VALLEY RAFTER			
Span Ft.	Length Ft. In.	Span In.	Lgth. In.	Span Ft.	Length Ft. In.	Span In.	Lgth. In.
1..	.9⅝	¼..	¼	1..	.11⅜	¼..	¼
2..	1.7¼	½..	⅜	2..	1.10⅝	½..	½
3..	2.4⅞	¾..	⅝	3..	2.10	¾..	¾
4..	3.2⅜	1..	¾	4..	3.9¼	1..	1
5..	4.0	¼..	1	5..	4.8⅝	¼..	⅛
6..	4.9⅝	½..	¼	6..	5.8	½..	⅜
7..	5.7¼	¾..	⅜	7..	6.7¼	¾..	⅝
8..	6.4⅞	2..	⅝	8..	7.6⅝	2..	⅞
9..	7.2½	¼..	¾	9..	8.5⅞	¼..	2⅛
10..	8.0	½..	2	10..	9.5¼	½..	⅜
11..	8.9⅝	¾..	¼	11..	10.4⅝	¾..	⅝
12..	9.7¼	3..	⅜	12..	11.3⅞	3..	⅞
13..	10.4⅞	¼..	⅝	13..	12.3¼	¼..	3⅛
14..	11.2½	½..	¾	14..	13.2½	½..	¼
15..	12.0⅛	¾..	3	15..	14.1⅞	¾..	½
16..	12.9⅝	4..	¼	16..	15.1¼	4..	¾
17..	13.7¼	¼..	⅜	17..	16.0½	¼..	4
18..	14.4⅞	½..	⅝	18..	16.11⅞	½..	¼
19..	15.2½	¾..	¾	19..	17.11⅛	¾..	½
20..	16.0⅛	5..	4	20..	18.10½	5..	¾
21..	16.9¾	¼..	¼	21..	19.9⅞	¼..	5
22..	17.7⅜	½..	⅜	22..	20.9⅛	½..	¼
23..	18.4⅞	¾..	⅝	23..	21.8½	¾..	⅜
24..	19.2½	6..	¾	24..	22.7⅞	6..	⅝
25..	20.0⅛	¼..	5	25..	23.7⅛	¼..	⅞
26..	20.9¾	½..	¼	26..	24.6½	½..	6⅛
27..	21.7⅜	¾..	⅜	27..	25.5¾	¾..	⅜
28..	22.4⅞	7..	⅝	28..	26.5⅛	7..	⅝
29..	23.2½	¼..	¾	29..	27.4⅜	¼..	⅞
30..	24.0⅛	½..	6	30..	28.3¾	½..	7⅛
31..	24.9¾	¾..	¼	31..	29.3⅛	¾..	⅜
32..	25.7⅜	8..	⅜	32..	30.2⅜	8..	½
33..	26.5	¼..	⅝	33..	31.1¾	¼..	¾
34..	27.2½	½..	¾	34..	32.1	½..	8
35..	28.0⅛	¾..	7	35..	33.0⅜	¾..	¼
36..	28.9¾	9..	¼	36..	33.11¾	9..	½
37..	29.7⅜	¼..	⅜	37..	34.11	¼..	¾
38..	30.5	½..	⅝	38..	35.10⅜	½..	9
39..	31.2⅝	¾..	¾	39..	36.9⅝	¾..	¼
40..	32.0¼	10..	8	40..	37.9	10..	½
41..	32.9¾	¼..	¼	41..	38.8⅜	¼..	⅝
42..	33.7⅜	½..	⅜	42..	39.7⅝	½..	⅞
43..	34.5	¾..	⅝	43..	40.7	¾.10⅛	
44..	35.2⅝	11..	¾	44..	41.6¼	11..	⅜
45..	36.0¼	¼..	9	45..	42.5⅝	¼..	⅝
46..	36.9⅞	½..	¼	46..	43.4⅞	½..	⅞
47..	37.7⅜	¾..	⅜	47..	44.4¼	¾.11⅛	
48..	38.5	12..	⅝	48..	45.3⅝	12..	⅜
49..	39.2⅝			49..	46.2⅞		
50..	40.0¼			50..	47.2¼		

Spaced In.	Length Ft. In.
1..	1⅝
2..	3¼
3..	4⅞
4..	6½
5..	8⅛
6..	9¾
7..	11½
8..1	1⅛
9..	2¾
10..	4⅜
11..	6
12..	7⅝
13..	9¼
14..	10⅞
15..2	0½
16..	2⅛
17..	3¾
18..	5⅜
19..	7
20..	8⅝
21..	10¼
22..3	0
23..	1⅝
24..	3¼
25..	4⅞
26..	6½
27..	8⅛
28..	9¾
29..	11⅜
30..4	1
31..	2⅝
32..	4¼
33..	5⅞
34..	7½
35..	9⅛
36..	10¾
37..5	0½
38..	2⅛
39..	3¾
40..	5⅜
41..	7
42..	8⅝
43..	10¼
44..	11⅞
45..6	1½
46..	3⅛
47..	4¾
48..	6⅜

15½ & 12 — 52¼°

EXPLANATION

Common Rafter

Width of building..........25'5¼"
Find length of Common Rafter.
Answer:
Under Span, ft. find 25' = 20' 5"
    "   " In. "   5¼" =   4¼"

Total length Common Rft. 20' 9¼"

When rafters overhang, add both overhangs to width of building. Use total span as before.

To get length of rafter by its run: doubling the run gives the span. Proceed as before.

Tables give full length. Allow for half thickness of ridge.

Spans over 50', as 60', add lengths of 50' & 10' spans together.

Hip Rafter

If common rafter span is 25'5¼", Hip rafter is 24'4¼" long. Measure length of Hip on center of top edge. If Hip is unbacked (top edge square), see Index. If edge is backed (beveled), see Index.

Allow for half thickness of ridge.

Jack Rafters

Spaced 27" apart are 3'8⅛" different in length. Measure length on center of top edge. Cut short equal to half thickness of hip.

CUTS FOR STEEL SQUARE.

The first figure is always the cut.

Common Rafter	Purlin Rafter
Plumb 15½- 12	Roof Sheathing
Level. 12 - 15½	Plumb 15½- 19⅝
	Cross. 12 - 19⅝

Hip Rafter	Valley Shingles
Plumb 15½- 17	Cross. 12 - 19⅝
Level. 17 - 15½	Set bevel on
Side.. 11½- 8½	butt end.
Backing15½- 23	
Set bevel to	Mitre-Box Cuts
last named.	for Gable Moulds
	Plumb 15½- 12
Jack Rafter	Mitre. 19⅝- 12
Plumb 15½- 12	
Level. 12 - 15½	Bisection of
Side.. 19⅝- 12	15½- 12=11¾- 24

For full explanation see Index.

COMMON RAFTER

Span Ft.	Length Ft. In.	Span In.	Lgth. In.
1	.9¾	¼	¼
2	1. 7⅝	½	⅜
3	2. 5⅜	¾	⅝
4	3. 3¼	1	⅞
5	4. 1	¼	1
6	4.10¾	½	¼
7	5. 8⅝	¾	⅜
8	6. 6⅜	2	⅝
9	7. 4¼	¼	⅞
10	8. 2	½	2
11	8.11¾	¾	¼
12	9. 9⅝	3	½
13	10. 7⅜	¼	⅝
14	11. 5¼	½	⅞
15	12. 3	¾	3
16	13. 0⅞	4	¼
17	13.10⅝	¼	½
18	14. 8⅜	½	⅝
19	15. 6¼	¾	⅞
20	16. 4	5	4⅛
21	17. 1⅞	¼	¼
22	17.11⅝	½	½
23	18. 9⅜	¾	¾
24	19. 7¼	6	⅞
25	20. 5	¼	5⅛
26	21. 2⅞	½	¼
27	22. 0⅝	¾	½
28	22.10⅜	7	¾
29	23. 8¼	¼	⅞
30	24. 6	½	6⅛
31	25. 3⅞	¾	⅜
32	26. 1⅝	8	½
33	26.11⅜	¼	¾
34	27. 9¼	½	⅞
35	28. 7	¾	7⅛
36	29. 4⅞	9	⅜
37	30. 2⅝	¼	½
38	31. 0½	½	¾
39	31.10¼	¾	8
40	32. 8	10	⅛
41	33. 5⅞	¼	⅜
42	34. 3⅝	½	⅝
43	35. 1½	¾	¾
44	35.11¼	11	9
45	36. 9	¼	⅛
46	37. 6⅞	½	⅜
47	38. 4⅝	¾	⅝
48	39. 2½	12	¾
49	40. 0¼		
50	40.10		

HIP OR VALLEY RAFTER

Span Ft.	Length Ft. In.	Span In.	Lgth. In.
1	.11½	¼	¼
2	1.11	½	½
3	2.10½	¾	¾
4	3.10	1	1
5	4. 9½	¼	¼
6	5. 9	½	⅜
7	6. 8½	¾	⅝
8	7. 7⅞	2	⅞
9	8. 7⅜	¼	2⅛
10	9. 6⅞	½	⅜
11	10. 6⅜	¾	⅝
12	11. 5⅞	3	⅞
13	12. 5⅜	¼	3⅛
14	13. 4⅞	½	⅜
15	14. 4⅜	¾	⅝
16	15. 3⅞	4	⅞
17	16. 3⅜	¼	4⅛
18	17. 2⅞	½	¼
19	18. 2⅜	¾	½
20	19. 1⅞	5	¾
21	20. 1⅜	¼	5
22	21. 0⅞	½	¼
23	22. 0⅜	¾	½
24	22.11¾	6	¾
25	23.11¼	¼	6
26	24.10¾	½	¼
27	25.10¼	¾	½
28	26. 9¾	7	¾
29	27. 9¼	¼	7
30	28. 8¾	½	⅛
31	29. 8¼	¾	⅜
32	30. 7¾	8	⅝
33	31. 7¼	¼	⅞
34	32. 6¾	½	8⅛
35	33. 6¼	¾	⅜
36	34. 5¾	9	⅝
37	35. 5¼	¼	⅞
38	36. 4¾	½	9⅛
39	37. 4¼	¾	⅜
40	38. 3⅝	10	⅝
41	39. 3⅛	¼	⅞
42	40. 2⅝	½	10
43	41. 2⅛	¾	¼
44	42. 1⅝	11	½
45	43. 1⅛	¼	¾
46	44. 0⅝	½	11
47	45. 0⅛	¾	¼
48	45.11⅝	12	½
49	46.11⅛		
50	47.10⅝		

Spaced In.	Length Ft. In.
1..	1 5/8
2..	3 3/8
3..	5
4..	6 5/8
5..	8 3/8
6..	10
7..	11 5/8
8..1	1 3/8
9..	3
10..	4 5/8
11..	6 3/8
12..	8
13..	9 5/8
14..	11 3/8
15..2	1
16..	2 5/8
17..	4 3/8
18..	6
19..	7 5/8
20..	9 3/8
21..	11
22..3	0 5/8
23..	2 3/8
24..	4
25..	5 5/8
26..	7 3/8
27..	9
28..	10 5/8
29..4	0 3/8
30..	2
31..	3 5/8
32..	5 3/8
33..	7
34..	8 5/8
35..	10 3/8
36..5	0
37..	1 5/8
38..	3 3/8
39..	5
40..	6 5/8
41..	8 3/8
42..	10
43..	11 5/8
44..6	1 3/8
45..	3
46..	4 5/8
47..	6 3/8
48..	8

16 & 12 — 53¼°

EXPLANATION

Common Rafter

Width of building..........30'10¼"
Find length of Common Rafter.
Answer:

Under Span, ft. find 30' = 25' 0"
" " In. " 10¼" = 8½"

Total length Common Rft. 25' 8½"

When rafters overhang, add both overhangs to width of building. Use total span as before.

To get length of rafter by its run: doubling the run gives the span. Proceed as before.

Tables give full length. Allow for half thickness of ridge.

Spans over 50', as 51', add lengths of 50' & 10' spans together.

Hip Rafter

If common rafter span is 30'10¼", Hip rafter is 29'11⅞" long. Measure length of Hip on center of top edge. If Hip is unbacked (top edge square), see Index. If edge is backed (beveled), see Index.

Allow for half thickness of ridge.

Jack Rafters

Spaced 32" apart are 4'5⅝" different in length. Measure length on center of top edge. Cut short equal to half thickness of hip.

CUTS FOR STEEL SQUARE.

The first figure is always the cut.

Common Rafter		Purlin Rafter Roof Sheathing	
Plumb	16 - 12		
Level.	12 - 16	Plumb	16 - 20
		Cross.	12 - 20

Hip Rafter		Valley Shingles	
Plumb	16 - 17	Cross.	12 - 20
Level.	17 - 16	Set bevel on	
Side..	11⅞- 8½	butt end.	
Backing	16 - 23⅜		

Set bevel to last named.

Mitre-Box Cuts for Gable Moulds	
Plumb	16 - 12
Mitre.	20 - 12

Jack Rafter			
Plumb	16 - 12		
Level.	12 - 16	Bisection of	
Side..	20 - 12	16- 12=11⅞- 24	

For full explanation see Index.

COMMON RAFTER

Span Ft.	Length Ft. In.	Span In.	Lgth. In.
1	.10	1/4	1/4
2	1. 8	1/2	3/8
3	2. 6	3/4	5/8
4	3. 4	1	7/8
5	4. 2	1/4	1
6	5. 0	1/2	1/4
7	5.10	3/4	1/2
8	6. 8	2	5/8
9	7. 6	1/4	7/8
10	8. 4	1/2	2 1/8
11	9. 2	3/4	1/4
12	10. 0	3	1/2
13	10.10	1/4	3/4
14	11. 8	1/2	7/8
15	12. 6	3/4	3 1/8
16	13. 4	4	3/8
17	14. 2	1/4	1/2
18	15. 0	1/2	3/4
19	15.10	3/4	4
20	16. 8	5	1/8
21	17. 6	1/4	3/8
22	18. 4	1/2	5/8
23	19. 2	3/4	3/4
24	20. 0	6	5
25	20.10	1/4	1/4
26	21. 8	1/2	3/8
27	22. 6	3/4	5/8
28	23. 4	7	7/8
29	24. 2	1/4	6
30	25. 0	1/2	1/4
31	25.10	3/4	1/2
32	26. 8	8	5/8
33	27. 6	1/4	7/8
34	28. 4	1/2	7 1/8
35	29. 2	3/4	1/4
36	30. 0	9	1/2
37	30.10	1/4	3/4
38	31. 8	1/2	7/8
39	32. 6	3/4	8 1/8
40	33. 4	10	3/8
41	34. 2	1/4	1/2
42	35. 0	1/2	3/4
43	35.10	3/4	9
44	36. 8	11	1/8
45	37. 6	1/4	3/8
46	38. 4	1/2	5/8
47	39. 2	3/4	3/4
48	40. 0	12	10
49	40.10		
50	41. 8		

HIP or VALLEY RAFTER

Span Ft.	Length Ft. In.	Span In.	Lgth. In.
1	.11 5/8	1/4	1/4
2	1.11 3/8	1/2	1/2
3	2.11	3/4	3/4
4	3.10 5/8	1	1
5	4.10 1/4	1/4	1/4
6	5.10	1/2	1/2
7	6. 9 5/8	3/4	3/4
8	7. 9 1/4	2	2
9	8. 9	1/4	1/4
10	9. 8 5/8	1/2	3/8
11	10. 8 1/4	3/4	5/8
12	11. 8	3	7/8
13	12. 7 5/8	1/4	3 1/8
14	13. 7 1/4	1/2	3/8
15	14. 6 7/8	3/4	5/8
16	15. 6 5/8	4	7/8
17	16. 6 1/4	1/4	4 1/8
18	17. 5 7/8	1/2	3/8
19	18. 5 5/8	3/4	5/8
20	19. 5 1/4	5	7/8
21	20. 4 7/8	1/4	5 1/8
22	21. 4 5/8	1/2	3/8
23	22. 4 1/4	3/4	5/8
24	23. 3 7/8	6	7/8
25	24. 3 1/2	1/4	6 1/8
26	25. 3 1/4	1/2	3/8
27	26. 2 7/8	3/4	1/2
28	27. 2 1/2	7	3/4
29	28. 2 1/4	1/4	7
30	29. 1 7/8	1/2	1/4
31	30. 1 1/2	3/4	1/2
32	31. 1 1/8	8	3/4
33	32. 0 7/8	1/4	8
34	33. 0 1/2	1/2	1/4
35	34. 0 1/8	3/4	1/2
36	34.11 7/8	9	3/4
37	35.11 1/2	1/4	9
38	36.11 1/8	1/2	1/4
39	37.10 7/8	3/4	1/2
40	38.10 1/2	10	3/4
41	39.10 1/8	1/4	10
42	40. 9 3/4	1/2	1/4
43	41. 9 1/2	3/4	1/2
44	42. 9 1/8	11	3/4
45	43. 8 3/4	1/4	7/8
46	44. 8 1/2	1/2	11 1/8
47	45. 8 1/8	3/4	3/8
48	46. 7 3/4	12	5/8
49	47. 7 1/2		
50	48. 7 1/8		

JACK RAFTER

Spaced In.	Length Ft.	In.
1..		1¾
2..		3⅜
3..		5⅛
4..		6¾
5..		8½
6..		10¼
7..		11⅞
8..	1	1⅝
9..		3¼
10..		5
11..		6¾
12..		8⅜
13..		10⅛
14..		11¾
15..	2	1½
16..		3¼
17..		4⅞
18..		6⅝
19..		8¼
20..		10
21..		11¾
22..	3	1⅜
23..		3⅛
24..		4¾
25..		6½
26..		8¼
27..		9⅞
28..		11⅝
29..	4	1¼
30..		3
31..		4¾
32..		6⅜
33..		8⅛
34..		9¾
35..		11½
36..	5	1¼
37..		2⅞
38..		4⅝
39..		6¼
40..		8
41..		9¾
42..		11⅜
43..	6	1⅛
44..		2¾
45..		4½
46..		6¼
47..		7⅞
48..		9⅝

16½ & 12 — 54°

EXPLANATION

Common Rafter

Width of building...........**42′3½″**
Find length of Common Rafter.

Answer:

Under **Span, ft.** find 42′ = 35′ 8½″
" " **in.** " 3½″ = 3″

Total length Common Rft. **35′11½″**

When rafters overhang, add both overhangs to width of building. Use total span as before.

To get length of rafter by its run: doubling the run gives the span. Proceed as before.

Tables give full length. **Allow for** half thickness of ridge.

Spans over 50′, as 60′, **add lengths** of 50′ & 10′ spans together.

Hip Rafter

If common rafter span **is 42′3½″,** Hip rafter is 41′8½″ long. Measure length of Hip on center of top edge. If Hip is unbacked (top edge square), see Index. If edge is backed (beveled), see Index.

Allow for half thickness of ridge.

Jack Rafters

Spaced 25″ apart are **3′6½″** different in length. Measure length on center of top edge. Cut short equal to half thickness of hip.

CUTS FOR STEEL SQUARE.

The first figure is always the cut.

Common Rafter

Plumb 16½- 12
Level. 12 - 16½

Hip Rafter

Plumb 8¼- 8½
Level. 8½- 8¼
Side.. 11⅞- 8½
Backing 16½- 23⅝
Set bevel to last named.

Jack Rafter

Plumb 16½- 12
Level. 12 - 16½
Side.. 20⅜- 12

Purlin Rafter Roof Sheathing

Plumb 16½- 20⅜
Cross. 12 - 20⅜

Valley Shingles

Cross. 12 - 20⅜
Set bevel on butt end.

Mitre-Box Cuts for Gable Moulds

Plumb 16½- 12
Mitre. 20⅜- 12

Bisection of

16½- 12=12⅛- 24

For full explanation see **Index.**

COMMON RAFTER				HIP or VALLEY RAFTER			
Span Ft.	Length Ft. In.	Span In.	Lgth. In.	Span Ft.	Length Ft. In.	Span In.	Lgth. In.
1	.10¼	¼	¼	1	.11⅞	¼	¼
2	1. 8⅜	½	⅜	2	1.11⅝	½	½
3	2. 6⅝	¾	⅝	3	2.11½	¾	¾
4	3. 4¾	1	⅞	4	3.11⅜	1	1
5	4. 3	¼	1⅛	5	4.11⅛	¼	1¼
6	5. 1¼	½	1¼	6	5.11	½	1½
7	5.11¾	¾	1½	7	6.10⅞	¾	1¾
8	6. 9⅝	2	1¾	8	7.10⅝	2	2
9	7. 7¾	¼	1⅞	9	8.10½	¼	2¼
10	8. 6	½	2⅛	10	9.10⅜	½	2½
11	9. 4¼	¾	2⅜	11	10.10⅛	¾	2¾
12	10. 2⅜	3	2½	12	11.10	3	3
13	11. 0⅝	¼	2¾	13	12. 9⅞	¼	3¼
14	11.10⅞	½	3	14	13. 9¾	½	3½
15	12. 9	¾	3¼	15	14. 9½	¾	3¾
16	13. 7¼	4	3⅜	16	15. 9⅜	4	4
17	14. 5⅜	¼	3⅝	17	16. 9¼	¼	4¼
18	15. 3⅝	½	3⅞	18	17. 9	½	4⅜
19	16. 1⅞	¾	4	19	18. 8⅞	¾	4⅝
20	17. 0	5	4¼	20	19. 8¾	5	4⅞
21	17.10¼	¼	4½	21	20. 8½	¼	5⅛
22	18. 8¾	½	4⅝	22	21. 8⅜	½	5⅜
23	19. 6⅝	¾	4⅞	23	22. 8¼	¾	5⅝
24	20. 4⅞	6	5⅛	24	23. 8	6	5⅞
25	21. 3	¼	5⅜	25	24. 7⅞	¼	6⅛
26	22. 1¼	½	5½	26	25. 7¾	½	6⅜
27	22.11⅜	¾	5¾	27	26. 7½	¾	6⅝
28	23. 9⅝	7	6	28	27. 7⅜	7	6⅞
29	24. 7¾	¼	6⅛	29	28. 7¼	¼	7⅛
30	25. 6	½	6⅜	30	29. 7	½	7⅜
31	26. 4¼	¾	6⅝	31	30. 6⅞	¾	7⅝
32	27. 2⅜	8	6¾	32	31. 6¾	8	7⅞
33	28. 0⅝	¼	7	33	32. 6½	¼	8⅛
34	28.10⅞	½	7¼	34	33. 6⅜	½	8⅜
35	29. 9	¾	7½	35	34. 6¼	¾	8⅝
36	30. 7¼	9	7⅝	36	35. 6	9	8⅞
37	31. 5⅜	¼	7⅞	37	36. 5⅞	¼	9⅛
38	32. 3⅝	½	8⅛	38	37. 5¾	½	9⅜
39	33. 1⅞	¾	8¼	39	38. 5½	¾	9⅝
40	34. 0	10	8½	40	39. 5⅜	10	9⅞
41	34.10¼	¼	8¾	41	40. 5¼	¼	10⅛
42	35. 8½	½	8⅞	42	41. 5	½	10⅜
43	36. 6⅝	¾	9⅛	43	42. 4⅞	¾	10⅝
44	37. 4⅞	11	9⅜	44	43. 4¾	11	10⅞
45	38. 3	¼	9⅝	45	44. 4⅝	¼	11⅛
46	39. 1¼	½	9¾	46	45. 4⅜	½	11⅜
47	39.11½	¾	10	47	46. 4¼	¾	11⅝
48	40. 9⅝	12	10¼	48	47. 4⅛	12	11⅞
49	41. 7⅞			49	48. 3⅞		
50	42. 6			50	49. 3¾		

Spaced In.	Length Ft. In.
1..	1¾
2..	3½
3..	5¼
4..	6⅞
5..	8⅝
6..	10⅜
7 1..	0⅛
8..	1⅞
9..	3⅝
10..	5⅜
11..	7⅛
12..	8¾
13..	10½
14..2	0¼
15..	2
16..	3¾
17..	5½
18..	7¼
19..	9
20..	10⅝
21..3	0⅜
22..	2⅛
23..	3⅞
24..	5⅝
25..	7⅜
26..	9⅛
27..	10⅞
28..4	0½
29..	2¼
30..	4
31..	5¾
32..	7½
33..	9¼
34..	11
35..5	0¾
36..	2⅜
37..	4⅛
38..	5⅞
39..	7⅝
40..	9⅜
41..	11⅛
42..6	0⅞
43..	2⅝
44..	4¼
45..	6
46..	7¾
47..	9½
'48..	11¼

17 & 12 — 54¾°

EXPLANATION

Common Rafter

Width of building............32'3"
Find length of Common Rafter.
Answer:
Under **Span**, ft. find 32' = 27' 9"
    "   in. "   3" =   2⅝"

Total length Common Rft. 27'11⅝"

When rafters overhang, add both overhangs to width of building. Use total span as before.

To get length of rafter by its run: doubling the run gives the span. Proceed as before.

Tables give full length. Allow for half thickness of ridge.

Spans over 50', as 60', add lengths of 50' & 10' spans together.

Hip Rafter

If common rafter span is 32'3", Hip rafter is 32'3⅜" long. Measure length of Hip on center of top edge. If Hip is unbacked (top edge square), see Index. If edge is backed (beveled), see Index.

Allow for half thickness of ridge.

Jack Rafters

Spaced 24" apart are 3'5⅝" different in length. Measure length on center of top edge. Cut short equal to half thickness of hip.

CUTS FOR STEEL SQUARE.

The first figure is always the cut.

Common Rafter	Purlin Rafter Roof Sheathing
Plumb 17 - 12	Plumb 17 - 20¾
Level. 12 - 17	Cross. 12 - 20¾

Hip Rafter	Valley Shingles
Plumb 8½- 8½	Cross. 12 - 20¾
Level. 8½- 8½	Set bevel on
Side.. 12 - 8½	butt end.
Backing17 - 24	
Set bevel to last named.	**Mitre-Box Cuts for Gable Moulds**
	Plumb 17 - 12
Jack Rafter	Mitre. 20¾- 12
Plumb 17 - 12	
Level. 12 - 17	**Bisection of**
Side.. 20¾- 12	17- 12=12¼- 24

For full explanation see Index.

COMMON RAFTER

Span Ft.	Length Ft. In.	Span In.	Lgth In.
1	.10⅜	¼	¼
2	1. 8¾	½	⅜
3	2. 7¼	¾	⅝
4	3. 5⅝	1	⅞
5	4. 4	¼	1⅛
6	5. 2⅜	½	¼
7	6. 0⅞	¾	½
8	6.11¼	2	¾
9	7. 9⅝	¼	2
10	8. 8	½	⅛
11	9. 6½	¾	⅜
12	10. 4⅞	3	⅝
13	11. 3¼	¼	⅞
14	12. 1⅝	½	3
15	13. 0⅛	¾	¼
16	13.10½	4	½
17	14. 8⅞	¼	⅝
18	15. 7¼	½	⅞
19	16. 5⅝	¾	4⅛
20	17. 4⅛	5	⅜
21	18. 2½	¼	½
22	19. 0⅞	½	¾
23	19.11¼	¾	5
24	20. 9¾	6	¼
25	21. 8⅛	¼	⅜
26	22. 6½	½	⅝
27	23. 4⅞	¾	⅞
28	24. 3⅜	7	6⅛
29	25. 1¾	¼	¼
30	26. 0⅛	½	½
31	26.10½	¾	¾
32	27. 9	8	7
33	28. 7⅜	¼	⅛
34	29. 5¾	½	⅜
35	30. 4⅛	¾	⅝
36	31. 2½	9	¾
37	32. 1	¼	8
38	32.11⅜	½	¼
39	33. 9¾	¾	½
40	34. 8⅛	10	⅝
41	35. 6⅝	¼	⅞
42	36. 5	½	9⅛
43	37. 3⅜	¾	⅜
44	38. 1¾	11	½
45	39. 0¼	¼	¾
46	39.10⅝	½	10
47	40. 9	¾	¼
48	41. 7⅜	12	⅜
49	42. 5¾		
50	43. 4¼		

HIP or VALLEY RAFTER

Span Ft.	Length Ft. In.	Span In.	Lgth In.
1	1. 0	¼	¼
2	2. 0	½	½
3	3. 0	¾	¾
4	4. 0	1	1
5	5. 0	¼	¼
6	6. 0⅛	½	½
7	7. 0⅛	¾	¾
8	8. 0⅛	2	2
9	9. 0⅛	¼	¼
10	10. 0⅛	½	½
11	11. 0⅛	¾	¾
12	12. 0⅛	3	3
13	13. 0⅛	¼	¼
14	14. 0⅛	½	½
15	15. 0⅛	¾	¾
16	16. 0⅛	4	4
17	17. 0⅛	¼	¼
18	18. 0¼	½	½
19	19. 0¼	¾	¾
20	20. 0¼	5	5
21	21. 0¼	¼	¼
22	22. 0¼	½	½
23	23. 0¼	¾	¾
24	24. 0¼	6	6
25	25. 0¼	¼	¼
26	26. 0¼	½	½
27	27. 0¼	¾	¾
28	28. 0¼	7	7
29	29. 0¼	¼	¼
30	30. 0⅜	½	½
31	31. 0⅜	¾	¾
32	32. 0⅜	8	8
33	33. 0⅜	¼	¼
34	34. 0⅜	½	½
35	35. 0⅜	¾	¾
36	36. 0⅜	9	9
37	37. 0⅜	¼	¼
38	38. 0⅜	½	½
39	39. 0⅜	¾	¾
40	40. 0⅜	10	10
41	41. 0⅜	¼	¼
42	42. 0⅜	½	½
43	43. 0½	¾	¾
44	44. 0½	11	11
45	45. 0½	¼	¼
46	46. 0½	½	½
47	47. 0½	¾	¾
48	48. 0½	12	12
49	49. 0½		
50	50. 0½		

Spaced In.	Length Ft. In.
1..	1¾
2..	3½
3..	5¼
4..	7⅛
5..	8⅞
6..	10⅝
7..1	0⅜
8..	2⅛
9..	3⅞
10..	5⅝
11..	7½
12..	9¼
13..	11
14..2	0¾
15..	2½
16..	4¼
17..	6
18..	7⅞
19..	9⅝
20..	11⅜
21..3	1⅛
22..	2⅞
23..	4⅝
24..	6⅜
25..	8¼
26..	10
27..	11¾
28..4	1½
29..	3¼
30..	5
31..	6⅞
32..	8⅝
33..	10⅜
34..5	0⅛
35..	1⅞
36..	3⅝
37..	5⅜
38..	7¼
39..	9
40..	10¾
41..6	0½
42..	2¼
43..	4
44..	5¾
45..	7⅝
46..	9⅜
47..	11⅛
48..7	0⅞

17½ & 12 — 55½°

EXPLANATION

Common Rafter

Width of building..........48′2¼″
Find length of Common Rafter.
Answer:

Under **Span**, ft. find 48′ = 42′ 5¼″
    "   "   in. "   2¼″ =   2″

Total length Common Rft. 42′ 7¼″

When rafters overhang, add both overhangs to width of building. Use total span as before.

To get length of rafter by its run: doubling the run gives the span. Proceed as before.

Tables give full length. Allow for half thickness of ridge.

Spans over 50′, as 60′, add lengths of 50′ & 10′ spans together.

Hip Rafter

If common rafter span is 48′2¼″, Hip rafter is 48′11¼″ long. Measure length of Hip on center of top edge. If Hip is unbacked (top edge square), see Index. If edge is backed (beveled), see Index.

Allow for half thickness of ridge.

Jack Rafters

Spaced 37″ apart are 5′3⅜″ different in length. Measure length on center of top edge. Cut short equal to half thickness of hip.

CUTS FOR STEEL SQUARE.

The first figure is always the cut.

Common Rafter	Purlin Rafter Roof Sheathing
Plumb 17½ - 12	Plumb 17½ - 21¼
Level. 12 - 17½	Cross. 12 - 21¼

Hip Rafter	Valley Shingles
Plumb 8¾- 8½	
Level. 8½- 8¾	Cross. 12 - 21¼
Side.. 12¼- 8½	Set bevel on
Backing 8¾- 12¼	butt end.

Set bevel to last named.

Jack Rafter	Mitre-Box Cuts for Gable Moulds
	Plumb 17½- 12
Plumb 17½- 12	Mitre. 21¼- 12
Level. 12 - 17½	
Side.. 21¼- 17½	Bisection of 17½- 12=12½- 24

For full explanation see Index.

COMMON RAFTER

Span Ft.	Length Ft. In.	Span In.	Lgth In.
1..	.10⅝	¼..	¼
2..	1. 9¼	½..	½
3..	2. 7⅞	¾..	⅝
4..	3. 6½	1..	⅞
5..	4. 5	¼..	1⅛
6..	5. 3⅝	½..	⅜
7..	6. 2¼	¾..	½
8..	7. 0⅞	2..	¾
9..	7.11½	¼..	2
10..	8.10⅛	½..	¼
11..	9. 8¾	¾..	⅜
12..	10. 7⅜	3..	⅝
13..	11. 5⅞	¼..	⅞
14..	12. 4½	½..	3⅛
15..	13. 3⅛	¾..	⅜
16..	14. 1¾	4..	½
17..	15. 0⅜	¼..	¾
18..	15.11	½..	4
19..	16. 9⅝	¾..	¼
20..	17. 8¼	5..	⅜
21..	18. 6¾	¼..	⅝
22..	19. 5⅜	½..	⅞
23..	20. 4	¾..	5⅛
24..	21. 2⅝	6..	¼
25..	22. 1¼	¼..	½
26..	22.11⅞	½..	¾
27..	23.10½	¾..	6
28..	24. 9⅛	7..	¼
29..	25. 7⅝	¼..	⅜
30..	26. 6¼	½..	⅝
31..	27. 4⅞	¾..	⅞
32..	28. 3½	8..	7⅛
33..	29. 2⅛	¼..	¼
34..	30. 0¾	½..	½
35..	30.11⅜	¾..	¾
36..	31.10	9..	8
37..	32. 8½	¼..	⅛
38..	33. 7⅛	½..	⅜
39..	34. 5¾	¾..	⅝
40..	35. 4⅜	10..	⅞
41..	36. 3	¼..	9
42..	37. 1⅝	½..	¼
43..	38. 0¼	¾..	½
44..	38.10⅞	11..	¾
45..	39. 9⅜	¼..	10
46..	40. 8	½..	⅛
47..	41. 6⅝	¾..	⅜
48..	42. 5¼	12..	⅝
49..	43. 3⅞		
50..	44. 2½		

HIP or VALLEY RAFTER

Span Ft.	Length Ft. In.	Span In.	Lgth In.
1..	1. 0¼	¼..	¼
2..	2. 0⅜	½..	½
3..	3. 0⅝	¾..	¾
4..	4. 0¾	1..	1
5..	5. 1	¼..	¼
6..	6. 1⅛	½..	½
7..	7. 1⅜	¾..	¾
8..	8. 1½	2..	2
9..	9. 1¾	¼..	¼
10..	10. 1⅞	½..	½
11..	11. 2⅛	¾..	¾
12..	12. 2¼	3..	3
13..	13. 2½	¼..	¼
14..	14. 2⅝	½..	½
15..	15. 2⅞	¾..	¾
16..	16. 3	4..	4
17..	17. 3¼	¼..	⅜
18..	18. 3⅜	½..	⅝
19..	19. 3⅝	¾..	⅞
20..	20. 3¾	5..	5⅛
21..	21. 4	¼..	⅜
22..	22. 4⅛	½..	⅝
23..	23. 4⅜	¾..	⅞
24..	24. 4½	6..	6⅛
25..	25. 4¾	¼..	⅜
26..	26. 4⅞	½..	⅝
27..	27. 5⅛	¾..	⅞
28..	28. 5¼	7..	7⅛
29..	29. 5½	¼..	⅜
30..	30. 5⅝	½..	⅝
31..	31. 5⅞	¾..	⅞
32..	32. 6	8..	8⅛
33..	33. 6¼	¼..	⅜
34..	34. 6⅜	½..	⅝
35..	35. 6⅝	¾..	⅞
36..	36. 6¾	9..	9⅛
37..	37. 7	¼..	⅜
38..	38. 7⅛	½..	⅝
39..	39. 7⅜	¾..	⅞
40..	40. 7½	10..	10⅛
41..	41. 7¾	¼..	⅜
42..	42. 7⅞	½..	⅝
43..	43. 8⅛	¾..	⅞
44..	44. 8¼	11..	11⅛
45..	45. 8½	¼..	⅜
46..	46. 8⅝	½..	⅝
47..	47. 8⅞	¾..	⅞
48..	48. 9	12..	12⅛
49..	49. 9¼		
50..	50. 9⅜		

18 & 12 — 56¼°

EXPLANATION

Common Rafter

Width of building...........38'7¾"
Find length of Common Rafter.
Answer:
Under Span, ft. find 38' = 34' 3"
  "   " in. " 7¾" = 7"

Total length Common Rft. 34'10"

When rafters overhang, add both overhangs to width of building. Use total span as before.

To get length of rafter by its run: doubling the run gives the span. Proceed as before.

Tables give full length. Allow for half thickness of ridge.

Spans over 50', as 60', add lengths of 50' & 10' spans together.

Hip Rafter

If common rafter span is 38'7¾", Hip rafter is 39'10" long. Measure length of Hip on center of top edge. If Hip is unbacked (top edge square), see Index. If edge is backed (beveled), see Index.

Allow for half thickness of ridge.

Jack Rafters

Spaced 32" apart are 4'9¾" different in length. Measure length on center of top edge. Cut short equal to half thickness of hip.

CUTS FOR STEEL SQUARE.

The first figure is always the cut.

Common Rafter		Purlin Rafter Roof Sheathing	
Plumb	18 - 12	Plumb	18 - 21⅝
Level.	12 - 18	Cross.	12 - 21⅝

Hip Rafter		Valley Shingles	
Plumb	9 - 8½	Cross.	12 - 21⅝
Level.	8½ - 9	Set bevel on	
Side..	12⅜ - 8½	butt end.	
Backing 9 - 12⅜			

Set bevel to last named.

Mitre-Box Cuts for Gable Moulds	
Plumb	18 - 12
Mitre.	21⅝- 12

Jack Rafter			
Plumb	18 - 12		
Level.	12 - 18	**Bisection of**	
Side..	21⅝ - 12	18- 12=12¾- 24	

For full explanation see Index.

COMMON RAFTER				HIP or VALLEY RAFTER			
Span Ft.	Length Ft. In.	Span In.	Lgth. In.	Span Ft.	Length Ft. In.	Span In.	Lgth. In.
1..	.10⅞	¼..	¼	1..	1. 0⅜	¼..	¼
2..	1. 9⅝	½..	½	2..	2. 0¾	½..	½
3..	2. 8½	¾..	⅝	3..	3. 1⅛	¾..	¾
4..	3. 7¼	1 ..	⅞	4..	4. 1½	1 ..	1
5..	4. 6⅛	¼..	1⅛	5..	5. 1⅞	¼..	¼
6..	5. 4⅞	½..	⅜	6..	6. 2¼	½..	½
7..	6. 3¾	¾..	⅝	7..	7. 2⅝	¾..	¾
8..	7. 2½	2 ..	¾	8..	8. 3	2 ..	2
9..	8. 1⅜	¼..	2	9..	9. 3⅜	¼..	⅜
10..	9. 0⅛	½..	¼	10..	10. 3⅝	½..	⅝
11..	9.11	¾..	½	11..	11. 4⅛	¾..	⅞
12..	10. 9¾	3 ..	¾	12..	12. 4⅜	3 ..	3⅛
13..	11. 8⅝	¼..	⅞	13..	13. 4¾	¼..	⅜
14..	12. 7⅜	½..	3⅛	14..	14. 5¼	½..	⅝
15..	13. 6¼	¾..	⅜	15..	15. 5½	¾..	⅞
16..	14. 5⅛	4 ..	⅝	16..	16. 5⅞	4 ..	4⅛
17..	15. 3⅞	¼..	⅞	17..	17. 6¼	¼..	⅜
18..	16. 2¾	½..	4	18..	18. 6⅝	½..	⅝
19..	17. 1½	¾..	¼	19..	19. 7	¾..	⅞
20..	18. 0⅜	5 ..	½	20..	20. 7⅜	5 ..	5⅛
21..	18.11⅞	¼..	¾	21..	21. 7¾	¼..	⅜
22..	19.10	½..	5	22..	22. 8⅛	½..	⅝
23..	20. 8¾	¾..	⅛	23..	23. 8½	¾..	⅞
24..	21. 7⅝	6 ..	⅜	24..	24. 8⅞	6 ..	6⅛
25..	22. 6⅜	¼..	⅝	25..	25. 9¼	¼..	½
26..	23. 5¼	½..	⅞	26..	26. 9⅝	½..	¾
27..	24. 4	¾..	6⅛	27..	27.10	¾..	7
28..	25. 2⅞	7 ..	¼	28..	28.10⅜	7 ..	¼
29..	26. 1⅝	¼..	½	29..	29.10¾	¼..	½
30..	27. 0½	½..	¾	30..	30.11⅛	½..	¾
31..	27.11⅜	¾..	7	31..	31.11½	¾..	8
32..	28.10⅛	8 ..	¼	32..	32.11⅞	8 ..	¼
33..	29. 9	¼..	⅜	33..	34. 0⅛	¼..	½
34..	30. 7¾	½..	⅝	34..	35. 0½	½..	¾
35..	31. 6⅝	¾..	⅞	35..	36. 0⅞	¾..	9
36..	32. 5⅜	9 ..	8⅛	36..	37. 1¼	9 ..	¼
37..	33. 4¼	¼..	⅜	37..	38. 1⅝	¼..	½
38..	34. 3	½..	⅝	38..	39. 2	½..	¾
39..	35. 1⅞	¾..	¾	39..	40. 2⅜	¾..	10
40..	36. 0⅝	10 ..	9	40..	41. 2¾	10 ..	¼
41..	36.11½	¼..	¼	41..	42. 3⅛	¼..	½
42..	37.10¼	½..	½	42..	43. 3½	½..	⅞
43..	38. 9⅛	¾..	¾	43..	44. 3⅞	¾..	11⅛
44..	39. 7⅞	11 ..	⅞	44..	45. 4¼	11 ..	⅜
45..	40. 6¾	¼..	10⅛	45..	46. 4⅝	¼..	⅝
46..	41. 5⅝	½..	⅜	46..	47. 5	½..	⅞
47..	42. 4⅜	¾..	⅝	47..	48. 5⅜	¾..	12⅛
48..	43. 3¼	12 ..	⅞	48..	49. 5¾	12 ..	⅜
49..	44. 2			49..	50. 6⅛		
50..	45. 0⅞			50..	51. 6½		

18½ & 12 — 57°

EXPLANATION

Common Rafter

Width of building..........47′5½″
Find length of Common Rafter.
Answer:

Under **Span**, ft. find	47′	= 43′ 2¼″
" " in. "	5½″ =	5″

Total length Common Rft. 43′ 7¼″

When rafters overhang, add both overhangs to width of building. Use total span as before.
To get length of rafter by its run: doubling the run gives the span. Proceed as before.

Tables give full length. Allow for half thickness of ridge.

Spans over 50′, as 60′, add lengths of 50′ & 10′ spans together.

Hip Rafter

If common rafter span is 47′5½″, Hip rafter is 49′7¾″ long. Measure length of Hip on center of top edge. If Hip is unbacked (top edge square), see Index. If edge is backed (beveled), see Index.

Allow for half thickness of ridge.

Jack Rafters

Spaced 23″ apart are 3′6¼″ different in length. Measure length on center of top edge. Cut short equal to half thickness of hip.

CUTS FOR STEEL SQUARE.

The first figure is always the cut.

Common Rafter			Purlin Rafter Roof Sheathing
Plumb	18½ - 12		
Level.	12 - 18½		Plumb 18½ - 22
			Cross. 12 - 22

Hip Rafter		
Plumb	9¼ -	8½
Level.	8½ -	9¼
Side..	12½ -	8½
Backing 9¼ - 12½

Set bevel to last named.

Valley Shingles
Cross. 12 - 22
Set bevel on butt end.

Jack Rafter		
Plumb	18½ - 12	
Level.	12 - 18½	
Side..	22 - 12	

Mitre-Box Cuts for Gable Moulds
Plumb 18½ - 12
Mitre. 22 - 12

Bisection of
18½- 12=12⅞- 24

For full explanation see Index.

COMMON RAFTER

Span Ft.	Length Ft. In.
1..	.11
2..	1.10
3..	2. 9⅛
4..	3. 8⅛
5..	4. 7⅛
6..	5. 6⅛
7..	6. 5⅛
8..	7. 4¼
9..	8. 3¼
10..	9. 2¼
11..	10. 1¼
12..	11. 0¼
13..	11.11⅜
14..	12.10⅜
15..	13. 9⅜
16..	14. 8⅜
17..	15. 7⅜
18..	16. 6½
19..	17. 5½
20..	18. 4½
21..	19. 3½
22..	20. 2½
23..	21. 1⅝
24..	22. 0⅝
25..	22.11⅝
26..	23.10⅝
27..	24. 9¾
28..	25. 8¾
29..	26. 7¾
30..	27. 6¾
31..	28. 5¾
32..	29. 4⅞
33..	30. 3⅞
34..	31. 2⅞
35..	32. 1⅞
36..	33. 0⅞
37..	34. 0
38..	34.11
39..	35.10
40..	36. 9
41..	37. 8
42..	38. 7⅛
43..	39. 6⅛
44..	40. 5⅛
45..	41. 4⅛
46..	42. 3⅛
47..	43. 2¼
48..	44. 1¼
49..	45. 0¼
50..	45.11¼

Span In.	Lgth In.
¼..	¼
½..	½
¾..	¾
1 ..	⅞
¼..	1⅛
½..	⅜
¾..	⅝
2 ..	⅞
¼..	2⅛
½..	¼
¾..	½
3 ..	¾
¼..	3
½..	¼
¾..	½
4 ..	⅝
¼..	⅞
½..	4⅛
¾..	⅜
5 ..	⅝
¼..	⅞
½..	5
¾..	¼
6 ..	½
¼..	¾
½..	6
¾..	¼
7 ..	⅜
¼..	⅝
½..	⅞
¾..	7¹⅛
8 ..	⅜
¼..	⅝
½..	¾
¾..	8
9 ..	¼
¼..	½
½..	¾
¾..	⅞
10 ..	9⅛
¼..	⅜
½..	⅝
¾..	⅞
11 ..	10⅛
¼..	⅜
½..	½
¾..	¾
12 ..	11

HIP or VALLEY RAFTER

Span Ft.	Length Ft. In.
1..	1. 0½
2..	2. 1⅛
3..	3. 1⅝
4..	4. 2¼
5..	5. 2¾
6..	6. 3⅜
7..	7. 3⅞
8..	8. 4⅜
9..	9. 5
10..	10. 5½
11..	11. 6⅛
12..	12. 6⅝
13..	13. 7⅛
14..	14. 7¾
15..	15. 8¼
16..	16. 8⅞
17..	17. 9⅜
18..	18.10
19..	19.10½
20..	20.11
21..	21.11⅝
22..	23. 0⅛
23..	24. 0¾
24..	25. 1¼
25..	26. 1¾
26..	27. 2⅜
27..	28. 2⅞
28..	29. 3½
29..	30. 4
30..	31. 4⅝
31..	32. 5⅛
32..	33. 5⅝
33..	34. 6¼
34..	35. 6¾
35..	36. 7⅜
36..	37. 7⅞
37..	38. 8½
38..	39. 9
39..	40. 9½
40..	41.10⅛
41..	42.10⅝
42..	43.11⅛
43..	44.11¾
44..	46. 0¼
45..	47. 0⅞
46..	48. 1⅜
47..	48. 2
48..	50. 2½
49..	51. 3⅛
50..	52. 3⅝

Span In.	Lgth In.
¼..	¼
½..	½
¾..	¾
1 ..	1
¼..	¼
½..	⅝
¾..	⅞
2 ..	2⅛
¼..	⅜
½..	⅝
¾..	⅞
3 ..	3⅛
¼..	⅜
½..	⅝
¾..	⅞
4 ..	4⅛
¼..	½
½..	¾
¾..	5
5 ..	¼
¼..	½
½..	¾
¾..	6
6 ..	¼
¼..	½
½..	¾
¾..	7⅛
7 ..	⅜
¼..	⅝
½..	⅞
¾..	8¼
8 ..	⅜
¼..	⅝
½..	⅞
¾..	9⅛
9 ..	⅜
¼..	⅝
½..	10
¾..	¼
10 ..	½
¼..	¾
½..	11
¾..	¼
11 ..	½
¼..	¾
½..	12
¾..	¼
12 ..	½

19 & 12 — 57¾°

EXPLANATION

Common Rafter

Width of building..........38'4¾"
Find length of Common Rafter.

Answer:

Under Span, ft. find	38'	= 35' 7"
" " in. "	4¾" =	4½

Total length Common Rft. 35'11½"

When rafters overhang, add both overhangs to width of building. Use total span as before.

To get length of rafter by its run: doubling the run gives the span. Proceed as before.

Tables give full length. Allow for half thickness of ridge.

Spans over 50', as 60', add lengths of 50' & 10' spans together.

Hip Rafter

If common rafter span is 38'4¾", Hip rafter is 40'9" long. Measure length of Hip on center of top edge. If Hip is unbacked (top edge square), see Index. If edge is backed (beveled), see Index.

Allow for half thickness of ridge.

Jack Rafters

Spaced 31" apart are 4'10" different in length. Measure length on center of top edge. Cut short equal to half thickness of hip.

CUTS FOR STEEL SQUARE

The first figure is always the cut.

Common Rafter		Purlin Rafter Roof Sheathing	
Plumb	19 - 12	Plumb 19 - 22½	
Level.	12 - 19	Cross. 12 - 22½	

Hip Rafter		Valley Shingles	
Plumb	9½- 8½	Cross. 12 - 22½	
Level.	8½- 9½	Set bevel on	
Side..	12¾- 8½	butt end.	
Backing	9½- 12¾		
Set bevel to		Mitre-Box Cuts	
last named.		for Gable Moulds	
		Plumb 19 - 12	
Jack Rafter		Mitre. 22½- 12	
Plumb	19 - 12		
Level.	12 - 19	Bisection of	
Side..	22½- 12	19- 12=13⅛ - 24	

For full explanation see Index.

COMMON RAFTER

Span Ft.	Length Ft. In.	Span In.	Lgth. In.
1	11¼	¼	¼
2	1.10½	½	½
3	2. 9¾	¾	¾
4	3. 9	1	⅞
5	4. 8¼	¼	1⅛
6	5. 7⅜	½	⅜
7	6. 6⅝	¾	⅝
8	7. 5⅞	2	⅞
9	8. 5⅛	¼	2⅛
10	9. 4⅜	½	⅜
11	10. 3⅝	¾	⅝
12	11. 2⅞	3	¾
13	12. 2⅛	¼	3
14	13. 1¼	½	¼
15	14. 0½	¾	½
16	14.11¾	4	¾
17	15.11	¼	4
18	16.10¼	½	¼
19	17. 9½	¾	½
20	18. 8¾	5	⅝
21	19. 8	¼	⅞
22	20. 7¼	½	5⅛
23	21. 6⅜	¾	⅜
24	22. 5⅝	6	⅝
25	23. 4⅞	¼	⅞
26	24. 4⅛	½	6⅛
27	25. 3⅜	¾	⅜
28	26. 2⅝	7	½
29	27. 1⅞	¼	¾
30	28. 1⅛	½	7
31	29. 0⅜	¾	¼
32	29.11½	8	½
33	30.10¾	¼	¾
34	31.10	½	8
35	32. 9¼	¾	¼
36	33. 8½	9	⅜
37	34. 7¾	¼	⅝
38	35. 7	½	⅞
39	36. 6¼	¾	9⅛
40	37. 5½	10	⅜
41	38. 4⅝	¼	⅝
42	39. 3⅞	½	⅞
43	40. 3⅛	¾	10⅛
44	41. 2⅜	11	¼
45	42. 1⅝	¼	½
46	43. 0⅞	½	¾
47	44. 0⅛	¾	11
48	44.11⅜	12	¼
49	45.10⅝		
50	46. 9¾		

HIP OR VALLEY RAFTER

Span Ft.	Length Ft. In.	Span In.	Lgth. In.
1	1. 0¾	¼	¼
2	2. 1½	½	½
3	3. 2¼	¾	¾
4	4. 3	1	1
5	5. 3¾	¼	⅜
6	6. 4⅜	½	⅝
7	7. 5⅛	¾	⅞
8	8. 5⅞	2	2⅛
9	9. 6⅝	¼	⅜
10	10. 7⅜	½	⅝
11	11. 8⅛	¾	⅞
12	12. 8⅞	3	3⅛
13	13. 9⅝	¼	½
14	14.10⅜	½	¾
15	15.11⅛	¾	4
16	16.11¾	4	¼
17	18. 0½	¼	½
18	19. 1¼	½	¾
19	20. 2	¾	5
20	21. 2¾	5	¼
21	22. 3½	¼	⅝
22	23. 4¼	½	⅞
23	24. 5	¾	6⅛
24	25. 5¾	6	⅜
25	26. 6½	¼	⅝
26	27. 7⅛	½	7
27	28. 7⅞	¾	⅛
28	29. 8⅝	7	⅜
29	30. 9⅜	¼	¾
30	31.10⅛	½	8
31	32.10⅞	¾	¼
32	33.11⅝	8	½
33	35. 0⅜	¼	¾
34	36. 1⅛	½	9
35	37. 1⅞	¾	¼
36	38. 2½	9	½
37	39. 3¼	¼	⅞
38	40. 4	½	10⅛
39	41. 4¾	¾	⅜
40	42. 5½	10	⅝
41	43. 6¼	¼	⅞
42	44. 7	½	11⅛
43	45. 7¾	¾	⅜
44	46. 8½	11	⅝
45	47. 9¼	¼	12
46	48. 9⅞	½	¼
47	49.10⅝	¾	½
48	50.11⅜	12	¾
49	52. 0⅛		
50	53. 0⅞		

JACK RAFTER

Spaced In.	Length Ft.	In.
1..		1⅞
2..		3⅞
3..		5¾
4..		7⅝
5..		9½
6..		11½
7..	1	1⅜
8..		3¼
9..		5⅛
10..		7⅛
11..		9
12..		10⅞
13..	2	0¾
14..		2¾
15..		4⅝
16..		6½
17..		8⅜
18..		10⅜
19..	3	0¼
20..		2⅛
21..		4⅛
22..		6
23..		7⅞
24..		9¾
25..		11¾
26..	4	1⅝
27..		3½
28..		5⅜
29..		7⅜
30..		9¼
31..		11⅛
32..	5	1
33..		3
34..		4⅞
35..		6¾
36..		8¾
37..		10⅝
38..	6	0½
39..		2⅜
40..		4⅜
41..		6¼
42..		8⅛
43..		10
44..	7	0
45..		1⅞
46..		3¾
47..		5⅝
48..		7⅝

19½ & 12 — 58½°

EXPLANATION

Common Rafter

Width of building...........40′4¼″
Find length of Common Rafter.

Answer:

Under Span, ft. find	40′	= 38′ 1⅞″
" " in. "	4¼″ =	4″
Total length Common Rft.		38 5⅞″

When rafters overhang, add both overhangs to width of building. Use total span as before.

To get length of rafter by its run: doubling the run gives the span. Proceed as before.

Tables give full length. Allow for half thickness of ridge.

Spans over 50′, as 60′, add lengths of 50′ & 10′ spans together.

Hip Rafter

If common rafter span is 40′4¼″, Hip rafter is 43′5⅝″ long. Measure length of Hip on center of top edge. If Hip is unbacked (top edge square), see Index. If edge is backed (beveled), see Index.

Allow for half thickness of ridge.

Jack Rafters

Spaced 27″ apart are 4′3½″ different in length. Measure length on center of top edge. Cut short equal to half thickness of hip.

CUTS FOR STEEL SQUARE.

The first figure is always the cut.

Common Rafter

Plumb 19½- 12
Level. 12 - 19½

Hip Rafter

Plumb 9¾- 8½
Level. 8½- 9¾
Side.. 12⅞- 8½
Backing 9¾- 12⅞
Set bevel to last named.

Jack Rafter

Plumb 19½- 12
Level. 12 - 19½
Side.. 22⅞- 12

Purlin Rafter Roof Sheathing

Plumb 19½- 22⅞
Cross. 12 - 22⅞

Valley Shingles

Cross. 12 - 22⅞
Set bevel on butt end.

Mitre-Box Cuts for Gable Moulds

Plumb 19½- 12
Mitre. 22⅞- 12

Bisection of

19½- 12=13¼- 24

For full explanation see Index.

COMMON RAFTER				HIP OR VALLEY RAFTER		
Span Ft.	Length Ft. In.	Span In.	Lgth. In.	Span Ft.	Length Ft. In.	Span In.	Lgth. In.
1..	.11½	¼..	¼	1..	1. 0⅞	¼..	¼
2..	1.10⅞	½..	½	2..	2. 1⅞	½..	½
3..	2.10⅜	¾..	¾	3..	3. 2¾	¾..	⅞
4..	3. 9¾	1 ..	1	4..	4. 3¾	1 ..	1⅛
5..	4. 9¼	¼..	¼	5..	5. 4⅝	¼..	⅜
6..	5. 8¾	½..	⅜	6..	6. 5½	½..	⅝
7..	6. 8⅛	¾..	⅝	7..	7. 6½	¾..	⅞
8..	7. 7⅝	2 ..	⅞	8..	8. 7⅜	2 ..	2⅛
9..	8. 7	¼..	2⅛	9..	9. 8⅜	¼..	⅜
10..	9. 6½	½..	⅜	10..	10. 9¼	½..	⅝
11..10.	5⅞	¾..	⅝	11..11.	10⅛	¾..	3
12..11.	5⅜	3 ..	⅞	12..12.	11⅛	3 ..	¼
13..12.	4⅞	¼..	3⅛	13..14.	0	¼..	½
14..13.	4¼	½..	⅜	14..15.	1	½..	¾
15..14.	3¾	¾..	⅝	15..16.	1⅞	¾..	4
16..15.	3⅛	4 ..	⅞	16..17.	2¾	4 ..	¼
17..16.	2⅝	¼..	4	17..18.	3¾	¼..	⅝
18..17.	2⅛	½..	¼	18..19.	4⅝	½..	⅞
19..18.	1½	¾..	½	19..20.	5⅝	¾..	5⅛
20..19.	1	5 ..	¾	20..21.	6½	5 ..	⅜
21..20.	0⅜	¼..	5	21..22.	7⅜	¼..	⅝
22..20.	11⅞	½..	¼	22..23.	8⅜	½..	⅞
23..21.	11¼	¾..	½	23..24.	9¼	¾..	6¼
24..22.	10¾	6 ..	¾	24..25.	10¼	6 ..	½
25..23.	10¼	¼..	6	25..26.	11⅛	¼..	¾
26..24.	9⅝	½..	¼	26..28.	0	½..	7
27..25.	9⅛	¾..	⅜	27..29.	1	¾..	¼
28..26.	8½	7 ..	⅝	28..30.	1⅞	7 ..	½
29..27.	8	¼..	⅞	29..31.	2⅞	¼..	¾
30..28.	7½	½..	7⅛	30..32.	3¾	½..	8⅛
31..29.	6⅞	¾..	⅜	31..33.	4⅝	¾..	⅜
32..30.	6⅜	8 ..	⅝	32..34.	5⅝	8 ..	⅝
33..31.	5¾	¼..	¾	33..35.	6½	¼..	¾
34..32.	5¼	½..	8⅛	34..36.	7½	½..	9⅛
35..33.	4¾	¾..	⅜	35..37.	8⅜	¾..	⅜
36..34.	4⅛	9 ..	⅝	36..38.	9¼	9 ..	¾
37..35.	3⅝	¼..	⅞	37..39.	10¼	¼..	10
38..36.	3	½..	9	38..40.	11⅛	½..	¼
39..37.	2½	¾..	¼	39..42.	0⅛	¾..	½
40..38.	1⅞	10 ..	½	40..43.	1	10 ..	¾
41..39.	1⅜	¼..	¾	41..44.	1⅞	¼..	11
42..40.	0⅞	½..	10	42..45.	2⅞	½..	¼
43..41.	0¼	¾..	¼	43..46.	3¾	¾..	⅝
44..41.	11¾	11 ..	½	44..47.	4¾	11 ..	⅞
45..42.	11⅛	¼..	¾	45..48.	5⅝	¼..	12⅛
46..43.	10⅝	½..	11	46..49.	6½	½..	⅜
47..44.	10⅛	¾..	¼	47..50.	7½	¾..	⅝
48..45.	9½	12 ..	½	48..51.	8⅜	12 ..	⅞
49..46.	9			49..52.	9⅜		
50..47.	8⅜			50..53.	10¼		

JACK RAFTER Spaced In.	Length Ft. In.
1..	2
2..	3⅞
3..	5⅞
4..	7¾
5..	9¾
6..	11⅝
7..1	1⅝
8..	3½
9..	5½
10..	7⅜
11..	9⅜
12..	11⅜
13..2	1¼
14..	3¼
15..	5⅛
16..	7⅛
17..	9
18..	11
19..3	0⅞
20..	2⅞
21..	4⅞
22..	6¾
23..	8¾
24..	10⅝
25..4	0⅝
26..	2½
27..	4½
28..	6⅜
29..	8⅜
30..	10¼
31..5	0¼
32..	2¼
33..	4⅛
34..	6⅛
35..	8
36..	10
37..	11⅞
38..6	1⅞
39..	3¾
40..	5¾
41..	7¾
42..	9⅝
43..	11⅝
44..7	1½
45..	3½
46..	5⅜
47..	7⅜
48..	9¼

20 & 12 — 59°

EXPLANATION

Common Rafter

Width of building...........35′7¼″
Find length of Common Rafter.

Answer:

Under **Span, ft.** find	35′	= 34′ 0⅛″
" " **in.** "	7¼″ =	7″
Total length Common Rft.		34′ 7⅛″

When rafters overhang, add both overhangs to width of building. Use total span as before.

To get length of rafter by its run: doubling the run gives the span. Proceed as before.

Tables give full length. Allow for half thickness of ridge.

Spans over 50′, as 60′, add lengths of 50′ & 10′ spans together.

Hip Rafter

If common rafter span is 35′7¼″, Hip rafter is 38′10⅞″ long. Measure length of Hip on center of top edge. If Hip is unbacked (top edge square), see Index. If edge is backed (beveled), see Index.

Allow for half thickness of ridge.

Jack Rafters

Spaced 34″ apart are 5′6⅛″ different in length. Measure length on center of top edge. Cut short equal to half thickness of hip.

CUTS FOR STEEL SQUARE.

The first figure is always the cut.

Common Rafter
Plumb 20 - 12
Level. 12 - 20

Hip Rafter
Plumb 10 - 8½
Level. 8½ - 10
Side.. 13⅛ - 8½
Backing 10 - 13⅛
Set bevel to last named.

Jack Rafter
Plumb 20 - 12
Level. 12 - 20
Side.. 23⅜ - 12

Purlin Rafter Roof Sheathing
Plumb 20 - 23⅜
Cross. 12 - 23⅜

Valley Shingles
Cross. 12 - 23⅜
Set bevel on butt end.

Mitre-Box Cuts for Gable Moulds
Plumb 20 - 12
Mitre. 23⅜ - 12

Bisection of
20- 12=13½- 24

For full explanation see Index.

Span Ft.	Length Ft. In.	Span In.	Lgth. In. In.	Span Ft.	Length Ft. In.	Span In.	Lgth. In. In.
1..	.115/8			1..	1. 11/8		
2..	1.113/8	1/4.. 1/4		2..	2. 21/4	1/4.. 1/4	
3..	2.11	1/2.. 1/2		3..	3. 33/8	1/2.. 1/2	
4..	3.105/8	3/4.. 3/4		4..	4. 41/2	3/4.. 7/8	
5..	4.101/4	1 ..1		5..	5. 55/8	1 ..11/8	
6..	5.10	1/4.. 1/4		6..	6. 63/4	1/4.. 3/8	
7..	6.95/8	1/2.. 1/2		7..	7. 73/4	1/2.. 5/8	
8..	7.91/4	3/4.. 3/4		8..	8. 87/8	3/4.. 7/8	
9..	8.9	2 ..2		9..	9.10	2 ..21/8	
10..	9.85/8	1/4.. 1/4		10..	10.111/8	1/4.. 1/2	
11..	10.81/4	1/2.. 3/8		11..	12. 01/4	1/2.. 3/4	
12..	11.8	3/4.. 5/8		12..	13. 13/8	3/4.. 3	
13..	12.75/8	3 ..7/8		13..	14. 21/2	3 ..1/4	
14..	13.71/4	1/4.. 31/8		14..	15. 35/8	1/4.. 1/2	
15..	14.67/8	1/2.. 3/8		15..	16. 43/4	1/2.. 3/4	
16..	15.63/8	3/4.. 5/8		16..	17. 57/8	3/4.. 41/8	
17..	16.61/4	4 ..7/8		17..	18. 7	4 ..3/8	
18..	17.57/8	1/4.. 41/8		18..	19. 81/8	1/4.. 5/8	
19..	18.55/8	1/2.. 3/8		19..	20. 91/4	1/2.. 7/8	
20..	19.51/4	3/4.. 5/8		20..	21.101/4	3/4.. 51/8	
21..	20.47/8	5 ..7/8		21..	22.113/8	5 ..1/2	
22..	21.41/2	1/4.. 51/8		22..	24. 01/2	1/4.. 3/4	
23..	22.41/4	1/2.. 3/8		23..	25. 15/8	1/2.. 6	
24..	23.37/8	3/4.. 5/8		24..	26. 23/4	3/4.. 1/4	
25..	24.31/2	6 ..7/8		25..	27. 37/8	6 ..1/2	
26..	25.31/4	1/4.. 61/8		26..	28. 5	1/4.. 7/8	
27..	26.27/8	1/2.. 3/8		27..	29. 61/8	1/2.. 71/8	
28..	27.21/2	3/4.. 1/2		28..	30. 71/4	3/4.. 3/8	
29..	28.21/4	7 ..3/4		29..	31. 83/8	7 ..5/8	
30..	29.17/8	1/4.. 7		30..	32. 91/2	1/4.. 7/8	
31..	30.11/2	1/2.. 1/4		31..	33.101/2	1/2.. 81/4	
32..	31.11/8	3/4.. 1/4		32..	34.115/8	3/4.. 1/2	
33..	32.07/8	8 ..3/4		33..	36. 03/4	8 ..3/4	
34..	33.01/2	1/4.. 8		34..	37. 17/8	1/4.. 9	
35..	34.01/8	1/2.. 1/4		35..	38. 3	1/2.. 1/4	
36..	34.117/8	3/4.. 1/4		36..	39. 41/8	3/4.. 5/8	
37..	35.111/4	9 ..3/4		37..	40. 51/4	9 ..7/8	
38..	36.111/8	1/4.. 9		38..	41. 63/8	1/4..101/4	
39..	37.107/8	1/2.. 1/4		39..	42. 71/2	1/2.. 3/8	
40..	38.101/2	3/4.. 1/4		40..	43. 85/8	3/4.. 5/8	
41..	39.101/8	10 ..3/4		41..	44. 93/4	10 ..7/8	
42..	40.93/4	1/4.. 10		42..	45.107/8	1/4..111/4	
43..	41.91/2	1/2.. 1/4		43..	47. 0	1/2.. 1/2	
44..	42.91/8	3/4.. 1/4		44..	48. 1	3/4.. 3/4	
45..	43.83/4	11 ..3/4		45..	49. 21/8	11 ..12	
46..	44.81/2	1/4.. 11		46..	50. 31/4	1/4.. 1/4	
47..	45.81/8	1/2.. 1/8		47..	51. 43/8	1/2.. 5/8	
48..	46.73/4	3/4.. 3/8		48..	52. 51/2	3/4.. 7/8	
49..	47.71/2	12 ..5/8		49..	53. 65/8	12 ..131/8	
50..	48.71/8			50..	54. 73/4		

Spaced In.	Length Ft. In.
1..	2
2..	4
3..	6
4..	7⅞
5..	9⅞
6..	11⅞
7..1	1⅞
8..	3⅞
9..	5⅞
10..	7¾
11..	9¾
12..	11¾
13..2	1¾
14..	3¾
15..	5¾
16..	7⅝
17..	9⅝
18..	11⅝
19..3	1⅝
20..	3⅝
21..	5⅝
22..	7½
23..	9½
24..	11½
25..4	1½
26..	3½
27..	5½
28..	7⅜
29..	9⅜
30..	11⅜
31..5	1⅜
32..	3⅜
33..	5⅜
34..	7¼
35..	9¼
36..	11¼
37..6	1¼
38..	3¼
39..	5¼
40..	7⅛
41..	9⅛
42..	11⅛
43 7..1⅛	
44..	3⅛
45..	5⅛
46..	7
47..	9
48..	11

20½ & 12 — 59¾°

EXPLANATION
Common Rafter

Width of building...........49'4½"
Find length of Common Rafter.

Answer:

Under Span, ft. find 49' = 48' 6"
"   " in. "   4½" =   4½=

Total length Common Rft. 48'10½"

When rafters overhang, add both overhangs to width of building. Use total span as before.

To get length of rafter by its run: doubling the run gives the span. Proceed as before.

Tables give full length. Allow for half thickness of ridge.

Spans over 50', as 60', add lengths of 50' & 10' spans together.

Hip Rafter

If common rafter span is 49'4½", Hip rafter is 54'9" long. Measure length of Hip on center of top edge. If Hip is unbacked (top edge square), see Index. If edge is backed (beveled), see Index.

Allow for half thickness of ridge.

Jack Rafters

Spaced 23" apart are 3'9½" different in length. Measure length on center of top edge. Cut short equal to half thickness of hip.

CUTS FOR STEEL SQUARE.

The first figure is always the cut.

Common Rafter	Purlin Rafter Roof Sheathing
Plumb 20½- 12	
Level. 12 - 20½	Plumb 20½- 23¾
	Cross. 12 - 23⅜

Hip Rafter	Valley Shingles
Plumb 10¼- 8½	Cross. 12 - 23¾
Level. 8½- 10¼	Set bevel on
Side.. 13¼- 8½	butt end.
Backing10¼- 13¼	
Set bevel to	Mitre-Box Cuts
last named.	for Gable Moulds
	Plumb 20½- 12
Jack Rafter	Mitre. 23¾- 12
Plumb 20½- 12	
Level. 12 - 20½	Bisection of
Side.. 23¾- 12	20½- 12=13⅝- 24

For full explanation see Index.

COMMON RAFTER

Span Ft.	Length Ft. In.	Span In.	Lgth. In.
1	.11 7/8	1/4	1/4
2	1.11 3/4	1/2	1/2
3	2.11 5/8	3/4	3/4
4	3.11 1/2	1	1
5	4.11 3/8	1/4	1/4
6	5.11 1/4	1/2	1/2
7	6.11 1/8	3/4	3/4
8	7.11	2	2
9	8.10 7/8	1/4	1/4
10	9.10 3/4	1/2	1/2
11	10.10 5/8	3/4	3/4
12	11.10 1/2	3	3
13	12.10 3/8	1/4	1/4
14	13.10 1/4	1/2	1/2
15	14.10 1/8	3/4	3/4
16	15.10	4	4
17	16. 9 7/8	1/4	1/4
18	17. 9 3/4	1/2	1/2
19	18. 9 5/8	3/4	3/4
20	19. 9 1/2	5	5
21	20. 9 3/8	1/4	1/4
22	21. 9 1/4	1/2	1/2
23	22. 9 1/8	3/4	3/4
24	23. 9	6	6
25	24. 8 7/8	1/4	1/4
26	25. 8 3/4	1/2	3/8
27	26. 8 5/8	3/4	3/4
28	27. 8 1/2	7	7/8
29	28. 8 3/8	1/4	7 1/8
30	29. 8 1/4	1/2	3/8
31	30. 8 1/4	3/4	5/8
32	31. 8 1/8	8	7/8
33	32. 8	1/4	8 1/8
34	33. 7 7/8	1/2	3/8
35	34. 7 3/4	3/4	5/8
36	35. 7 5/8	9	7/8
37	36. 7 1/2	1/4	9 1/8
38	37. 7 3/8	1/2	3/8
39	38. 7 1/4	3/4	5/8
40	39. 7 1/8	10	7/8
41	40. 7	1/4	10 1/8
42	41. 6 7/8	1/2	3/8
43	42. 6 3/4	3/4	5/8
44	43. 6 5/8	11	7/8
45	44. 6 1/2	1/4	11 1/8
46	45. 6 3/8	1/2	3/8
47	46. 6 1/4	3/4	5/8
48	47. 6 1/8	12	7/8
49	48. 6		
50	49. 5 7/8		

HIP OR VALLEY RAFTER

Span Ft.	Length Ft. In.	Span In.	Lgth. In.
1	1. 1 1/4	1/4	1/4
2	2. 2 5/8	1/2	1/2
3	3. 3 7/8	3/4	7/8
4	4. 5 1/4	1	1 1/8
5	5. 6 1/2	1/4	3/8
6	6. 7 7/8	1/2	5/8
7	7. 9 1/8	3/4	2
8	8.10 1/2	2	1/4
9	9.11 3/4	1/4	1/2
10	11. 1 1/8	1/2	3/4
11	12. 2 3/8	3/4	3
12	13. 3 5/8	3	3/8
13	14. 5	1/4	5/8
14	15. 6 1/4	1/2	7/8
15	16. 7 5/8	3/4	4 1/8
16	17. 8 7/8	4	3/8
17	18.10 1/4	1/4	3/4
18	19.11 1/2	1/2	5
19	21. 0 7/8	3/4	1/4
20	22. 2 1/8	5	1/2
21	23. 3 1/2	1/4	7/8
22	24. 4 3/4	1/2	6 1/8
23	25. 6	3/4	3/8
24	26. 7 3/8	6	5/8
25	27. 8 5/8	1/4	7/8
26	28.10	1/2	7 1/4
27	29.11 1/4	3/4	1/2
28	31. 0 5/8	7	3/4
29	32. 1 7/8	1/4	8
30	33. 3 1/4	1/2	3/8
31	34. 4 1/2	3/4	5/8
32	35. 5 3/4	8	7/8
33	36. 7 1/8	1/4	9 1/8
34	37. 8 3/8	1/2	3/8
35	38. 9 3/4	3/4	3/4
36	39.11	9	10
37	41. 0 3/8	1/4	1/4
38	42. 1 5/8	1/2	1/2
39	43. 3	3/4	3/4
40	44. 4 1/4	10	11 1/8
41	45. 5 5/8	1/4	3/8
42	46. 6 7/8	1/2	5/8
43	47. 8 1/8	3/4	7/8
44	48. 9 1/2	11	12 1/4
45	49.10 3/4	1/4	1/2
46	51. 0 1/8	1/2	3/4
47	52. 1 3/8	3/4	13
48	53. 2 3/4	12	1/4
49	54. 4		
50	55. 5 3/8		

Spaced In.	Length Ft. In.
1..	2
2..	4
3..	6
4..	8⅛
5..	10⅛
6	1..0⅛
7..	2⅛
8..	4⅛
9..	6⅛
10..	8⅛
11..	10⅛
12	2..0¼
13..	2¼
14..	4¼
15..	6¼
16..	8¼
17..	10¼
18	3..0¼
19..	2¼
20..	4⅜
21..	6⅜
22..	8⅜
23..	10⅜
24..4	0⅜
25..	2⅜
26..	4⅜
27..	6⅜
28..	8½
29..	10½
30..5	0½
31..	2½
32..	4½
33..	6½
34..	8½
35..	10½
36..6	0⅝
37..	2⅝
38..	4⅝
39..	6⅝
40..	8⅝
41..	10⅝
42..7	0⅝
43..	2⅝
44..	4¾
45..	6¾
46..	8¾
47..	10¾
48..8	0¾

21 & 12   60¼°

EXPLANATION

Common Rafter

Width of building...........43'4½"
Find length of Common Rafter.
Answer:
Under Span, ft. find 43' = 43' 4"
"   "   in. "   4½" =   4½"

Total length Common Rft. 43' 8½"

When rafters overhang, add both overhangs to width of building. Use total span as before.

To get length of rafter by its run: doubling the run gives the span. Proceed as before.

Tables give full length. Allow for half thickness of ridge.

Spans over 50', as 60', add lengths of 50' & 10' spans together.

Hip Rafter

If common rafter span is 43'4½", Hip rafter is 48'9½" long. Measure length of Hip on center of top edge. If Hip is unbacked (top edge square), see Index. If edge is backed (beveled), see Index.

Allow for half thickness of ridge.

Jack Rafters

Spaced 32" apart are 5'4½" different in length. Measure length on center of top edge. Cut short equal to half thickness of hip.

CUTS FOR STEEL SQUARE.

The first figure is always the cut.

Common Rafter		Purlin Rafter Roof Sheathing	
Plumb	21 - 12		
Level.	12 - 21	Plumb 10½- 12⅛	
		Cross. 6- 12⅛	

Hip Rafter		Valley Shingles	
Plumb	10½- 8½	Cross. 6- 12⅛	
Level.	8½- 10½	Set bevel on	
Side..	13½- 8½	but end.	
Backing	10½- 13½		

Set bevel to last named.

Mitre-Box Cuts for Gable Moulds

Plumb 21 - 12
Mitre. 12⅛- 6

Jack Rafter	
Plumb	21 - 12
Level.	12 - 21
Side..	12⅛- 6

Bisection of

21- 12=13¾- 24

For full explanation see Index.

COMMON RAFTER				HIP or VALLEY RAFTER			
Span Ft.	Length Ft. In.	Span In.	Lgth. In.	Span Ft. In.	Length Ft. In.	Span In.	Lgth. In.
1..	1. 0⅛	¼..	¼	1..	1. 1½	¼..	¼
2..	2. 0⅛	½..	½	2..	2. 3	½..	⅝
3..	3. 0¼	¾..	¾	3..	3. 4½	¾..	⅞
4..	4. 0⅜	1 ..	1	4..	4. 6	1 ..	1⅛
5..	5. 0½	¼..	¼	5..	5. 7½	¼..	⅜
6..	6. 0½	½..	½	6..	6. 9	½..	¾
7..	7. 0⅝	¾..	¾	7..	7.10½	¾..	2
8..	8. 0¾	2 ..	2	8..	9. 0	2 ..	¼
9..	9. 0⅞	¼..	¼	9..	10. 1½	¼..	½
10..	10. 0⅞	½..	½	10..	11. 3	½..	⅞
11..	11. 1	¾..	¾	11..	12. 4½	¾..	3⅛
12..	12. 1⅛	3 ..	3	12..	13. 6	3 ..	⅜
13..	13. 1¼	¼..	¼	13..	14. 7½	¼..	⅝
14..	14. 1¼	½..	½	14..	15. 9	½..	⅞
15..	15. 1⅜	¾..	¾	15..	16.10½	¾..	4¼
16..	16. 1½	4 ..	4	16..	18. 0	4 ..	½
17..	17. 1⅝	¼..	¼	17..	19. 1½	¼..	¾
18..	18. 1⅝	½..	½	18..	20. 3	½..	5
19..	19. 1¾	¾..	¾	19..	21. 4½	¾..	⅜
20..	20. 1⅞	5 ..	5	20..	22. 6	5 ..	⅝
21..	21. 2	¼..	¼	21..	23. 7½	¼..	⅞
22..	22. 2	½..	½	22..	24. 9	½..	6⅛
23..	23. 2⅛	¾..	¾	23..	25.10½	¾..	½
24..	24. 2¼	6 ..	6	24..	27. 0	6 ..	¾
25..	25. 2⅜	¼..	¼	25..	28. 1½	¼..	7
26..	26. 2⅜	½..	½	26..	29. 3	½..	¼
27..	27. 2½	¾..	¾	27..	30. 4½	¾..	⅝
28..	28. 2⅝	7 ..	7	28..	31. 6	7 ..	⅞
29..	29. 2¾	¼..	¼	29..	32. 7½	¼..	8⅛
30..	30. 2¾	½..	½	30..	33. 9	½..	⅜
31..	31. 2⅞	¾..	⅞	31..	34.10½	¾..	¾
32..	32. 3	8 ..	8⅛	32..	36. 0	8 ..	9
33..	33. 3⅛	¼..	⅜	33..	37. 1½	¼..	¼
34..	34. 3⅛	½..	⅝	34..	38. 3	½..	½
35..	35. 3¼	¾..	⅞	35..	39. 4½	¾..	⅞
36..	36. 3⅜	9 ..	9⅛	36..	40. 6	9 .	10⅛
37..	37. 3½	¼..	⅜	37..	41. 7½	¼..	⅜
38..	38. 3½	½..	⅝	38..	42. 9	½..	⅝
39..	39. 3⅝	¾..	⅞	39..	43.10½	¾.	11
40..	40. 3¾	10 .	10⅛	40..	45. 0	10 ..	¼
41..	41. 3⅞	¼..	⅜	41..	46. 1½	¼..	½
42..	42. 3⅞	½..	⅝	42..	47. 3	½..	¾
43..	43. 4	¾..	⅞	43..	48. 4½	¾.	12⅛
44..	44. 4⅛	11 .	11⅛	44..	49. 6	11 ..	⅜
45..	45. 4¼	¼..	⅜	45..	50. 7½	¼..	⅝
46..	46. 4¼	½..	⅝	46..	51. 9	½..	⅞
47..	47. 4⅜	¾..	⅞	47..	52.10½	¾.	13¼
48..	48. 4½	12 .	12⅛	48..	54. 0	12 ..	½
49..	49. 4⅝			49..	55. 1½		
50..	50. 4⅝			50..	56. 3		

Spaced In.	Length Ft. In.
1..	2
2..	4⅛
3..	6⅛
4..	8¼
5..	10¼
6 1..	0¼
7..	2⅜
8..	4⅜
9..	6½
10..	8½
11..	10⅝
12..2	0⅝
13..	2⅝
14..	4¾
15..	6¾
16..	8⅞
17..	10⅞
18..3	0⅞
19..	3
20..	5
21..	7⅛
22..	9⅛
23..	11¼
24 4	1¼
25..	3¼
26..	5⅜
27..	7⅜
28..	9½
29..	11½
30..5	1½
31..	3⅝
32..	5⅝
33..	7¾
34..	9¾
35..	11⅞
36..6	1⅞
37..	3⅞
38..	6
39..	8
40..	10⅛
41..7	0⅛
42..	2⅛
43..	4¼
44..	6¼
45..	8⅜
46..	10⅜
47..8	0⅜
48..	2½

21½ & 12 — 61°

EXPLANATION

Common Rafter

Width of building..........45'5¼"
Find length of Common Rafter.
Answer:

Under Span, ft. find	45'	= 46' 2"
" " in. "	5¼" =	5⅜"

Total length Common Rft. 46' 7⅜"

When rafters overhang, add both overhangs to width of building. Use total span as before.

To get length of rafter by its run: doubling the run gives the span. Proceed as before.

Tables give full length. Allow for half thickness of ridge.

Spans over 50', as 60', add lengths of 50' & 10' spans together.

Hip Rafter

If common rafter span is 45'5¼", Hip rafter is 51'10¼" long. Measure length of Hip on center of top edge. If Hip is unbacked (top edge square), see Index. If edge is backed (beveled), see Index.

Allow for half thickness of ridge.

Jack Rafters

Spaced 28" apart are 4'9"½ different in length. Measure length on center of top edge. Cut short equal to half thickness of hip.

CUTS FOR STEEL SQUARE.

The first figure is always the cut.

Common Rafter	Purlin Rafter Roof Sheathing
Plumb 21½- 12	
Level. 12 - 21½	Plumb 10¾- 12¼
	Cross. 6 - 12¼

Hip Rafter	Valley Shingles
Plumb 10¾- 8½	Cross. 6 - 12¼
Level. 8½- 10¾	Set bevel on
Side.. 13¾- 8½	butt end.
Backing10¾- 13¾	
Set bevel to	**Mitre-Box Cuts**
last named.	**for Gable Moulds**
	Plumb 21½- 12
	Mitre. 12¼- 6

Jack Rafter	
Plumb 21½- 12	**Bisection of**
Level. 12 - 21½	
Side.. 12¼- 6	21½- 12=13⅞- 24

For full explanation see Index.

COMMON RAFTER

Span Ft.	Length Ft. In.	Span In.	Lgth. In.
1	1. 0¼	¼	¼
2	2. 0⅝	½	½
3	3. 0⅞	¾	¾
4	4. 1¼	1	1
5	5. 1½	¼	¼
6	6. 1⅞	½	½
7	7. 2⅛	¾	¾
8	8. 2½	2	2
9	9. 2¾	¼	¼
10	10. 3⅛	½	⅝
11	11. 3⅜	¾	⅞
12	12. 3¾	3	3⅛
13	13. 4	¼	⅜
14	14. 4⅜	½	⅝
15	15. 4⅝	¾	⅞
16	16. 5	4	4⅛
17	17. 5¼	¼	⅜
18	18. 5⅝	½	⅝
19	19. 5⅞	¾	⅞
20	20. 6¼	5	5⅛
21	21. 6½	¼	⅜
22	22. 6⅞	½	⅝
23	23. 7⅛	¾	⅞
24	24. 7½	6	6⅛
25	25. 7¾	¼	⅜
26	26. 8⅛	½	⅝
27	27. 8⅜	¾	⅞
28	28. 8¾	7	7⅛
29	29. 9	¼	⅜
30	30. 9⅜	½	¾
31	31. 9⅝	¾	8
32	32.10	8	¼
33	33.10¼	¼	½
34	34.10⅝	½	¾
35	35.10⅞	¾	9
36	36.11¼	9	¼
37	37.11½	¼	½
38	38.11⅞	½	¾
39	40. 0⅛	¾	10
40	41. 0½	10	¼
41	42. 0¾	¼	½
42	43. 1⅛	½	¾
43	44. 1⅜	¾	11
44	45. 1⅝	11	¼
45	46. 2	¼	½
46	47. 2¼	½	¾
47	48. 2⅝	¾	12
48	49. 2⅞	12	¼
49	50. 3¼		
50	51. 3½		

HIP OR VALLEY RAFTER

Span Ft.	Length Ft. In.	Span In.	Lgth. In.
1	1. 1¾	¼	¼
2	2. 3⅜	½	⅝
3	3. 5⅛	¾	⅞
4	4. 6¾	1	1⅛
5	5. 8½	¼	⅜
6	6.10⅛	½	¾
7	7.11⅞	¾	2
8	9. 1⅝	2	¼
9	10. 3¼	¼	⅝
10	11. 5	½	⅞
11	12. 6⅝	¾	3⅛
12	13. 8⅜	3	⅜
13	14.10	¼	¾
14	15.11¾	½	4
15	17. 1⅜	¾	¼
16	18. 3⅛	4	⅝
17	19. 4⅞	¼	⅞
18	20. 6½	½	5⅛
19	21. 8¼	¾	⅜
20	22. 9⅞	5	¾
21	23.11⅝	¼	6
22	25. 1¼	½	¼
23	26. 3	¾	⅝
24	27. 4¾	6	⅞
25	28. 6⅜	¼	7⅛
26	29. 8⅛	½	⅜
27	30. 9¾	¾	¾
28	31.11½	7	8
29	33. 1⅛	¼	¼
30	34. 2⅞	½	⅝
31	35. 4½	¾	⅞
32	36. 6¼	8	9⅛
33	37. 8	¼	⅜
34	38. 9⅝	½	¾
35	39.11⅜	¾	10
36	41. 1	9	¼
37	42. 2¾	¼	½
38	43. 4⅜	½	⅞
39	44. 6⅛	¾	11⅛
40	45. 7⅞	10	⅜
41	46. 9½	¼	¾
42	47.11¼	½	12
43	49. 0⅞	¾	¼
44	50. 2⅝	11	½
45	51. 4¼	¼	⅞
46	52. 6	½	13⅛
47	53. 7⅝	¾	⅜
48	54. 9⅜	12	¾
49	55.11⅛		
50	57. 0¾		

Spaced In.	Length Ft. In.
1..	2⅛
2..	4⅛
3..	6¼
4..	8⅜
5..	10½
6 1	0½
7..	2⅝
8..	4¾
9..	6¾
10..	8⅞
11..	1 0
12..2	1
13..	3⅛
14..	5¼
15..	7⅜
16..	9⅜
17..	11½
18..3	1⅝
19..	3⅝
20..	5¾
21..	7⅞
22..	10
23..4	0
24..	2⅛
25..	4¼
26..	6¼
27..	8⅜
28..	10½
29..5	0½
30..	2⅝
31..	4¾
32..	6⅞
33..	8⅞
34..	11
35..6	1⅛
36..	3⅛
37..	5¼
38..	7⅜
39..	9½
40..	11½
41..7	1⅝
42..	3¾
43..	5¾
44..	7⅞
45..	10
46..8	0
47..	2⅛
48..	4¼

22 & 12 — 61½°

EXPLANATION

Common Rafter

Width of building..........49'1¾"
Find length of Common Rafter.
　　Answer:

Under Span, ft. find 49'	= 51' 2"
"　　" in. " 1¾" =	1⅞"

Total length Common Rft. 51' 3⅞"

When rafters overhang, add both overhangs to width of building. Use total span as before.

To get length of rafter by its run: doubling the run gives the span. Proceed as before.

Tables give full length. Allow for half thickness of ridge.

Spans over 50', as 60', add lengths of 50' & 10' spans together.

Hip Rafter

If common rafter span is 49'1¾", Hip rafter is 56'10¾" long. Measure length of Hip on center of top edge. If Hip is unbacked (top edge square), see Index. If edge is backed (beveled), see Index.

Allow for half thickness of ridge.

Jack Rafters

Spaced 24" apart are 4'2⅛" different in length. Measure length on center of top edge. Cut short equal to half thickness of hip.

CUTS FOR STEEL SQUARE.

The first figure is always the cut.

Common Rafter		Purlin Rafter Roof Sheathing	
Plumb 22 - 12		Plumb 11 - 12½	
Level. 12 - 22		Cross. 6 - 12½	

Hip Rafter		Valley Shingles	
Plumb 11 - 8½		Cross. 6 - 12½	
Level. 8½- 11		Set bevel on	
Side.. 13⅞- 8½		butt end.	
Backing 11 - 13⅞			
Set bevel to		Mitre-Box Cuts	
last named.		for Gable Moulds	
		Plumb 22 - 12	

Jack. Rafter		Mitre. 12½- 6	
Plumb 22 - 12		Bisection of	
Level. 12 - 22		22- 12=14 - 24	
Side.. 12½- 6			

For full explanation see Index.

COMMON RAFTER

Span Ft.	Length Ft. In.	Span In.	Lgth. In.
1..	1. 0½	¼..	¼
2..	2. 1	½..	½
3..	3. 1⅝	¾..	¾
4..	4. 2⅛	1 ..	1
5..	5. 2⅝	¼..	¼
6..	6. 3⅛	½..	⅝
7..	7. 3¾	¾..	⅞
8..	8. 4¼	2 ..	2⅛
9..	9. 4¾	¼..	⅜
10..	10. 5¼	½..	⅝
11..	11. 5⅞	¾..	⅞
12..	12. 6⅜	3 ..	3⅛
13..	13. 6⅞	¼..	⅜
14..	14. 7⅜	½..	⅝
15..	15. 8	¾..	⅞
16..	16. 8½	4 ..	4⅛
17..	17. 9	¼..	½
18..	18. 9½	½..	⅝
19..	19. 10⅛	¾..	5
20..	20. 10⅝	5 ..	¼
21..	21. 11⅛	¼..	½
22..	22. 11⅝	½..	¾
23..	24. 0¼	¾..	6
24..	25. 0¾	6 ..	¼
25..	26. 1¼	¼..	½
26..	27. 1¾	½..	¾
27..	28. 2¼	¾..	7
28..	29. 2⅞	7 ..	¼
29..	30. 3⅜	¼..	⅝
30..	31. 3⅞	½..	⅞
31..	32. 4⅜	¾..	8⅛
32..	33. 5	8 ..	⅜
33..	34. 5½	¼..	⅝
34..	35. 6	½..	⅞
35..	36. 6½	¾..	9⅛
36..	37. 7⅛	9 ..	⅜
37..	38. 7⅝	¼..	⅝
38..	39. 8⅛	½..	⅞
39..	40. 8⅝	¾.	10⅛
40..	41. 9¼	10 ..	½
41..	42. 9¾	¼..	¾
42..	43. 10¼	½..	11
43..	44. 10¾	¾..	¼
44..	45. 11⅜	11 ..	½
45..	46. 11⅞	¼..	¾
46..	48. 0⅜	½.	12
47..	49. 0⅞	¾..	¼
48..	50. 1½	12 ..	½
49..	51. 2		
50..	52. 2½		

HIP OR VALLEY RAFTER

Span Ft.	Length Ft. In.	Span In.	Lgth. In.
1..	1. 1⅞	¼..	¼
2..	2. 3¾	½..	⅝
3..	3. 5⅝	¾..	⅞
4..	4. 7⅝	1 ..	1⅛
5..	5. 9½	¼..	½
6..	6. 11⅜	½..	¾
7..	8. 1¼	¾..	2
8..	9. 3⅛	2 ..	⅜
9..	10. 5	¼..	⅝
10..	11. 6⅞	½..	⅞
11..	12. 8⅞	¾.	3⅛
12..	13. 10¾	3 ..	½
13..	15. 0⅝	¼..	¾
14..	16. 2½	½..	4
15..	17. 4⅜	¾..	⅜
16..	18. 6¼	4 ..	⅝
17..	19. 8⅛	¼..	5
18..	20. 10⅛	½..	¼
19..	22. 0	¾..	½
20..	23. 1⅞	5 ..	¾
21..	24. 3¾	¼..	6⅛
22..	25. 5⅝	½..	⅜
23..	26. 7½	¾..	⅝
24..	27. 9⅜	6 ..	7
25..	28. 11⅜	¼..	¼
26..	30. 1¼	½..	½
27..	31. 3⅛	¾..	⅞
28..	32. 5	7 ..	8⅛
29..	33. 6⅞	¼..	⅜
30..	34. 8¾	½..	⅝
31..	35. 10⅝	¾..	9
32..	37. 0½	8 ..	¼
33..	38. 2½	¼..	½
34..	39. 4⅜	½..	⅞
35..	40. 6¼	¾.	10⅛
36..	41. 8⅛	9 ..	⅜
37..	42. 10	¼..	¾
38..	43. 11⅞	½.	11
39..	45. 1¾	¾..	¼
40..	46. 3¾	10 ..	⅝
41..	47. 5⅝	¼..	⅞
42..	48. 7½	½.	12⅛
43..	49. 9⅜	¾..	½
44..	50. 11¼	11 ..	¾
45..	52. 1⅛	¼.	13
46..	53. 3	½..	⅜
47..	54. 5	¾..	⅝
48..	55. 6⅞	12 ..	⅞
49..	56. 8¾		
50..	57. 10⅝		

JACK RAFTER	
Spaced	Length
In.	Ft. In.
1..	2⅛
2..	4¼
3..	6⅜
4..	8½
5..	10⅝
6..1	0¾
7..	2⅞
8..	5
9..	7⅛
10..	9¼
11..	11⅜
12..2	1½
13..	3⅝
14..	5¾
15..	7⅞
16..	10
17..3	0⅛
18..	2¼
19..	4⅜
20..	6½
21..	8⅝
22..	10¾
23..4	0⅞
24..	3
25..	5⅛
26..	7¼
27..	9⅜
28..	11½
29..5	1⅝
30..	3¾
31	5⅞
32..	8
33..	10⅛
34..6	0¼
35..	2⅜
36..	4½
37..	6⅝
38..	8¾
39..	10⅞
40..7	1
41..	3⅛
42..	5¼
43..	7⅜
44..	9½
45..	11⅝
46..8	1¾
47..	3⅞
48..	6

22½ & 12 — 62°

EXPLANATION

Common Rafter

Width of building..........48'4¼"
Find length of Common Rafter.
Answer:

Under Span, ft. find	48'	= 51' 0"
" " in. "	4¼" =	4½"

Total length Common Rft. 51' 4½"

When rafters overhang, add both overhangs to width of building. Use total span as before.

To get length of rafter by its run: doubling the run gives the span. Proceed as before.

Tables give full length. Allow for half thickness of ridge.

Spans over 50', as 60', add lengths of 50' & 10' spans together.

Allow for half thickness of ridge.

Hip Rafter

If common rafter span is 48'4¼", Hip rafter is 56'9⅜" long. Measure length of Hip on center of top edge. If Hip is unbacked (top edge square), see Index. If edge is backed (beveled), see Index.

Jack Rafters

Spaced 30" apart are 5'3¾" different in length. Measure length on center of top edge. Cut short equal to half thickness of hip.

CUTS FOR STEEL SQUARE.

The first figure is always the cut.

Common Rafter	Purlin Rafter
Plumb 22½- 12	**Roof Sheathing**
Level. 12 - 22½	Plumb 11¼- 12¾
	Cross. 6 - 12¾

Hip Rafter	
Plumb 11¼- 8½	**Valley Shingles**
Level. 8½- 11¼	Cross. 6 - 12¾
Side.. 14⅛- 8½	Set bevel on
Backing 11¼- 14⅛	butt end.
Set bevel to	
last named.	**Mitre-Box Cuts**
	for Gable Moulds
	Plumb 22½- 12
Jack Rafter	Mitre. 12¾- 6
Plumb 22½- 12	
Level. 12 - 22½	**Bisection of**
Side.. 12¾- 6	22½- 12=14⅛- 24

For full explanation see Index.

108

COMMON RAFTER

Span Ft.	Length Ft. In.	Span In.	Lgth. In.
1..	1. 0¾	¼ ..	¼
2..	2. 1½	½ ..	½
3..	3. 2¼	¾ ..	¾
4..	4. 3	1 ..	1⅛
5..	5. 3¾	¼ ..	⅜
6..	6. 4½	½ ..	⅝
7..	7. 5¼	¾ ..	⅞
8..	8. 6	2 ..	2⅛
9..	9. 6¾	¼ ..	⅜
10..	10. 7½	½ ..	⅝
11..	11. 8¼	¾ ..	⅞
12..	12. 9	3 ..	3¼
13..	13. 9¾	¼ ..	½
14..	14. 10½	½ ..	¾
15..	15. 11¼	¾ ..	4
16..	17. 0	4 ..	¼
17..	18. 0¾	¼ ..	½
18..	19. 1½	½ ..	¾
19..	20. 2¼	¾ ..	5
20..	21. 3	5 ..	⅜
21..	22. 3¾	¼ ..	⅝
22..	23. 4½	½ ..	⅞
23..	24. 5¼	¾ ..	6⅛
24..	25. 6	6 ..	⅜
25..	26. 6¾	¼ ..	⅝
26..	27. 7½	½ ..	⅞
27..	28. 8¼	¾ ..	7⅛
28..	29. 9	7 ..	⅜
29..	30. 9¾	¼ ..	¾
30..	31. 10½	½ ..	8
31..	32. 11¼	¾ ..	¼
32..	34. 0	8 ..	½
33..	35. 0¾	¼ ..	¾
34..	36. 1½	½ ..	9
35..	37. 2¼	¾ ..	¼
36..	38. 3	9 ..	⅝
37..	39. 3¾	¼ ..	⅞
38..	40. 4½	½ .	10⅛
39..	41. 5¼	¾ ..	⅜
40..	42. 6	10 ..	⅝
41..	43. 6¾	¼ ..	⅞
42..	44. 7½	½ .	11⅛
43..	45. 8¼	¾ ..	⅜
44..	46. 9	11 ..	⅝
45..	47. 9¾	¼ .	12
46..	48. 10½	½ ..	¼
47..	49. 11¼	¾ ..	½
48..	51. 0	12 ..	¾
49..	52. 0¾		
50..	53. 1½		

HIP OR VALLEY RAFTER

Span Ft.	Length Ft. In.	Span In.	Lgth. In.
1..	1. 2⅛	¼ ..	¼
2..	2. 4⅛	½ ..	⅝
3..	3. 6¼	¾ ..	⅞
4..	4. 8⅜	1 ..	1⅛
5..	5. 10½	¼ ..	½
6..	7. 0½	½ ..	¾
7..	8. 2⅝	¾ ..	2
8..	9. 4¾	2 ..	⅜
9..	10. 6⅞	¼ ..	⅝
10..	11. 8⅞	½ ..	⅞
11..	12. 11	¾ ..	3¼
12..	14. 1⅛	3 ..	½
13..	15. 3⅛	¼ ..	⅞
14..	16. 5¼	½ ..	4⅛
15..	17. 7⅜	¾ ..	⅜
16..	18. 9½	4 ..	¾
17..	19. 11½	¼ ..	5
18..	21. 1⅝	½ ..	¼
19..	22. 3¾	¾ ..	⅝
20..	23. 5⅞	5 ..	⅞
21..	24. 7⅞	¼ ..	6⅛
22..	25. 10	½ ..	½
23..	27. 0⅛	¾ ..	¾
24..	28. 2¼	6 ..	7
25..	29. 4¼	¼ ..	⅜
26..	30. 6⅜	½ ..	⅝
27..	31. 8½	¾ ..	⅞
28..	32. 10½	7 ..	8¼
29..	34. 0⅝	¼ ..	½
30..	35. 2¾	½ ..	¾
31..	36. 4⅞	¾ ..	9⅛
32..	37. 6⅞	8 ..	⅜
33..	38. 9	¼ ..	¾
34..	39. 11⅛	½ .	10
35..	41. 1¼	¾ ..	¼
36..	42. 3¼	9 ..	⅝
37..	43. 5⅜	¼ ..	⅞
38..	44. 7½	½ .	11⅛
39..	45. 9½	¾ ..	½
40..	46. 11⅝	10 ..	¾
41..	48. 1¾	¼ .	12
42..	49. 3⅞	½ ..	⅜
43..	50. 5⅞	¾ ..	⅝
44..	51. 8	11 ..	⅞
45..	52. 10⅛	¼ .	13¼
46..	54. 0¼	½ ..	½
47..	55. 2¼	¾ ..	¾
48..	56. 4⅜	12 .	14⅛
49..	57. 6½		
50..	58. 8½		

JACK RAFTER

Spaced In.	Length Ft. In.
1..	2¼
2..	4⅜
3..	6½
4..	8⅝
5..	10¾
6..1	1
7..	3⅛
8..	5¼
9..	7½
10..	9⅝
11..	11¾
12..2	2
13..	4⅛
14..	6¼
15..	8⅜
16..	10⅝
17..3	0¾
18..	2⅞
19..	5⅛
20..	7¼
21..	9⅜
22..	11½
23..4	1¾
24..	3⅞
25..	6
26..	8¼
27..	10⅜
28..5	0½
29..	2¾
30..	4⅞
31..	7
32..	9⅛
33..	11⅜
34..6	1½
35..	3⅝
36..	5⅞
37..	8
38..	10⅛
39..7	0¼
40..	2½
41..	4⅝
42..	6¾
43..	9
44..	11⅛
45..8	1¼
46..	3½
47..	5⅝
48..	7¾

23 & 12 — 62½°

EXPLANATION

Common Rafter

Width of building..........33′2½″
Find length of Common Rafter.
Answer:

Under Span, ft. find 33′ = 35′ 8″
"   "   in. "   2½″ =   2¾″

Total length Common Rft. 35′10¾″

When rafters overhang, add both overhangs to width of building. Use total span as before.

To get length of rafter by its run: doubling the run gives the span. Proceed as before.

Tables give full length. Allow for half thickness of ridge.

Spans over 50′, as 60′, add lengths of 50′ & 10′ spans together.

Hip Rafter

If common rafter span is 33′2½″, Hip rafter is 39′6⅝″ long. Measure length of Hip on center of top edge. If Hip is unbacked (top edge square), see Index. If edge is backed (beveled), see Index.

Allow for half thickness of ridge.

Jack Rafters

Spaced 22″ apart are 3′11½″ different in length. Measure length on center of top edge. Cut short equal to half thickness of hip.

CUTS FOR STEEL SQUARE.
The first figure is always the cut.

Common Rafter		Purlin Rafter Roof Sheathing	
Plumb	23 - 12	Plumb 11½- 13	
Level.	12 - 23	Cross. 6 - 13	

Hip Rafter		Valley Shingles	
Plumb	11½- 8½	Cross. 6 - 13	
Level.	8½- 11½	Set level on	
Side..	14¼- 8½	butt end.	
Backing	11½- 14¼		

Set bevel to last named.

Mitre-Box Cuts for Gable Moulds

Plumb 23 - 12
Mitre. 13 - 6

Jack Rafter	
Plumb	23 - 12
Level.	12 - 23
Side..	13 - 6

Bisection of
23- 12=14⅜- 24

For full explanation see Index.

COMMON RAFTER

Span Ft.	Length Ft. In.	Span In.	Lgth. In.
1	1. 1	1/4	1/4
2	2. 2	1/2	1/2
3	3. 2 7/8	3/4	3/4
4	4. 3 7/8	1	1 1/8
5	5. 4 7/8	1/4	3/8
6	6. 5 7/8	1/2	5/8
7	7. 6 3/4	3/4	7/8
8	8. 7 3/4	2	2 1/8
9	9. 8 3/4	1/4	3/8
10	10. 9 3/4	1/2	3/4
11	11. 10 5/8	3/4	3
12	12. 11 5/8	3	1/4
13	14. 0 5/8	1/4	1/2
14	15. 1 5/8	1/2	3/4
15	16. 2 5/8	3/4	4
16	17. 3 1/2	4	3/8
17	18. 4 1/2	1/4	5/8
18	19. 5 1/2	1/2	7/8
19	20. 6 1/2	3/4	5 1/8
20	21. 7 3/8	5	3/8
21	22. 8 3/8	1/4	5/8
22	23. 9 3/8	1/2	7/8
23	24. 10 3/8	3/4	6 1/4
24	25. 11 1/4	6	1/2
25	27. 0 1/4	1/4	3/4
26	28. 1 1/4	1/2	7
27	29. 2 1/4	3/4	1/4
28	30. 3 1/4	7	5/8
29	31. 4 1/8	1/4	7/8
30	32. 5 1/8	1/2	8 1/8
31	33. 6 1/8	3/4	3/8
32	34. 7 1/8	8	5/8
33	35. 8	1/4	7/8
34	36. 9	1/2	9 1/8
35	37. 10	3/4	1/2
36	38. 11	9	3/4
37	39. 11 7/8	1/4	10
38	41. 0 7/8	1/2	1/4
39	42. 1 7/8	3/4	1/2
40	43. 2 7/8	10	3/4
41	44. 3 3/4	1/4	11 1/8
42	45. 4 3/4	1/2	3/8
43	46. 5 3/4	3/4	5/8
44	47. 6 3/4	11	7/8
45	48. 7 3/4	1/4	12 1/8
46	49. 8 5/8	1/2	3/8
47	50. 9 5/8	3/4	3/4
48	51. 10 5/8	12	13
49	52. 11 5/8		
50	54. 0 1/2		

HIP OR VALLEY RAFTER

Span Ft.	Length Ft. In.	Span In.	Lgth In.
1	1. 2 1/4	1/4	1/4
2	2. 4 5/8	1/2	5/8
3	3. 6 7/8	3/4	7/8
4	4. 9 1/8	1	1 1/4
5	5. 11 1/2	1/4	1/2
6	7. 1 3/4	1/2	3/4
7	8. 4	3/4	2 1/8
8	9. 6 3/8	2	3/8
9	10. 8 5/8	1/4	5/8
10	11. 10 7/8	1/2	3
11	13. 1 1/4	3/4	1/4
12	14. 3 1/2	3	5/8
13	15. 5 3/4	1/4	7/8
14	16. 8 1/8	1/2	4 1/8
15	17. 10 3/8	3/4	1/2
16	19. 0 5/8	4	3/4
17	20. 3	1/4	5 1/8
18	21. 5 1/4	1/2	3/8
19	22. 7 1/2	3/4	5/8
20	23. 9 7/8	5	6
21	25. 0 1/8	1/4	1/4
22	26. 2 3/8	1/2	1/2
23	27. 4 3/4	3/4	7/8
24	28. 7	6	7 1/8
25	29. 9 1/4	1/4	1/2
26	30. 11 5/8	1/2	3/4
27	32. 1 7/8	3/4	8
28	33. 4 1/8	7	3/8
29	34. 6 1/2	1/4	5/8
30	35. 8 3/4	1/2	7/8
31	36. 11	3/4	9 1/4
32	38. 1 3/8	8	1/2
33	39. 3 5/8	1/4	7/8
34	40. 5 7/8	1/2	10 1/8
35	41. 8 1/4	3/4	3/8
36	42. 10 1/2	9	3/4
37	44. 0 3/4	1/4	11
38	45. 3 1/8	1/2	3/8
39	46. 5 3/8	3/4	5/8
40	47. 7 5/8	10	12
41	48. 10	1/4	1/4
42	50. 0 1/4	1/2	1/2
43	51. 2 1/2	3/4	3/4
44	52. 4 7/8	11	13 1/8
45	53. 7 1/8	1/4	3/8
46	54. 9 3/8	1/2	5/8
47	55. 11 3/4	3/4	14
48	57. 2	12	1/4
49	58. 4 1/4		
50	59. 6 5/8		

Spaced In.	Length Ft. In.
1..	2¼
2..	4⅜
3..	6⅝
4..	8¾
5..	11
6..1	1¼
7..	3⅜
8..	5⅝
9..	7¾
10..	10
11..2	0⅛
12..	2⅜
13..	4⅝
14..	6¾
15..	9
16..	11⅛
17..3	1⅜
18..	3⅝
19..	5¾
20..	8
21..	10⅛
22..4	0⅜
23..	2⅝
24..	4¾
25..	7
26..	9⅛
27..	11⅜
28 5..1	5⅝
29..	3¾
30..	6
31 ..	8⅛
32..	10⅜
33..6	0½
34..	2¾
35..	5
36..	7⅛
37..	9⅜
38..	11½
39..7	1¾
40..	4
41..	6⅛
42..	8⅜
43..	10½
44..8	0¾
45..	3
46..	5⅛
47..	7⅜
48..	9½

23½ & 12 — 63°

EXPLANATION

Common Rafter
Width of building..........36'2½"
Find length of Common Rafter.
Answer:
Under Span, ft. find 36' = 39' 7"
   "   " in. "   2½" =   2¾"

Total length Common Rft. 39' 9¾"

When rafters overhang, add both overhangs to width of building. Use total span as before.
To get length of rafter by its run: doubling the run gives the span. Proceed as before.
Tables give full length. Allow for half thickness of ridge.
Spans over 50', as 60', **add lengths** of 50' & 10' spans together.

Hip Rafter
If common rafter span is 36'2½", Hip rafter is 43'8¾" long. Measure length of Hip on center of top edge. If Hip is unbacked (top edge square), see Index. If edge is backed (beveled), see Index.
Allow for half thickness of ridge.

Jack Rafters
Spaced 26" part are 4'9⅛" different in length. Measure length on center of top edge. Cut short equal to half thickness of hip.

CUTS FOR STEEL SQUARE.
The first figure is always the cut.

Common Rafter	Purlin Rafter Roof Sheathing
Plumb 23½- 12	Plumb 11¾- 13¼
Level. 12 - 23½	Cross. 6 - 13¼

Hip Rafter	Valley Shingles
Plumb 11¾- 8½	Cross. 6 - 13¼
Level. 8½- 11¾	Set bevel on
Side.. 14½- 8½	butt end.
Backing 11¾- 14½	
Set bevel to	Mitre-Box Cuts
last named.	for Gable Moulds

Jack Rafter	Plumb 23½- 12
	Mitre. 13¼- 6
Plumb 23½- 12	
Level. 12 - 23½	Bisection of
Side.. 13¼- 6	23½- 12=14½- 24

For full explanation see Index.

COMMON RAFTER

Span Ft.	Length Ft. In.	Span In.	Lgth. In.
1	1. 1¼	¼	¼
2	2. 2⅜	½	½
3	3. 3⅝	¾	⅞
4	4. 4¾	1	1⅛
5	5. 6	¼	⅜
6	6. 7⅛	½	⅝
7	7. 8⅜	¾	⅞
8	8. 9½	2	2¼
9	9.10¾	¼	½
10	10.11⅞	½	¾
11	12. 1⅛	¾	3
12	13. 2⅜	3	¼
13	14. 3½	¼	⅝
14	15. 4¾	½	⅞
15	16. 5⅞	¾	4⅛
16	17. 7	4	⅜
17	18. 8¼	¼	⅝
18	19. 9½	½	5
19	20.10⅝	¾	¼
20	21.11⅞	5	½
21	23. 1	¼	¾
22	24. 2¼	½	6
23	25. 3½	¾	⅜
24	26. 4⅝	6	⅝
25	27. 5⅞	¼	⅞
26	28. 7	½	7⅛
27	29. 8¼	¾	⅜
28	30. 9⅜	7	⅝
29	31.10⅝	¼	8
30	32.11¾	½	¼
31	34. 1	¾	½
32	35. 2⅛	8	¾
33	36. 3⅜	¼	9⅛
34	37. 4⅝	½	⅜
35	38. 5¾	¾	⅝
36	39. 7	9	⅞
37	40. 8⅛	¼	10⅛
38	41. 9⅜	½	½
39	42.10½	¾	¾
40	43.11¾	10	11
41	45. 0⅞	¼	¼
42	46. 2⅛	½	½
43	47. 3¼	¾	⅞
44	48. 4½	11	12⅛
45	49. 5¾	¼	⅜
46	50. 6⅞	½	⅝
47	51. 8⅛	¾	⅞
48	52. 9¼	12	13⅛
49	53.10½		
50	54.11⅝		

HIP OR VALLEY RAFTER

Span Ft.	Length Ft. In.	Span In.	Lgth. In.
1	1. 2½	¼	⅜
2	2. 5	½	⅝
3	3. 7½	¾	⅞
4	4.10	1	1¼
5	6. 0½	¼	½
6	7. 3	½	⅞
7	8. 5½	¾	2⅛
8	9. 8	2	⅜
9	10.10½	¼	¾
10	12. 0⅞	½	3
11	13. 3⅜	¾	⅜
12	14. 5⅞	3	⅝
13	15. 8⅜	¼	⅞
14	16.10⅞	½	4¼
15	18. 1⅜	¾	½
16	19. 3⅞	4	⅞
17	20. 6⅜	¼	5⅛
18	21. 8⅞	½	⅜
19	22.11⅜	¾	¾
20	24. 1⅞	5	6
21	25. 4⅜	¼	⅜
22	26. 6⅞	½	⅝
23	27. 9⅜	¾	7
24	28.11⅞	6	¼
25	30. 2⅜	¼	½
26	31. 4⅞	½	⅞
27	32. 7⅜	¾	8⅛
28	33. 9⅞	7	½
29	35. 0¼	¼	¾
30	36. 2¾	½	9
31	37. 5¼	¾	⅜
32	38. 7¾	8	⅝
33	39.10¼	¼	10
34	41. 0¾	½	¼
35	42. 3¼	¾	⅝
36	43. 5¾	9	⅞
37	44. 8¼	¼	11⅛
38	45.10¾	½	½
39	47. 1¼	¾	¾
40	48. 3¾	10	12⅛
41	49. 6¼	¼	⅜
42	50. 8¾	½	⅝
43	51.11¼	¾	13
44	53. 1¾	11	¼
45	54. 4¼	¼	⅝
46	55. 6¾	½	⅞
47	56. 9¼	¾	14¼
48	57.11¾	12	½
49	59. 2⅛		
50	60. 4⅝		

Spaced In.	Length Ft. In.
1	2¼
2	4½
3	6¾
4	9
5	11⅛
6	1 1⅜
7	3⅝
8	5⅞
9	8⅛
10	10⅜
11	2 0⅝
12	2⅞
13	5⅛
14	7¼
15	9½
16	11¾
17	3 2
18	4¼
19	6½
20	8¾
21	11
22	4 1¼
23	3⅜
24	5⅝
25	7⅞
26	10⅛
27	5 0⅜
28	2⅝
29	4⅞
30	7⅛
31	9⅜
32	11½
33	6 1¾
34	4
35	6¼
36	8½
37	10¾
38	7 1
39	3¼
40	5½
41	7⅝
42	9⅞
43	8 0⅛
44	2⅜
45	4⅝
46	6⅞
47	9¼
48	11⅜

24 & 12 — 63½°

EXPLANATION

Common Rafter

Width of building..........46'4½"
Find length of Common Rafter.
Answer:

Under **Span**, ft. find 46' = 51' 5⅛"
"   "   in. "   4½" =   5"

Total length Common Rft. 51'10⅛"
When rafters overhang, add both
overhangs to width of building.
Use total span as before.
To get length of rafter by its run:
doubling the run gives the span.
Proceed as before.
Tables give full length. Allow for
half thickness of ridge.
Spans over 50', as 60', add lengths
of 50' & 10' spans together.

Hip Rafter

If common rafter span is 46'4½",
Hip rafter is 56'9½" long. Measure length of Hip on center of top
edge. If Hip is unbacked (top edge
square), see Index. If edge is
backed (beveled) see Index.
Allow for half thickness of ridge.

Jack Rafters

Spaced 24" apart are 4'5⅝" different in length. Measure length
on center of top edge. Cut short
equal to half thickness of hip.

CUTS FOR STEEL SQUARE.

The first figure is always the cut.

Common Rafter	Purlin Rafter Roof Sheathing
Plumb 24 - 12	
Level. 12 - 24	Plumb 12 - 13⅜
	Cross. 6 - 13⅜

Hip Rafter	Valley Shingles
Plumb 12 - 8½	Cross. 6 - 13⅜
Level. 8½ - 12	Set bevel on
Side.. 14¾ - 8½	butt end.
Backing 12 - 14¾	
Set bevel to	Mitre-Box Cuts
last named.	for Gable Moulds

	Plumb 24 - 12
	Mitre. 13⅜ - 6

Jack Rafter	
Plumb 24 - 12	Bisection of
Level. 12 - 24	24- 12=14⅝- 24
Side.. 13⅜ - 6	

For full explanation see **Index.**

COMMON RAFTER

Span Ft.	Length Ft. In.	Span In.	Lgth. In.
1..	1. 1⅜	¼..	¼
2..	2. 2⅞	½..	⅝
3..	3. 4¼	¾..	⅞
4..	4. 5⅝	1 ..	1⅛
5..	5. 7⅛	¼..	⅜
6..	6. 8½	½..	⅝
7...	7. 9⅞	¾..	2
8..	8. 11⅜	2 ..	¼
9..	10. 0¾	¼..	½
10..	11. 2⅛	½..	¾
11..	12. 3⅝	¾..	3⅛
12..	13. 5	3 ..	⅜
13..	14. 6⅜	¼..	⅝
14..	15. 7⅞	½..	⅞
15..	16. 9¼	¾..	4¼
16..	17. 10⅝	4 ..	½
17..	19. 0⅛	¼..	¾
18..	20. 1½	½..	5
19..	21. 2⅞	¾..	¼
20..	22. 4⅜	5 ..	⅝
21..	23. 5¾	¼..	⅞
22..	24. 7⅛	½..	6⅛
23..	25. 8⅝	¾..	⅜
24..	26. 10	6 ..	¾
25..	27. 11⅜	¼..	7
26..	29. 0⅞	½..	¼
27..	30. 2¼	¾..	½
28..	31. 3⅝	7 ..	⅞
29..	32. 5⅛	¼..	8⅛
30..	33. 6½	½..	⅜
31..	34. 7⅞	¾..	⅝
32..	35. 9⅜	8 ..	9
33..	36. 10¾	¼..	¼
34..	38. 0⅛	½..	½
35..	39. 1⅝	¾..	¾
36..	40. 3	9 .	10
37..	41. 4⅜	¼..	⅜
38..	42. 5⅞	½..	⅝
39..	43. 7¼	¾..	⅞
40..	44. 8⅝	10 .	11⅛
41..	45. 10⅛	¼..	½
42..	46. 11½	½..	¾
43..	48. 0⅞	¾.	12
44..	49. 2⅜	11 ..	¼
45..	50. 3¾	¼..	⅝
46..	51. 5⅛	½..	⅞
47..	52. 6⅝	¾.	13⅛
48..	53. 8	12 ..	⅜
49..	54. 9⅜		
50..	55. 10⅞		

HIP OR VALLEY RAFTER

Span Ft.	Length Ft. In.	Span In.	Lgth. In
1..	1. 2¾	¼..	¼
2..	2. 5⅜	½..	⅝
3..	3. 8⅛	¾..	⅞
4..	4. 10¾	1 ..	1¼
5..	6. 1½	¼..	½
6..	7. 4⅛	½..	⅞
7..	8. 6⅞	¾..	2⅛
8..	9. 9⅝	2 ..	½
9..	11. 0¼	¼..	¾
10..	12. 3	½..	3⅛
11..	13. 5⅝	¾..	⅜
12..	14. 8⅜	3 ..	⅝
13..	15. 11	¼..	4
14..	17. 1¾	½..	¼
15..	18. 4½	¾..	⅝
16..	19. 7⅛	4 ..	⅞
17..	20. 9⅞	¼..	5¼
18..	22. 0½	½..	½
19..	23. 3¼	¾..	⅞
20..	24. 6	5 ..	6⅛
21..	25. 8⅝	¼..	⅜
22..	26. 11⅜	½..	¾
23..	28. 2	¾..	7
24..	29. 4¾	6 ..	⅜
25..	30. 7⅜	¼..	⅝
26..	31. 10⅛	½..	8
27..	33. 0⅞	¾..	¼
28..	34. 3½	7 ..	⅝
29..	35. 6¼	¼..	⅞
30..	36. 8⅞	½..	9⅛
31..	37. 11⅝	¾..	½
32..	39. 2¼	8 ..	¾
33..	40. 5	¼.	10⅛
34..	41. 7¾	½..	⅜
35..	42. 10⅜	¾..	¾
36..	44. 1⅛	9 .	11
37..	45. 3¾	¼..	⅜
38..	46. 6½	½..	⅝
39..	47. 9⅛	¾.	12
40..	48. 11⅞	10 ..	¼
41..	50. 2⅝	¼..	½
42..	51. 5¼	½..	⅞
43..	52. 8	¾.	13⅛
44..	53. 10⅝	11 ..	½
45..	55. 1⅜	¼..	¾
46..	56. 4	½.	14⅛
47..	57. 6¾	¾..	⅜
48..	58. 9½	12 ..	⅝
49..	60. 0⅛		
50..	61. 2⅞		

PROBLEMS TO BE SOLVED WITH THE
"FULL LENGTH ROOF FRAMER"

Examine the book for a few minutes and read pages 7 to 14 and then solve these problems. The answers are at the end.

Practice writing down problems of your own and see how quickly you can solve them.

Roof framing is the most fascinating and interesting part of a building as well as the most difficult. An expert roof framer is always looked upon with great respect by his employer and fellow mechanic.

The three objects in writing this book were to have it *simple, unquestionably accurate* and as *brief* and *small* as possible for *pocket size.*

The pitch of a roof is printed on the building plans as so many inches of rise to 12″ of run. The 12″ of run is standard and is always used, as 6″ and 12″, meaning 6″ of rise to 12″ of run. Also 6½ and 12, 7 and 12, 7½ and 12, 8 and 12 and so on from ½ and 12 up to 24 and 12. The plan might call for any of these 48 different pitches and the mechanic must be prepared to frame any roof at short notice.

PROBLEM ONE

A building is 33′ 7¾″ wide. The pitch is 7½ and 12. It is a gable roof and has neither Hip, Valley or Jack rafters. Find the length and cuts for the Common rafters. (Pages 7 and 48.)

PROBLEM TWO

A building is 29′ 9¼″ wide. The pitch is 9½ and 12. The rafters project or overhang 1′ 11″ on each side of the building line (measuring out level).

This is another gable roof with only Common rafters. Find the location of the seat cut (pages 9 and 56) and then the entire length (page 56).

PROBLEM THREE

A building is 31′ 5¼″ wide. The pitch is 17½ and 12. The rafters overhang 2′ 1″ (measuring

116

out level). This building is "L" shaped and has Hip, Valley and Jack rafters, as well as Common rafters. The Jack rafters are spaced 28″ apart. Find the location of the seat cut of the Common, Hip and Valley rafters (pages 9 and 88) and then the entire lengths (page 88).

PROBLEM FOUR

A porch projects 9′ 6″ from the main building. It is to be covered with a 6½ and 12 lean-to or half span roof which rests against the side of the main building (page 11). The porch rafters overhang 24″. There are hip rafters on the porch corners. Find the location of the seat cut of the Hip and Common rafters (pages 11 and 44). Then find the entire lengths (page 44). The Jack rafters are spaced 24″ apart.

ANSWERS TO THE ABOVE PROBLEMS
PROBLEM ONE

Common rafter length	19′	10⅛″

PROBLEM TWO

Common rafter to seat cut	18′	11¾″
Common rafter length	21′	5⅛″

PROBLEM THREE

Common rafter to seat cut	27′	9½″
Common rafter length	31′	5¾″
Hip and Valley to seat cut	31′	11¼″
Hip and Valley length	36′	2″
Jack rafter length	4′	1½″

Jack rafter seat cut same as for
  Common rafter.

PROBLEM FOUR

Common rafter seat cut	10′	9⅝″
Common rafter length	13′	1″
Hip and Valley seat cut	14′	4⅝″
Hip and Valley length	17′	5″
Jack rafter length	2′	3¼″

Jack rafter seat cut same as for
  Common rafter.

JACK RAFTER AGAINST HIP

Amount cut off the length of Jack. Half thickness of Hip. See pp. 10, 13. Figs. 9, 15, 20. Jack is 2'4⅞" long. Pitch is 8" rise and 12" run. Hip is 1⅝. See table below. Column one. Rise 8. Col. 2, Hip 1⅝ thick. Allowance in Col. 2 is 1⅜". The Jack is now 2'3½" long. From dotted line, Figs. 9, 15.

HIP RAFTER AGAINST RIDGE

Amount cut off the length of Hip. Half thickness of Ridge. See pp. 13, 18. Figures 15, 37. The Hip is 16'5". Pitch is 8 rise to 12" run. Ridge is 1⅝. See table below. Column one. Rise 8" and in Col. 5 is 1¼", the amount to reduce length. The Hip is now 16'3¾" long. The Valley is also 16'3¾". Dotted line Figs. 15, 37, 38.

JACKS against Hip			HIPS against Ridge		
Thickness			**Thickness**		
Rise	1⅝"	1⅞"	¾"	1⅝"	1⅞"
2	1⅛	1⅜	½	1⅛	1⅜
4	1¼	1⅜	½	1⅛	1⅜
6	1¼	1½	½	1¼	1⅜
8	1⅜	1⅝	⅝	1¼	1½
10	1½	1¾	⅝	1⅜	1½
12	1⅝	1⅞	⅝	1⅜	1⅝
14	1¾	2	¾	1½	1⅝
16	1⅞	2¼	¾	1⅝	1¾

COMMON RAFTER AGAINST RIDGE

See page 13, Fig. 11. At dotted line is length taken from tables. The cutoff is half the thickness of your ridge.